SO THIS WAS HER ENEMY.

Black hair, black clothes, face arrogantly boned and burned to a dark brown by sun and wind. This then was the six-foot pirate who ruled his moorland province. This was the devil who had sent her father to the pillory. And if gossip were to be believed, he had sullied his reputation with enough brutality to make him an outlaw.

Lord Ventnor took Mary's arm. "You are the sauciest young woman I have ever met. How dare you be so impudent to me!"

Mary pulled away defiantly. "I am not well schooled in servility—any more than you are in courtesy, my lord!"

Ventnor threw back his head and roared with laughter. "You look the prim little town miss—but act like a vixen." He gripped her arm firmly.

"And you're still the young woman I'm to bring back for slaughter..."

THE VIXEN'S REVENGE

Paula Allardyce

PLAYBOY PRESS
PAPERBACKS

THE VIXEN'S REVENGE

Copyright © 1957 by Paula Allardyce

Cover illustration by Gerry Hoover: Copyright © 1979 by PEI Books, Inc.

Published simultaneously in the United States and Canada by Playboy Press Paperbacks, New York, New York. Printed in the United States of America. Library of Congress Catalog Card Number: 79-89961. Originally published as *The Lady and the Pirate* in Great Britain in 1957 by Ward, Lock & Co., Ltd.

Books are available at quantity discounts for promotional and industrial use. For further information, write our sales promotion agency: Ventura Associates, 40 East 49th Street, New York, New York 10017.

ISBN: 0-872-16607-4

First Playboy Press Paperbacks printing March 1980.

CONTENTS

Oh, it's owre the Border awa', awa',
It's owre the Border awa', awa',
We'll on and march to Carlisle ha',
Wi' its yetts, its castles, an' a' an' a',
Wi' a hundred pipers an' a' an' a',
We'll up and gie them a blaw, a blaw.

JACOBITE SONG

This one is for three *very* special people,

TOM E. HUFF, who over the months has given me so much encouragement and who told me repeatedly that the second book is the hardest . . . Tom, you're absolutely right!

HOWARD BUSBEE, my husband, my favorite critic, my favorite proofreader, my favorite fan, and my mainstay.

And finally, ROSIE, who keeps me on the right track, and drops those little gems of wisdom at precisely the right time.

I Prologue

Derby: September, 1745

"It is not," Aunt Briarcliffe was saying, "as if Mary is going to find a husband easily."

Mary sighed, but did not otherwise stir. She had heard this many times before. She looked rather wearily at her aunt—"She looks like a big-beaked bird with a fringe," Nan had once said, which was naughty of her, for at twelve one should surely have respect for one's elders—but the remark was not inaccurate, and Mary suddenly wished to smile, though God knows there was little enough humor in the situation.

She was a girl with a strong sense of duty. She organized sewing meetings for papa's parishioners, took Sunday school, and lectured her small sister on her unladylike behavior. But there was another side of her—Nan called it her diary side—and this now studied her relatives without flattery.

Mr. Briarcliffe was really growing excessively fat. If he worked a little more at his silk mills it would not have harmed him; his face was colored like the port wine he so indulged in. He stood by the mantelpiece like a pompous alderman, one fat beringed hand gesticulating. Cousin Horace sat behind him, drowned in boredom. He was a stupid boy, well-meaning, but uncouth and addicted to horseplay. He was afraid of Mary, for all she was a year younger, but this did not prevent his continually trying to kiss her, which exasperated her beyond endurance. He teased Nan, too. He meant no harm. To him big girls were to be kissed and little girls to be teased. It never entered his head that a young lady of twelve could possess any personal pride. But then the trouble with Horace—this

11

was Mary in one of her backsliding moments—was that there was too much vacant space within his mind, and everything that penetrated was dashed to pieces. So he derided Nan, pulled her ringlets, tickled her, and once even dared to pick her up and swing her high in his arms. When he received a bony fist full in the eye, he was quite aggrieved. But even then he did not understand, and still grabbed at Nan when he could, and poked fun at her, saying she was like her sister, she would never find a beau, such skinny pieces they were, the two of them.

But it was true, Mary knew well enough, that she was unlikely to find a husband. The marriage market was a market like any other, especially in these money-minded days. Even now at eighteen she was small, thin and pale, with brown hair and eyes that were in no way exceptional. And of course she had no dowry. Besides, she often thought that she was not made for love; she had never experienced it. She found the young men who kissed her tedious; when they quoted poetry she wanted to laugh. She had sometimes comforted and advised the young girls who came to her, weeping because they were not loved enough or perhaps because they had been loved too well. She was very sorry for them, but could never visualize herself in any similar situation. Besides, the grand passions did not fit in with a white, witch's face; this was what Horace termed it once when she had rebuffed him. "And," he had added, "you have a witch's tongue, too, cousin. A man don't like a wife who's too sharp; it makes him feel uncomfortable." Well—that was true too, she supposed. A sharp face and a sharp tongue led inevitably to the lozenged arms of spinsterhood. But it was a pity to inflict all this on papa, who was really not responsible for his daughter's unhappy sense of the ridiculous, nor for her lack of flesh in the proper places, neither.

She raised her head to look at him. The tears sprang to her eyes. She could laugh at the romantic young men, but she loved her father with all her heart and soul. Darling, darling papa—it was cruel to nag at him so. Her heart twinged in angry pity as she saw how he seemed to have shrunk these past few weeks. The wicked rents in his ears had healed, but there was a wound in him now that would

never heal again. The face which had never looked unkindly at her did not look unkindly now. It held still its
old irony and comprehension, but there was a flat, trans-
parent pallor to it, and the eyes, the wise, quizzical eyes,
tended sometimes in moments of abstraction to stare as if
they were seeing again the horror that always lay below
the surface. A violent protectiveness throbbed within
Mary, to be followed by the rage that papa would not tol-
erate—"It is never worthwhile being angry," he had said
to her once when she was no older than Nan was now, "It
only expends energy that should be reserved for something else."—"I cannot help it," the twelve-year-old Mary
had sobbed, "I hate and I want to kill." Now, six years
later, it was the same. She hated, and she wanted to kill.
It was so cruel, so unfair. Such things should not happen.
It was not only that her father had never done any harm;
the same no doubt could be said of Uncle George, with his
vast silk mills in Derby, and the innumerable people he
employed. But then Uncle George had never done much
good, either, and papa had done good all his life, practiced
every minute of the day what he preached in his sabbath
sermons.

That this should happen to him—— To be whirled into
the political vortex, papa, whose only word for the Pretender's son—"my Chevalier," Nan called him, but then
Nan, bless her, was preposterously romantic—had been
that he was a foolish boy who would doubtless end by killing off more of his countrymen than the English could
achieve in a hundred years. And after that to have this
unbelievably hideous humiliation inflicted on him——
Mary's pale face grew set and hard. He bore no grudge
for what had happened; even now there was no hatred in
his heart. But his daughter possessed a very different disposition. One day, she thought, I will find out who was
responsible, and when I do——

"Look at her!" cried Aunt Briarcliffe. "Look at her,
Edward! If you make faces like that, miss, you'll have the
gentlemen running to get away from you. Such a shrew!
If you was my daughter, I'd not permit these tantrums,
indeed I'd not. What's got into the girl? Been drinking
vinegar?"

Horace at this spluttered into one of his great, vulgar, horselaughs. He had tried to kiss his cousin earlier in the day, and had been most properly set down. "What she needs," he said, "is a bit of cuddling. All women turn sour if they don't have a bit of cuddling, now and then."

"Horrie!" exclaimed his mother.

Mr. Vernon looked up. He did not even glance at his nephew. He smiled at Mary. "You must forgive her," he said, "it has not been too easy for any of us. And you know, Hetty, I do not believe I could endure a coy miss of a daughter who simpered and becked and bowed, as if she were making a permanent Court entrance. Mary, my love, come here a moment."

Mary rose to her feet obediently. Now that she was standing, one could see how slight and small she was. The plain dark gown made of her a shadow, framed by the glow of the lamp. She sat down on the arm of her father's chair, and smiled back at him, her sharp face grown soft in tenderness.

"Thank you, papa," she said. Her eyes flickered from Aunt Briarcliffe to Horace, then back again. "It is true," she said in her voice which was so deceptively gentle, "that I have never been in love. I do not believe I ever shall be. It seems to destroy both judgment and reason, and that I find distasteful. But I do not believe that cuddling, as you so genteelly term it, Horace, would make me smile any more than I do now. And if I must find myself a beau, I swear I'll choose better than an overgrown boy who pulled the wings off flies when he was a baby, and now prefers to pull the petticoats of any local girl who will endure him. But thank you for the suggestion, cousin. It is vastly obliging of you. And indeed it makes me smile, so you have accomplished your purpose."

"Mary!" said her father, taking her hand in his. In his eyes was the ironic half-smile, reproachful yet amused, that even now she could provoke in him, as if he were bewildered by this waspish little daughter who drew her sword on the smallest provocation.

Aunt Briarcliffe had turned up her eyes, and was tut-tutting and fanning herself. Mary, who could now only see her in some ornithological guise, thought she resembled a hen about to lay an egg. "Well!" she said. "Well! Really—— Of course, if you choose to put up with this kind of thing, brother—— When I was young, I swear a girl wasn't permitted to speak so free. Papa would have stopped it quick enough, and well you know it. But you was always soft, soft as butter."

Horace burst out, "If you talk to me like that again, Mary, I'll—I'll——"

"Yes?" she said.

He went very red beneath her cool, reflective glance. He mumbled, "You need a set down. 'Pon honor, you do. And one day some man's going to give it you. And good luck to him. And I don't see what you've got to be so proud of. Especially now when——"

"That will do, son," said Mr. Briarcliffe, speaking for almost the first time that evening. "That will do." But the look he cast at Mary was not friendly. He adored his boy and in his heart agreed entirely with what he had just said.

However, Horace was too stung to remain silent. His temperament was a sulky one. He laughed a great deal, and often too loudly, but the faintest slur on his vanity was something to be avenged. He was sadly affronted. He had not missed the contempt in his cousin's eyes. He said, his voice a growl, "Well, you need not worry about me. I wouldn't cuddle you, not if you was the last girl in the world. No, mama, I will speak. Why shouldn't I? She's always so confounded rude to me."

"Oh, poor Horace!" sighed Mary. They had after all been brought up together, and she could never really think of him as fully grown.

"I suppose," he said savagely, "I'm not good enough for you. I suppose your feather head is full of missish fancies. I suppose you think you'll marry a lord, or something high-flown like that. Well, you won't, you know. You'll just die an old maid, and serve you right. What sort of man do you think would put up with you, for God's sake?"

Mary, in her turn, was a little stung. She had no respect for Horace's opinions, and she would have been the first to admit that she was likely to stay unwed. But to hear this from a young man was somehow hurtful; she found that her lower lip was beginning to tremble. She said, very coldly, "The question is, perhaps, what kind of man I would put up with." Then she forced herself to smile at him; the wide, derisive grin made her look startlingly like her sister, Nan. "Oh, I'll have the whole of it, Horace. He shall be tall and dark and handsome, and a lord into the bargain. And if I cannot have him, I'll be the old maid as you prophesy, and why not? There are worser things. Will you be angry with me, papa, if I do not make a good match?"

"I think," said her father, "that I could endure it."

" 'Faith, he'll have to," snapped Aunt Briarcliffe. "You're a plaguy girl, Mary. I've no patience with you. And there's no call to be so rude to poor Horrie. I'm sure he's a good boy. But all this is beside the point, and now, Mary, you'll please to hold that nasty tongue of yours, for what I have to say is important. And you, Horrie, you can be quiet, too. God knows, the situation is serious enough without all this silly bickering."

Horace said nothing, but the look he cast at his mother from beneath his brows was not agreeable. He had always detested his nickname. The one good thing he could say for Mary was that she never used it. He wished now he had not been so rude. His eyes slid sideways to her. She was, pox take it, anything but pretty, but her figure was neat enough, and there was a kind of style to her, after all, despite that don't-touch air of hers. He was consumed with a violent desire to seize hold of her, and kiss that maddening composure away. A lord, indeed! He was as good as any bloody lord, wasn't he? Certain vague, clumsy plannings began to stir in his mind. But his mother was well away now—God, how women prattled—so he huddled into his chair, his round, youthful face very sulky indeed, his foot tapping, his hands stuck into his pockets.

"Now!" said Aunt Briarcliffe firmly. "George and I are quite agreed that you must come back to London with us. Is that not so, Mr. Briarcliffe?"

"Yes, my love," replied her husband, looking solemn and portentous. He was a vast, rubicund man. One day Horace would be exactly like him.

"You cannot think to stay here. You have no living. No church. And precious little money."

Oh cruel, cruel, thought Mary. Her hand tightened round her father's. Yet it was as if he scarcely listened. His eyes stared ahead; his face was grave and composed.

"And all the neighbors talking, too. It's not right for the girls. Nan needs good schooling, and Mary, for all the stuff she talks, needs a good husband. You'll not find either here. There's no Derby man would look at the daughter of an unfrocked clergyman, and one accused of high treason, at that."

"Aunt——" began Mary, nearly choking.

Aunt Briarcliffe ignored her. "One has to face facts, Edward. I believe in facing facts, and speaking my mind, too. I daresay it's not your fault, but you'll have to see that the situation is an impossible one. Everybody knows about it. Everybody whispers behind our backs. Mr. Briarcliffe even remarked it at the mills, and after all, he's scarce a Derby man, these days, now we have our London house, and mix in good society. Did you not remark it, Mr. Briarcliffe?"

"Yes, indeed, my love," said her husband.

"You see! And if you stay, things will get worse and worse. There's no good denying it, Edward! You was always a dreamer, I know, but this is the time to be practical. Of course, I do not believe, myself, that the Pretender's son will ever march near England, not with dear Marshal Wade, and General Sir John Cope on the lookout for him, but he's doing pretty well in Scotland—oh, pretty well—and there's horrid stories going about, and they say the mad Ventnors have come to town, and everyone knows what nasty popish creatures they are, and they'd not be here if there wasn't something going on, what with their all being as mad as Bedlamites, and the eldest boy such a wild, savage creature that they say he don't even wear a wig, like a proper Christian gentleman, and him a lord and all——"

"Hetty," interposed Mr. Vernon gently, his quiet voice piercing the torrent of sound, "Hetty. I do not believe that one must wear a wig in order to be a Christian. The Ventnors are an old Derbyshire family, and as good as one is like to meet. I remember the old lord very well. It was before your time, my dear," he added to Mary who, consumed with a desire to wring her aunt's neck, was sitting rigidly at his side. "He once attended service at my church. I remember we talked afterwards, and the little boy was with him, the one that now inherits the title. A fine little lad, self-possessed and well-mannered beyond his years——"

"All that is as may be," interrupted his sister, "but he'd not married his cook, then. Such a shocking thing! Why, they say they never go up to London, now, as they did in her ladyship's day, but live at Wardwick Hall, in the middle of the moors, and there's such goings-on that scarce any servants will stay with them. And Ventnor, himself—why, he's supposed to be possessed of the devil, and the stories told of him are too shocking to relate. I believe he killed someone. A poor girl who came there as companion. Is that not so, Mr. Briarcliffe?"

"I believe, my love, it is."

"And he bullies the life out of his younger brother. Of course, it's not to be wondered at, what with the Hall standing all alone on those horrid moors, with nothing but wind and rain, and no genteel company at all."

Horace said—for once, Mary was in entire agreement with him—"I don't see what this has to do with Uncle Edward, mama."

"Of course it's to do with your uncle." Aunt Briarcliffe paused perceptibly to consider why. She went on in great triumph, "It's to show him what wild Jacobites they are, and now Ventnor is in Derby, and that means mischief if anything does, and perhaps it means that the Pretender's son may get here after all, and if he does, Edward, you know very well what will happen to you. I know you do not care about yourself, but at least you should think of Mary and poor little Nan. They don't want to hear people calling their father a traitor, and who knows, if that abominable popish boy came here, what would happen."

Mr. Vernon said wearily, "I do not believe that any more could happen than has already done so."

"Well, I do believe it! Those Ventnors always bring trouble with them. They say he's sold his soul to Satan, long ago, and his familiar always accompanies him.

And——" Here Aunt Briarcliffe's voice sank to an awful whisper. "And, Edward, he was in Derby when you—when——"

Mr. Vernon said, his voice brittle, "Hetty, I must beg of you to be silent. The Ventnors have nothing to do with me. What you are insinuating is the grossest calumny, and that I will not permit in this house." As he said this, he released Mary's hand, and rose to his feet. He was a small man, but at that moment surprisingly formidable. "You tell me that his lordship was in Derby on the day when I was put in the pillory." He smiled into her shocked face. "Why, sister, must I not speak the word? It was the pillory, and it is no shame of mine. If indeed it was his lordship that set me there, the shame is his, and I pity him for having to endure it. To inflict humiliation on another human being is a torment to the soul that nothing can eradicate. He is the sufferer, not I. But I do not believe that he could do such a thing. Why do you make such an accusation?"

"He's a Jacobite! I daresay he was not sorry to see the blame fixed elsewhere. And he *was* in Derby. The men at Mr. Briarcliffe's mills said so. You could not miss him, with all that black hair, and his devil's face, and him so tall, too——"

"You are being very dramatic," sighed Mr. Vernon. "There must after all have been a great many other people in Derby, at that time. Indeed a number of them were centered round me, if you remember—must I not say that, neither?" He looked down for a second at his daughter, whose head was bowed. "Very well. I'll not mention it again. Yet is is a strange belief that silence can erase memory. But we'll not mention the Ventnors, neither, sister. Have I not suffered enough from the false accusation that others should be made to suffer likewise?" His smile was ironic, a little bitter. "I swear his lordship's sole crime is that he does not wear a wig. Put a peruke on him, then, and he'll be as fine a Christian as any. But enough of the Ventnors. They have nothing to do with us. I have only one more thing to say. I am not leaving Derby. No!" He raised his hand, as his sister was about to burst into speech. "I am quite resolved. I am, as you say, a dishonored man, condemned as a traitor. My church and my living have been taken from me. But I cannot leave. This is my home. You would have me run away, Hetty. And to London—— What am I to do in London?"

"What are you to do here?" cried his sister. "Oh, Mr. Briarcliffe, why do you not say something, instead of just standing there?"

Mr. Briarcliffe started, then, red in the face, brooded. "I think," he said at last, "that Edward should come to London." And with this pronouncement he cleared his throat and took a vast pinch of snuff.

"You see!" said his wife triumphantly. "You see! Mr. Briarcliffe is always right. You must come to London. You must think of the girls. Why, when I was Mary's age, I would not have thought a day worthy of the name if it had not ended in dancing, and I vow the beaux were thick as flies upon my doorstep."

"Aunt," said Mary in a clear, cold voice, "I am not interested in dancing."

"You unnatural girl!"

"Nor, indeed, in beaux——"

"Ho, ho!" said Horace derisively.

"——And I believe my father's decision is entirely the right one. Papa," said Mary, "we will all stay in Derby together. If people wish to speak ill of us, why—let them do so. I do not need the kind of life my aunt plans for me. Why," she cried in sudden vehemence, "I should be bored to death."

"Stuff!" said Horace, "Fiddle!"

"Bored to death, Horace! You all tell me I'm not pretty. I know I am not. What would I do in town? Flutter my fan? Say, La, sir, and Fie, sir, and make big eyes? They'd all laugh at me for the country miss I am, and well I'd deserve it. I tell you, aunt, I'd be happier at your Wardwick Hall that you speak of so severely, with the wind and the rain and the moors for company. And your unwigged lord thrown in as make-weight! At least, if he's sold his soul to the devil, he must have more to talk about than pretty nothings. I've always held the devil to be an intelligent being, otherwise he'd scarce have the wit to catch men's souls."

"This is blasphemy," cried her aunt, then her uncle stepped forward, saying in his slow, pompous voice, "Now, child, now. You do not really mean this."

"But I do, I do! And if it's blasphemy, I am sorry, but I would rather talk an hour with your devil-lord than all the quality of London put together, for they think of nothing but gaming and drinking and duelling, and even if I could find a husband among them, he would be no good to me, for I need more than a man to give me his name."

"He'd give you brats, too," said Horace, "and that'd keep you quiet." He added, "It would be about the only thing that would." But as he said this, he stared at her with renewed interest, for there was a color to her cheeks, and a flame in her eyes, as if a candle were lit inside her.

"Horrie!" cried his mother again. "I vow if you talk so nasty, I'll box your ears. Edward, are you going to let the girl be so plaguy silly, and do nothing about it?"

"Why," said Mr. Vernon, turning towards his daughter, "it seems I have no choice, my dear Hetty." His hand came up to stroke Mary's hair. "She has said that she prefers the company of the damned. How can I, who am also of that number, gainsay her?"

"And what," said his sister icily, "are you going to do about money, Edward? If I may ask, that is."

"You may always ask, my dear. I do not know. I am afraid I have never given the matter much consideration."

"I can always work," said Mary. She gave her father an almost frantic look. She loved him so very dearly, and it was wicked that he should be tortured in this way; she knew only too well that his calm was a surface thing.

"Vastly genteel, I'm sure," cried Aunt Briarcliffe with prodigious sarcasm and, when Horace with one of his great guffaws that always made Mary jump, demanded, "And what, pray, would you do, cousin? Take a post as companion?"—his mother suffered this to pass without rebuke, and went on, "A pretty thing, I must say, when my own niece talks of going out to work as if she—as if she were some mill girl. And what about Nan? Has either of you ever thought of her, poor little child?"

"I have thought of little else," replied Mr. Vernon, sitting down suddenly. He put a hand to his forehead. "You mean kindly, Hetty. And you too, George. You are very good friends. If Nan would go with you, I should be glad for her. But she will not. You know that. She would not stir without Mary."

"Then I think it is exceeding selfish of Mary not to come with us."

"Or indeed without me. I could send her away, of course. But she would not be happy. And neither," added Mr. Vernon a little grimly, "would you. Nan is a young lady who makes her wishes felt. Is that not so, Mary? She is not such a meek, chastened and pliable character as yourself."

"No, papa," said Mary. A faint smile of perfect comprehension passed between father and daughter.

"It would be ungenerous of me, then, to send her to London. I know you would do everything to make her happy, and I know, too, that in a month's time you would be begging me to remove her."

"If you think I'm not capable of dealing with a twelve-year-old child—— After all, I brought up Horace."

"Yes," said Mr. Vernon reflectively. He turned his calm gaze upon his nephew who wriggled a little in his chair. "Yes. You have, as you say, brought up Horace." He surveyed the boy for a second. "But nonetheless I should not care to saddle you with Nan. Indeed, she is as wild as the young Jacobite lord you have been speaking of. Perhaps they could make a match of it. I feel they would be well-suited. Though of course the disparity in age—— He must be nearing thirty, if my reckoning is correct. It will have to be you, Mary. Do you feel you could endure a diabolical husband who lives on the moors, and wears no peruke?"

"For your sake, papa," said Mary meekly, "I would do my best."

"You might at least after a time persuade him to cut his hair."

"Really, Edward," cried his sister, "I simply do not

understand you. How can you joke at such a moment——
Mr. Briarcliffe!"

"Yes, my love?"

"Oh!" she wailed, infuriated suddenly by this stolid
acquiescence. "Oh! Really, men are quite unendurable."
And she glared, first at her husband and then at her
brother, bewildered that even in the face of disaster Mr.
Vernon should preserve his strange, ironic detachment
and jest in this unseemly manner with his daughter.

Mr. Vernon remarked—a vein was throbbing in his
temple, but only Mary noticed it—"I feel that after all
this, we are in need of some refreshment. Mary, my
dear, do you think you could persuade the girl to bring
us in some wine and cakes?" He added to his sister, "We
are sadly reduced in domestic staff, but our Hannah is
a good girl and refuses to leave us despite the neighbors
who warn her three times a day that I am likely either to
cut her throat or convert her to popery—I cannot quite
make out which is considered the worser fate."

Aunt Briarcliffe looked at him, then abandoned the
struggle. She sat down heavily beside her husband who,
feeling that he should make some remark, announced:
"For September it is really prodigious cold, prodigious
cold. They say this has been the worst summer for five
years—nothing like it since 1740——"

"I will see to the wine, papa," said Mary, "and then
I must say goodnight to Nan."

"Is she not asleep yet?" demanded Aunt Braircliffe.
"It is past nine o'clock. I never permitted Horace to be
awake after nine o'clock."

"It is a pity," said Mr. Vernon mildly, "to inculcate
these childish habits for, if well-grounded, they tend to
continue into maturity."

Horace, who had sunk into an apathy of boredom,
jerked up his head at this, and Mary slipped out of the
room and into the kitchen.

Hannah, whom Mr. Vernon referred to as a girl, was a
woman of over forty. She came from the Derbyshire
dales, a long way from the town where she had arrived,
some twenty years back with a sickly baby in her arms,

and no wedding ring on her finger. Mary at that point had not yet been born, but she remembered her mother's describing how thin and gaunt Hannah had been, and how, after a few weeks in the Vernon household, the buttons of her dress had popped off, one by one. The baby had died, and Hannah now was a stout, strapping woman, who would have championed the family with her life-blood, and who was their friend, rather than a servant. She stood there, arms folded, the hair, dampened by the heat from the oven, flat across her forehead. She said ominously in the strong accent of her county, "What's your aunt been saying, the silly old faggot?"

"Oh," said Mary with a sigh, "she has been saying a great deal too much, and I could gladly take a rolling-pin to her. It is a pity that our sex talks before it thinks, for I believe she truly means well. These cakes look delicious, Hannah. I'll take one up to Nan."

"Has she been a-worriting *him?*"

"Oh yes. She's been worrying us all. Is it not strange," said Mary, picking up one of the newly baked cakes, and biting a piece out of it, "that she is papa's sister? One would not believe they came from the same family. Oh well. We'll not see them again for a long time, I fancy." She looked up at Hannah. "I think I shall have to find myself a post as companion or governess. Can you not see me? Yes, my lady, no, my lady, a footstool for your poor feet, my lady. Reading the Bible in the daytime, and keeping decently to my own room when there's company. Arranging flowers and bowing my head over an embroidery frame—— It'll not be my fault if after six months of this a thread of my sewing silk gets caught across the staircase so that my lady catches her heel in it and comes a-tumbling down. And I swear she'd not even leave me her old teapot."

"How you talk," said Hannah. "Are you eating all those cakes, yourself?"

Mary started guiltily. "Oh, dear. No, of course not. They are for the company. Take them in, Hannah dear. Stuff them into my aunt's wide mouth so that she cannot talk so much, and pour the wine down Horace's throat so that the next time he tries to kiss me, he'll not see his target." Then she cracked her small hands together. "How cruel they are! Oh, I know they mean to be kind, but to sit there and · hear them uttering cruelty after cruelty—— It would perhaps be as well if I were away for a little."

"They say," remarked Hannah, "that the old woman up at Wardwick Hall is advertising for a companion. She'll be lucky. No one in their senses'd go there, with the winter snows to coop them in, and all on 'em tenpence ha'penny in the shilling, and wild as killer dogs into the bargain."

"Wardwick Hall?" Mary, at the door, turned. "That's where the Ventnors live. The mad Ventnors."

"Ay. And a fine devil's brood, too." Here Hannah, to Mary's astonishment, crossed herself.

"That is very popish," she said, then, a gleam in her eye. "So they want a companion, do they?"

"Now, Miss Mary——"

"I only asked the question. I did not offer myself as victim. Only," said Mary, her voice vague, "they sound so charming. Do you think I could tame them, Hannah? Whistle them to heel? They must have some humanity in them."

"Precious little," grumbled Hannah.

"Ah, of course, he does not wear a wig, the poor damned soul. And a Jacobite into the bargain—— What is the latest news, by the way? But Nan will tell me that, for she is as Jacobite as the Ventnors, and sleeps with a white rose beneath her pillow."

"Miss Mary, I know nothing about Jacobites, and care less, but will you please leave those cakes alone——"

"I only wanted a couple for Nan. And one more for myself. It is not good for my uncle and aunt to eat too much, for they are over fat, already." And with this, Mary left the kitchen, and went upstairs to the bedroom which her small sister shared with her.

Nan greeted her with a cry of welcome, and received delightedly the cakes that Mary dropped into her hands. She was more sturdily built than her sister, with darker hair, bolder eyes and a bright red in her cheeks, but shared the same high-boned, pointed face. There would

be no difficulty in finding a husband for Nan; not even
Aunt Briarcliffe could prophesy disaster.

"You look cross," she said, pulling Mary down beside
her on the bed. "It's Aunt Briarcliffe. Or Horace. Has he
been trying to kiss you again? You should give him a
leveler. That would teach him. I did."

"So I was informed! Papa, poor soul, must feel ac-
sursed with his two ladylike daughters. What with you
using your fists like the *haut-ton* in the ring, and me——"
Her face tightened so that in some strange way it
resembled Aunt Briarcliffe's. "In my young days a gal
was not permitted to speak so free."

Nan began to giggle; at Mary's look of stern reproach
she only giggled the more. "What else did she say? Oh
tell me, tell me. Did she get all miffed? And Horace——
Did he say nothing?"

"Oh, he said I'd never find myself a husband. And
that," said Mary, "is very true. Though one does not always care to hear it set forth so plain."

"You could marry anyone you wished," said Nan.
"Anyone. Only you never fall in love. Why do you never
fall in love?"

"I prefer to keep my independence," said Mary. "It
seems to me that to fall in love must be like getting drunk;
one no longer has control over oneself. I should not like
that. I do not wish to place myself at someone's mercy.
Besides, who would fall in love with me? I am not pretty."

"What stuff? There's no one in the Assembly ballrooms
who's a patch on you."

"You rate our Derby beauties low, Nan. You're talking
nonsense, child. And so am I, for I told Aunt Briarcliffe
I'd marry a lord, and a tall, dark, handsome one at that.
Poor man! The aristocracy must already be shaking in its
shoes."

"It's shaking all right," said Nan, taking a fierce bite
out of her cake, "Oh, how it's shaking! But not half so
much as it'll shake shortly, gemini, no."

"I gather from this that the Pretender's son is now on
the outskirts of Derby."

"Not yet. But he will be." And Nan began to sing,

"Oh Charlie is my darling,
The Young Chevalier!"

Then, at the look on her sister's face she broke off, whispering, "Oh, I'm sorry, I'm sorry—I forgot. Do you think anyone heard? Oh, Mary!" The tears were beginning to trickle down her cheeks. "Look out of the window. Please."

"Don't be such a goose," said Mary, hugging her. Yet she rose to her feet, and stood by the window for a second, parting the curtains. She thought with great bitterness, a fine world indeed, where little girls must see their fathers pilloried, where they are afraid to sing a foolish song. She said gently, "Be careful, darling. You know how it is. People are stupid and thoughtless, and there are so many rumors about, these days. But never mind. There is no one there." And even as she said this, had the strange impression that someone was. She listened. But there was complete silence. She drew the curtains again, and came back to the bed. She said briskly, "Well, what is the news? What is the Pretender's son doing now? Still eating babies for breakfast?"

"Mary!"

"And ravaging the countryside with his wild petticoat men?"

"He is behaving with the utmost courtesy and consideration. And everyone says how kind and handsome he is."

"Naturally. And where is he now, the pretty boy?"

"Only near Prestonpans. That's all."

"Well, of course that would mean a great deal more to me if I knew where Prestonpans was. And what about General Sir John Cope? Is he not near Prestonpans, too?"

"I should imagine so."

"And will they not meet?"

"Of course they'll meet. And that will be the end of Johnny Cope."

"Johnny Cope she calls him! The impudence of it. How sure you are that the Pretender's son will win."

"The Chevalier, please."

"The Pretender's son!"

"Well," said Nan, shifting her ground of argument, "he

made 'em run like hares at Colt Bridge. A whole regiment of dragoons flying like mad before a dozen Scottish pipers —— If only I'd been there to see."

"I expect they did not like the noise," said Mary, then before her sister could reply, said thoughtfully, "It will be strange if he does beat Cope. For I believe he is now not so far from the Border. How strange it is, Nan. No, I'm being serious. I care nothing for Pretenders, nor for Hanoverians, neither. You know that. If it had not been for—for what happened to us, I'd not think of the matter at all. But now it's important. It is David against Goliath, is it not? I do not really like David any more than I do Goliath, but in one's heart one cannot but feel for the little man. Yet it may be an ill day for us if David reaches Derby."

Nan said nothing. Her color was a little faded. She stared at her sister who sat there motionless on the side of the bed. She said at last in a small, ill-assured voice, "That letter they found in papa's study—— What did it say, Mary? You never told me."

"It said enough to hang us all."

"But why should they think it was papa? No one could imagine he would ever do anything wrong."

"It was addressed to 'V'. Just the capital letter. And it was in the secret drawer of his writing desk. It was natural enough," said Mary, adding in a fierce low voice. "Somebody placed it there. Somebody who wished to avert suspicion from himself. And one day I will find out who that somebody was."

"What will you do?" whispered Nan, fascinated.

"Why, it will again be David against Goliath, will it not? A miserable, puling little David against a great——" Mary stopped. An odd, considering look appeared in her eyes, but the candlelight was too dim for Nan to discern it. She said, smiling, and in her normal voice, "You know, Nan, I am going to tell you something which is not important yet which interests me. I know why your handsome Chevalier has come so far, and may come even further."

"Why, then?"

"Because he is fighting for a cause, an ideal. I believe

him to be wrong—oh yes, my little Jacobite lady, I know
he is wrong. Yet he is fighting, nonetheless, as his heart
bids him—and we, we are fighting for nothing at all,
except to defend ourselves. One day, perhaps, when the
blows strike nearer home, we shall find ourselves in arms
for the ancient rights that the Stuarts have defiled—and
then, I fear, David will go home again—ow're the water,
Charlie, dear Charlie, brave Charlie—and not dine wi'
Maclean after all!"

"It is a lovely song!"

"Yes. They have the lovely songs. That is another ad-
vantage. But when I find my Goliath, Nan, he will have
no chance at all, because he is evil and stupid and beastly,
and I shall be fighting for papa, and that will give me the
strength of all Johnny Cope's army—and Wade's, too,
with Cumberland's thrown in."

"You'll be a Jacobite yet," said Nan who was growing
sleepy, and had not quite followed this.

"Then I'd best go before you convert me."

"Oh, stay—— Please, Mary!"

"Your eyes are half shut. Good night, darling. Sleep
well."

"Are you going back to Aunt Briarcliffe and that stuffy
old Horace?"

"Oh," said Mary, rather wearily; her face in the
candlelight looked pale and drawn—"I could not endure
them any more. They are so stupid, and I am grown
horrid in my old age."

"Old age! You're only eighteen."

"It's old enough. Old enough to despise stupidity. The
devil would be better, after all."

Nan did not understand a word of this, but her eyes
were indeed closing, and she lay back on the pillows in
silence.

"I shall go for a walk," continued Mary. "They can do
very well without me. Aunt Briarcliffe can tell papa how
big their London house is, and how many servants they
have, and how Lord This and Lady That came to take a
dish of tea with them—and Uncle George will say, Yes,
my love, at the appropriate intervals, and Horace will be

snoring, and who's to blame him? How would you like to go to London, Nan?"

"I would detest it."

"Why? It would be gay. Lots of people. You know you like people."

"I'd rather stay here."

Mary, smiling at the sleepy voice, kissed her sister's cheek, snuffed the candle and went towards the door.

"Mary!"

"Nan, go to sleep. What is it?"

"What did you mean when you said the devil would be better?"

Mary, a shadow by the door, moved in again to open the cupboard. "I suppose I need my cloak—— Oh, one could pit one's wits against the devil. It might be amusing. For a while. Though it would not be so amusing in the end, not if, as I am beginning to believe, his name begins with 'V'. Why, he don't even wear a wig to protect him——" She checked herself, and looked round. But Nan lay very still, her breathing soft and even.

She shut the door then, slipping her cloak over her shoulders, crept past the drawing room and out into the street.

The Vicarage—it needed a new name now, for the vicar was vicar no longer, and a new, red-faced man, so proud of his Oath of Abjuration that it was as if he had abjured all charity and tenderness as well as allegiance to the Stuarts, preached loudly where once papa had stood—was at the end of the town of Derby, near to where the Derwent flowed out into country, towards Breadsall. Mary knew the river bank well, and at that moment sadly needed its peace and solitude. There was anger, distress and a thirst for vengeance in her heart; she could not face papa when she was in such a mood. The late September night was cool and wild with a wind that bellied her cloak about her, and tore at the soft brown hair. But she was hardy, and the cold did not trouble her; the rough wind against her cheek revived her spirits.

She walked past the cottages, until she came to the further reaches of the river, black and sombre in the evening dark, with only a shred of moon to light herself by, and the stars blotted out with cloud. With a sigh of contentment she listened to the lazy water lapping against the bank, the hooting of a solitary owl, and the brittle rustle of the falling leaves. Then she heard a sound that pleased her not at all—the trampling of approaching and unmistakably masculine footsteps.

She was not afraid. But she grew extremely angry, because she wished to be alone and, when she perceived who it was, she was angrier than ever.

Her face pale with rage, she turned, her cloak whirling about her. "Oh, Horace," she said, in a most unwelcoming voice, "why have you come here?"

The young man said simply, "I came after you."

"Why? I do not want you. I wish to be alone."

"Well, I think that's deucedly unsociable of you," said Horace, coming up to her. He stumbled as he did so, for he was heavily built for his age, and the river bank slippery and uneven. "You're a fine one, Mary, I must say. You leave a fellow boxed-up with his aged relatives, and they are all talking about things that happened before I was born—fit to make me die of boredom. And they're stuffing themselves with little cakes, so they'll be sick in the morning, and I say, Mary, you really should get Uncle Edward to do something about his wine merchant—that canary's the vilest stuff, 'pon honor, it is!"

Mary, despite her annoyance, had to laugh at Horace's aggrieved tone, but regretted this immediately, for he at once moved nearer and caught at her hand. He said coaxingly—and now that he was at close quarters, it was plain that, however bad Mr. Vernon's wine might be, a great deal of it had gone down his throat—"Come on. Be friends with me. Why are you always so standoffish? Don't you like me at all?"

She nearly said, "No." The habits of childhood die hard, and it was difficult for her to think of Horace as anyone but the spoilt, stupid little boy with whom she had quarreled so incessantly. But she managed to say, dragging her hand from his, "I do not mean to be standoffish. Of course I like you, Horace, but I am very tired, and it's been such a tedious day, and I need to be alone for a little while."

This plea for pity was a mistake, as she saw too late. Horace said, "You poor little thing. My sainted mama would tire anyone."

"I did not mean that, and you know it perfectly well."

"Well, so she would. But you don't want to be alone, a sweet girl like you——"

"Horace, please don't be so silly!"

"Oh, come on, cousin. Give me a kiss, now. Just one. It'll not harm you and," added Horace ingenuously, "it would do me a prodigious amount of good."

Mary might normally have laughed at this, even given him the kiss he wanted, but now she was nearly in tears of exasperation. She had not till this moment realized how tired she was. She had walked alone, a valiant David planning the defeat of Goliath, thinking to turn the world the right way round for papa, and now she suddenly knew that she was nothing more imposing than a young girl of eighteen whose head was swimming with misery and exhaustion. For one of the few times in her valiant young life she wanted a shoulder to lean on, a hand to wipe away her tears. And instead she had to put up with a loutish young man grabbing at her waist with clumsy fingers, and dodging his head from side to side in a ludicrous fashion, in the effort to press his mouth down on hers. She cried out, a sob in her voice, "Oh go away, please go away. Why can you not leave me alone? You have been excessively rude all the evening, and now you have to come and pester me when I'm so tired I can scarce stand. You was always an odious boy. Do you not know that I cannot endure the sight of you?"

At that he released her. He said quietly, "What a beast you are!" Then, "But perhaps you'll not be so choosy later on. You didn't hear the news, did you? The rebels have just routed Cope's army at Prestonpans. The Pretender's son is now well on his way towards the Border. Are you not pleased, cousin? I should have thought you'd be overjoyed. Uncle Edward must be planting white rose bushes all over the garden. But it'll not last, you know, and you'll not look so proud, my girl, when papa lands himself on the gallows, and you are left without a penny. Perhaps you won't say no to kisses then—and you'll be lucky if you're offered any."

There would, of course, be no one in the morning more sorry about this than Horace. He was really a most good-natured boy, and if the catastrophe he prophesied had occurred, would have been the first to rush forward to help, with kisses or anything else. But he had never been able to take his drink, and now he was not only fuddled but badly stung in his vanity. Mary in her heart knew this, and knew too that she had said things equally unpardonable. But she was confused and unhappy; the temper that consumed her now was such that she would, if her strength had permitted, have struck him down. She fought for self-control. She was thankful that the dark obscured her face. She said at last in a choked voice, "Will you please go?" and made a frantic gesture with her hand as if to push him away.

That gesture was the last straw. Horace cried out in a loud, petulant voice, "I'll not go till I've had that kiss. You think you're too fine to kiss me, I suppose. But you're not. Why should you be? You're always so high and mighty, but you're no better than I am. Oh come on! You might as well give in and be done with it. I'm stronger than you are."

(Horace at thirteen, when Mary was twelve, crying out, "You give it me, I'll take it anyway, I'm stronger than you——")

But now he was fighting for something a little different than a book or a toy. He was quite beside himself with temper and hurt feelings. He gripped her in his arms in a bear-like hug, and pulled her against him. His violence alarmed her. She had not realized he was so strong. This was David and Goliath, indeed—with David getting very much the worst of it. She tried to disengage her hands, but her cloak was caught about her so that they were entangled in its folds. She twisted her head away from him, and cried out at the top of her voice, "Let me go at once! How dare you, how *dare* you——"

Horace had no intention of letting her go. Her struggling excited him very much. But above her crying he heard a strange, rapidly swelling noise like thunder, and this bewildered him so that his arms instinctively slackened. Mary managed to jerk herself free, sobbing with anger, fear and humiliation, her hair wild about her face. What happened then she was too dazed to take in. The thunder roared into the thudding of galloping hooves. The rider—she could not see him properly, but he was black and huge against the skyline—swept across the fields and crashed towards them so that, unable to move, she believed she would be mown down. She could not make a sound; she only stared with wide, appalled eyes. The rider passed within an inch of her, the proximity and the darkness giving him the likeness of some diabolical apparition; as he did so, his right hand with the crop in it swung out and caught Horace, equally aghast, between the shoulder blades with an energy that was certainly unghostly; the startled young man flung up his arms with a shriek and fell backwards with a great splash into the river.

Mary said in a faint gasp, "Oh, God!" She looked incredulously at Horace, floundering in the water, swimming to the bank as well as he could for the dragging weight of his sodden clothes—then, feeling as if she were entrapped in a nightmare, swung round to stare after the rider who had not paused for a second, and whom she caught a final glimpse of, crouching forward on his horse, making hell-for-leather for the open country. Behind her she heard the slithering sounds of Horace trying to haul himself up to the bank, gasping, spluttering and uttering such expressions as would have sent Aunt Briarcliffe into a fit of the hysterics.

Her rescuer—if she could so call him—had certainly not troubled himself further about her safety. But perhaps he knew that few men remain ardent after a ducking. She turned her wild eyes on Horace who, frantic with shock and rage, stood there most deplorably, with a pool of water gathering round him, wig over one eye, and only one boot. Then the laughter began to swell in her throat. She choked, swallowed, pressed her fingers against her mouth, but it was no use, no use at all. The hysterical mirth pealed from her. "Oh, Horace!" she gasped. "Oh, Horace! You look so funny!"

He gave her one look. She could not interpret it in the dark, but she could imagine it well enough. Then he turned and ran back along the path, in a strange, ludicrous, leaking progress, reduced to hopping because of his stockinged foot, and making unpleasant squelching noises as he went.

She wondered if he were hurt, but thought that he could not be at his rate of running. In any case, to ask him such a question would be the final insult. "Oh, poor Horace!" she said aloud. Her anger was gone. She felt somewhat as if it were she who had been thrown into the river. She turned slowly round and stared at the skyline where the rider had disappeared. It had all happened in a flash. She had not the faintest idea what he looked like. All that stayed with her was an impression of someone big above the ordinary, black and swift, and a great arm sweeping out. He had calculated the distance to the inch. A fraction nearer, and she would have been in the river too, or crushed beneath his horse's hooves. And not even to pause——

Mary grew aware that she was shivering with cold. A little weakly she began to retrace her footsteps. She thought of nothing now but this incredible adventure. How excited Nan would be. How she would laugh. Certainly, thought Mary, whose sense of the ridiculous was returning to her, this gentleman, whoever he may be, appears to have the strangest of occupations. Perhaps he was once crossed in love and must attack all courting couples as a point of principle; between his bouts of drowning lovers he will sit by himself in some gloomy turret, drinking himself to oblivion.

I wish, she thought, I had seen him more closely. Then she was exasperated by her own preoccupation, and even more so by the excited jolting of her heart. She paused to set her cloak to rights, smoothed back her hair, then came quietly into the house. She halted outside the drawing room door. The lamplight slitted beneath it still, but there was silence within, from which she deduced that Aunt Briarcliffe must have retired for the night.

She pushed the door open.

Her father was still sitting where she had left him. His dejected attitude knifed through her heart. But at the sound of her entry, he raised his head and smiled.

"Have they gone to bed?" asked Mary, still standing in the doorway.

"Yes. It appears," said Mr. Vernon, "that Horace had an unhappy accident and fell into the river. Your aunt is naturally beside herself with anxiety, and is soothing the invalid with brandy and hot possets, while your uncle stands beside her to soothe her." He looked up at her flushed face and still disarranged hair. "I did not feel I could add anything to the situation. But of course the river bank is slippery."

"Yes," said Mary. She suddenly giggled, then grew grave again as her father's reflective gaze traveled over her.

"Did you push him in?" he asked, as if this were the most natural thing in the world.

"Oh no, papa. He—he slipped." For some reason she did not want to tell him of the violent stranger. But she added with some hesitation, "He tried to kiss me."

"Oh well," said Mr. Vernon, "that is natural enough. He did not mention that to his mother, but that is natural, too. Are you coming in, my dear, or going to bed? I have no objection to your drowning your cousin, for I have always tried to be a tolerant father, but I have the gravest objection to draughts."

"I am coming in," said Mary, and did so, curling herself up on the rug by his feet, leaning back against his knee.

"He is not a bad lad," said her father. "There is no harm in Horace except perhaps that there is no harm in him. He will follow in your Uncle George's footsteps as he is already following in his waistline, do a little discreet gambling in London, a little indiscreet kissing in Derby, and settle down to a decent prosperous middle age. I think, however, Mary, it is only fair to warn you that if you decide to marry him, I shall at once disown you. I will endure Horace as a nephew, for we must all bear our crosses, but I will not have him as a son-in-law. There are, for reasonable men, limits to martyrdom."

"Very well, papa," she said, "I will never forgive you, but I will nurse my broken heart in silence."

He looked down at her, and she up at him. They both smiled. Then Mary said, "Papa——"

"Well?"

"Do you think the Pretender's son will reach Derby?"

"This is Nan's influence—— Yes. It is quite possible."

"And what will happen then?"

"Do you mean, what will happen to England, or what will happen to us?"

"Oh, England can look after itself. What will happen to you?"

"If your aunt heard you speaking in this scandalous manner, she would never match-make again."

"Do you mean," cried Mary, momentarily distracted, "that she really intends for me to marry Horace?"

"Don't disturb yourself, my dear. Your aunt has always intended, ever since I have known her. In any case, Horace may now possibly have other ideas, and he is quite as obstinate as she is."

"It is no good, papa," said Mary, "I am not going to tell you exactly what happened tonight."

"Is it not suitable for an old man to hear?"

"No! It is not. And you are trying to change the subject. What would happen to you if the Prince arrived here?"

Her father's voice changed; it was casual enough, yet there was a hint of despair in it. "It depends how long he stays here. I fancy we may all be swept up behind him like leaves in the wind. I know little of the young man. I believe him to be sincere, but I think in the end that only the bones of his adherents will be left. That is the worst of heroes, Mary. They make their gestures, but a spectre on a pale horse follows after them, and no one sees the death's head for the glory. You are too young to remember the flying man of Derby—it was eleven years ago. A fine fool who caught the eye of the town. His plan to entertain was to slide down a rope, one end of which was attached to the top of All Saints' steeple, and the other to the bottom of St. Mary-gate. And as if this were not enough, he was to draw a wheelbarrow after him, in which was a boy of thirteen. Oh, it was tremendous! How we cheered! It was as if he were falling perpendicular. And then, twenty yards before he reached the gates of the county hall, the rope broke. It might indeed be said that at that point our hero bore down all before him. The whole multitude was overwhelmed. Legs and arms went to destruction. There were a dozen injured and at least three killed. But not our hero. For him there was a pavement of bodies to roll over. He sneaked out of Derby, that very night. The deaths were, after all, not his concern, only his own skin. And that was not even punctured."

He fell silent, and so did his daughter who sat there, the fringe of the rug twisted between her fingers. She said at last, "Papa. Will you promise not to be angry if I say something?"

"I don't remember ever having beaten you more than twice in one day," said Mr. Vernon.

"Papa——"

"You are so be-fathering me, my darling, that I perceive this is serious, indeed. Well? I am tame. Pronounce."

"We have no money, have we?"

"The small sum that your mother left me. A hundred a year or so. I have never saved on my stipend. Your uncle makes me a small allowance. I have accepted it. It was kindly offered, and I did not wish Nan and you to starve. But I do not know how long it will continue."

"I would like to take a post, papa."

He did not receive this with cries of outraged horror. It was not his nature to do so. But she felt the involuntary movement of his knee, though he said calmly enough, "Is this necessary, do you think?"

"Yes, I think so. Would it distress you very much?"

"Your Aunt Briarcliffe will never recover."

"I do not care a rap for my Aunt Briarcliffe. But what do you think, papa? Please tell me. What do you think?"

"I should like to know first what kind of post you are proposing to take, before I give any opinion."

Mary was thankful that her back was turned. A bright flush began to spread over her cheeks. She said, "I wish to go as a companion. To—to the Ventnors."

"The Ventnors!" His voice rang out in astonishment.

"Yes. Oh, I did not mean at first to go to them. But I hear that Lady Ventnor is advertising for a companion and—and——"

He said dryly, "Ah yes, of course. You'll marry a lord. Dark, tall and handsome. Indeed, I believe Ventnor is all of that. They are a fine-looking stock. The old lord was the same. Some admixture of gypsy blood, I understand. They seem to have a fondness for marrying beneath them, so you should be encouraged."

"Papa, this is shameful! Do you really believe I would set my cap at him in such a way? Besides, I am not interested in marriage. Most men are such tedious creatures, and I suspect they only need us for breeding purposes." Then, "I'm sorry, papa. I did not mean to speak so. I—I feel—— Oh, I don't know what is the matter with me, this evening."

His arms came round her. He said nothing but held her close. She perceived how thin and frail he was; she thought wretchedly, I am distressing him, but I must go, and I can never tell him why——

He released her suddenly. "Well," he said, "there is such a thing as love, after all, and not all men are tedious. But I'll not dispute the matter with you. Instead we shall have a little wine. It will temper our emotion." He poured the wine out. His hand, she saw, was shaking. But he went on, "Have you already applied for this post?"

"No. I wanted your permission first."

"That is very dutiful of you, Mary. What will happen if I withhold it?"

"I suppose I should go, all the same." She looked sadly up at him, from beneath the penciled brows that were so like his own.

"I think," he said, "I must tell you a little more about the Ventnors. You will of course do as you choose. No! I am not speaking as an aggrieved parent. Sorrow is as absurd as anger. If you go, you go, and my blessing stays with you, whether you like it or not. But I think you should know a little more of where your decision is taking you."

"They may not want me."

"I do not think there will be so many applicants. I would not let your aunt continue, this evening, for she only repeats gossip. But there are many ugly stories about the family. His lordship not only wears his own hair, thus defying Christianity, but he is, so the world says, a black-avised pirate who rides the moor as if it were the devil's kingdom."

"There must be other such riders about," said Mary in a stifled voice.

He said in some surprise, "Perhaps. Why do you say that? But not—I repeat the town's talk—so many pirates with so fine a person, so long a pedigree, and so few of the world's scruples. Possibly," he added, "a peruke is the symbol of a conscience, and can extinguish devilment as the snuffer a candle. But my sermon days are over. And, daughter, I think I am softening in my wits, for I should have known that to tell you this would only enflame you the further."

She began to laugh. A wild excitement, like nothing she had ever known, held her. She felt indeed quite elevated, though she had only sipped at her wine. She turned her face to her father and he, staring at the flushed cheeks and bright eyes, exclaimed so that she nearly dropped her glass.

He said, in an odd, repressed voice, "Do you know, Mary, I do not think it would be at all wise for this un-wigged pirate to meet you?"

Mary thought this was true enough, but only said, "Why? I shall be a little plain girl reading aloud to her ladyship. He will not even notice me. Does he eat young women for breakfast, then, like the Pretender's son his babies? Tell me more about the family. They sound like something from the *Inferno*."

"I can only repeat what I hear," said her father. "Yet he was a fine little boy—— But his mother was alive, then. The present Lady Ventnor, as your aunt has told you, was the cook. Perhaps the old lord liked her cooking so well that he must needs eat her into the bargain. There is a stepbrother, Nicholas. A quiet boy, much under Ventnor's thumb. They say the thumb is not a gentle one. The family—in this your aunt is quite correct—are rabid Jacobites. And Wardwick Hall is set in isolation in the midst of the moors, beneath the shadow of Kinder Scout. If you go there, Mary, you will be very much alone."

"Do you think I would be afraid?"

"I am only afraid you might have cause to be. A man is termed a pirate when he rides against the law, and such a man is perforce dangerous." He said with sudden intensity, "Why do you wish to go there? The stories may be untrue. But the fact that they follow the Stuart cause is indisputable, and that has its own perils. There are other posts, are there not? Other old ladies. It would be difficult for you in Derby, but there is always London, and your aunt, however much she may disapprove of you, would be there to help if need be."

"I would not like London," said Mary, "and I fancy London would not like me. And I have always loved the moors. I am not afraid of pirates, I get on famously with old ladies, and I have a good reading voice, or so you always told me."

"You are a shocking girl," said her father, "headstrong, hot-tempered, outspoken and with the deplorable possession of a mind of your own. I can prophesy nothing for you but Gothic damnation. Nonetheless, I would not have another kind of daughter."

She cried joyfully, "I will write tonight."

"Does Nan know of this?"

"Not yet. I'll not tell her till I'm certain."

He said gravely, "You really could not endure the thought of staying with your Aunt Briarcliffe in London? I know she is a foolish woman in some ways, but she has a good heart, and she would do her best for you, and Nan, too. You do not lead much of a life here. I do not pretend that routs and balls and the playhouse are the sum total of existence, but they can add a little gaiety to it. It would not harm you to play the fine lady for a while, and I am sure you would do it very well."

"I see," said Mary. "We would dance and sing and be merry, while you, my dearest old man——"

He began to laugh. "I should box your ears for that."

"But you are my dearest old man, papa. My very dearest. And while we are making the very stars in the firmament flicker in the volume of our song, you would be sitting here, starving yourself, thinking of things that are best forgot, and with no naughty daughters to tease you back to life again."

"Hannah would never let me starve. And you'll scarce be teasing me from Kinder Scout."

"I'll be home for the holidays. And Nan will be here. There'll be no moping with Nan around."

"Good God, no," said her father in some exasperation. "What with the rebels defeating Cope at Prestonpans, I can see that my future will be scarce worth living. Well, Mary. You must have your way. I daresay you'll tame your pirate in the end. You have never lacked courage. You must take your diary with you. We shall all look forward to your account of high life on the moors."

"I will give you regular readings when I come back. I shall be well accustomed. You will find me far more dutiful."

"Then be dutiful now, and go to bed."

"Yes, papa." Then she flung her arms about him. "It will be all right in the end. You'll see. I promise it will."

He said wearily, in the fretful, aged voice that was sometimes his, these days, "This must have been very hard for you. I would give everything that I possess that it had not happened to you. You should not have to work. You are young——"

"You are talking like Aunt Briarcliffe."

"Oh, you are quite impossible! Worse even than Nan. Go to bed, before I take my stick to you." His voice was normal again, and his smile very tender.

They went upstairs together. She kissed him goodnight outside his room then, holding her candle absentmindedly so that the wax splashed on to the floor, went into her own.

But she did not sleep. She found herself listening, as she had listened every night after those dreadful, un-

believable days not so long ago. She remembered the stones
at the windows, the shattered glass, the obscene, menacing letters slipped beneath the door. Even then he had
said little. But at night the horrors had come upon him,
submerged the strong spirit in dream-wrecked sleep, so
that he had groaned and muttered, calling out things
she did not understand, naming people who had died long
ago—and once, as she would always remember, crying
out in a great voice the name of Mary's mother, and then,
"I cannot endure it, I cannot——" He was moaning a little
now. She could hear the faint sound across the landing.
She crept out of bed, and softly opened his door. He was
asleep, an old man who had aged some twenty years
in as many days. But the face, still and cold, was upturned to the ceiling, taut in its grief and anguish, and
as she looked, she said below her breath what he had
never said, "It is not fair, not fair——" pushing away
thoughts of a God she could no longer believe in, and
thinking with savage satisfaction of the vengeance she
would exact from a pirate who rode the moors and tramp-
led down the innocent in his path.

But when at last she slept, she dreamt not of revenge
but of another rider whom she had scarcely seen, who
had swept past her like a lightning flash, and in her dream
he gathered her up in his outflung arm and rode off
with her to some black, bleak moorland, with Kinder Scout
looking down upon them.

II The Companion

From the town of Derby to this moorland inn, in so brief
a space of time. To be waiting there at the *Jacob's Ladder*,
huddling against the cold in the new fleece-lined cloak
that Aunt Briarcliffe, protesting to the last—"This is so
ungenteel! That a niece of mine should *work* for her living!"—had given her———

Oh, God, how quickly the time had gone! It was the
beginning of November now, and she still could not believe it was all happening to her, though she was seated
in the stagecoach outside the George Inn, with her portmanteau, the new cloak and an enormous parcel of food
from Hannah who said ominously, "You was always
too thin. You'd best have one decent meal, anyways,
summat inside of you in case it's the last you get." She
had said goodbye to her father and Nan—Nan in tears,
floods and floods of tears, Nan like Niobe, a fountain of
grief, clinging round her neck, wailing, "Don't go, don't
go! They'll be horrid, I know they will, they're mad, they'll
ill-use you, they'll beat you———"

Her father said, calmly enough, "Well, Mary, you
cannot pretend you have not been warned. Hannah
prophesies you will be starved. Nan prophesies you will
be beaten."

"And what do you prophesy, papa?" she demanded,
half-laughing, yet not far from tears, herself.

He said, "Oh, I prophesy that you will carry all before
you, you will tame the mad Ventnors, discipline their
politics, and so terrorize his piratical lordship that he'll
not dare emerge into the light of day without his peruke,
and Kinder Scout, itself, will bow before you."

"I am a companion, sir, not a schoolmarm."

"There are various forms of instruction, and not all

44

of them involve the ferrule. But I'll leave you, daughter, for otherwise this brat of mine will necessitate an ark rather than the 'Derby Dilly' to carry you."

She watched them go. With them undeniably went home, warmth and safety. And as she sat there, mittened hands folded in her lap, and an ominous lump rising in her throat—she could hear Nan's sobbing halfway up the street—she saw a large square-built form emerging from the inn.

"Horace!" she cried, and flung open the door.

He stood there, looking up at her rather furtively, the embarrassed redness creeping into his face. She had not seen him since the episode on the river bank; he had left for London the next day without even saying goodbye to her. But he stood there now, and presently he blurted out, "Damme, I had to say goodbye, didn't I? And," he added with an unexpected flash of humor—probably a great deal of wine had gone to float this courage—"I thought I'd kiss you—oh, in a cousinly way, you know—and—and well, there ain't no river here——"

"Oh, Horace!" she cried again and, leaning forward, held up her face to him, her hands catching at the lapels of his coat.

"Pon honor," he cried, eyeing her, "I don't know if you deserve it. And my coat cost all of fifty guineas, so kindly don't ruin it for me."

"I deserve nothing," said Mary, "but please kiss me, Horace dear."

"I've a mind not to," said Horace.

"Then I shall have to kiss you," said Mary, and did so with fervor, at which he went so red that it seemed as if he would choke. But he put his arms about her, a little gingerly, and held her with such tenderness that at last the tears did come, and she began to cry against his padded shoulder.

He said, rather muffled, "I don't know why you have to go. You was always a mad girl."

"Well, they're mad, too," wept Mary, much comforted, "so we can all be in Bedlam together."

He shook his head. His eyes rested wistfully on the

slender nape revealed to him. But he only said, "Well,
I've brought something for you."

"A present? Oh, Horace——"

"Well, it's not exactly a present—— I mean, a present's
something pretty, ain't it?—a sort of gewgaw, the kind of
fustian girls like—— It's not what I'd call a present."

"But what is it?" Mary sat back and stared at him.

"Well, it's—— I'm giving it to you, all right. But it ain't
a *present*——"

"Oh, Horace, for pity's sake!"

He looked away from her. He rummaged for a moment
in his pocket. Then he laid on Mary's knee a small ivory-
hafted pistol.

She stared at him, speechless.

"I thought you might need it. It works. You put your
finger here—of course you don't want to have mittens on—
and you press so—— What the devil are you laughing at?
Of course if you're so deuced proud you can't take what
a fellow offers you——"

"I'm not proud, and it's sweet of you, but——" She
abandoned herself to laughter, then stopped suddenly.
The driver was climbing up into his seat; the passengers were ready; the "Derby Dilly" about to go. But it
was not only that. It was the realization that the small thing
her fingers had touched with apprehension was not a
toy; one pressure would put the most efficient period to
a man's life. And perhaps she would have need of it.
Up till now she had thought of herself as the avenger.
And now she saw that she was only a young girl, slight
and small, pitting her wits against a giant, a pirate, whose
fingers could squeeze the life from her. She was driving
into danger, perhaps a grave on the windswept moors.
Vengeance was, after all, two-edged.

She leant out to wave at Horace. She had never thought
to feel so fond of him, so sad to see him disappear. He
stood there in the inn yard, waving back, a stout ungainly
figure, like some forlorn schoolboy going back to the classroom.

But it was she who was going to the classroom. She
slipped the pistol into her reticule. Sitting very upright,
she watched the familiar landmarks vanish, one by one.

Exeter House, with its ferry at the end of the garden, and the branching chestnut, now bare of leaves, overlooking the river. The church spires of All Saints (where the mountebank had slid down his rope), St. Werburgh's and St. Alkmund's, with the twelfth century building of St. Michael's in between. Nan and her father would be home by now. But Nan would have stopped crying. She was a good child, and a brave one. She would take her responsibilities seriously, and know that now she must look after her father. She would grow motherly and rather bullying, saying, "Now, papa, sit by the fire and I'll bring you a glass of wine." If tears were to be shed, it would be only in the privacy of her room.

And no more tears for me, neither, thought Mary, raising her head and not even noticing the smile that one of the male passengers was bestowing on her. No more tears from now on. Oh, she thought, her fingers touching the hard bulge in her reticule, you little know, my fine pirate, what is coming to you, if what I believe is true—— You little know.

Of course it had not been all tears. Up till the end it had been magnificently exciting. The letter applying for the post, with a reference from the vicar of All Saints, and from Mr. Franceys, who was after all the best-known apothecary in Derby. Then the answer, written not by the old lady (perhaps she could not write?) but actually by the pirate, himself. His signature, a bold, masculine sprawl of "Ventnor" flung half across the page. Mary had studied that signature. It was her first sight of the enemy. If that black, defiant hand told its tale fairly, it indicated an opponent worthy of her steel. She examined it from every angle, reading into it all kinds of menace and evil. But the letter was abrupt and to the point. She was to take up her post on November 5th. On that day a hundred odd years ago, another gentleman had planned to blow up Parliament. It seemed an appropriate date of departure for Miss Mary Vernon, who was planning to blow a Jacobite plot sky-high, and it was not necessary to remember that Mr. Guido Fawkes had been by no means successful. And then the preparations, the packing, the constant scenes with Aunt Briarcliffe who kept on coming down from London and, when she did not come in person, bombarded her with letters: "My dearest Niece, I cannot comprehend, *I cannot,* why you should leave your *Home* and your dear *Father,* so *young* a Girl, and so *unnecessary,* when my Home is *always* at your Disposal! I can only *pray* you will not *regret* it, and *beg* of you to change your Mind before it is *too late*——"

Aunt Briarcliffe's letters were always a series of shrieks.

And Hannah, saying more and more grimly, "They are mad. And *he* is a devil. You must be out of your mind, Miss Mary. If I was your father, I'd lock you up on bread and water till you came to your senses."

"At least," Mary remarked to her father, "no one has any right to be astonished if I come to a bad end, for they are all waiting with shovelfuls of soil to cast on my grave." She added, for Mr. Vernon's eye was not altogether encouraging, "But it is all quite preposterous. This is 1745, not the Middle Ages, and the law takes exception to the doing away with of young women."

"The Romans camped beneath Kinder Scout," replied Mr. Vernon gravely, "and the Saxons before them. You will see their traces. The moors are old, Mary. They have seen the passing of century after century. They are not concerned with laws; they make their own, and so do those who inhabit them. I would wish you were not going but, since you are set on it, I will say nothing further." He added surprisingly, "Yet I feel quite sorry for Ventnor. I doubt he has ever been up against anyone like you."

That had been comforting, and towards the end she had needed comfort, God knows. Even Nan, once so set on the idea, had grown more and more dismal during the last week.

"Mary," she said, that last evening, sitting up in bed, "why must you go? It's so plaguy far, and so plaguy cold, and they live right on the moors. You'll not be able to dance. There'll be no young men."

"You're an empty-headed little girl," said Mary cheerfully. She wondered why children in their nightgowns must always look so pathetic. "I have not danced for some time now. The Assembly Ball Rooms do not make me welcome. In any case I do not need to dance, and I do not need young men. Is that all you think of?"

"If you stayed here," said Nan, "you'd meet that wonderful man again, who knocked Horace into the river. Oh, that I'd been there to see! How I would have laughed!"

"I am not sure if a habit of knocking people into rivers is a desirable trait in a husband. And why should I meet him again, pray? He did not show much wish to continue the acquaintance."

"Oh," said Nan, round-eyed, "I think it is fated. You will meet him again. I know it."

"It'll probably be me in the river, next time. Oh, let us stop talking of husbands and suchlike. There'll be time later for all that. After all, child, I'm only eighteen."

"I'll be married at eighteen. I'll not be an old maid like you."

"You're worse than Aunt Briarcliffe. Oh, Nan," said Mary, her voice beginning to crack, "you know I don't really want to leave you." She checked herself. She must never give Nan the faintest hint of her secret. "Only we do need the money so badly. We cannot continue to live on charity, and it does not look as if I'll make a rich marriage, or do any of the things that are expected of me. And now I shall be earning, and I shall save every penny of it, so when I come home again I can perhaps say to Aunt Briarcliffe, 'Thank you very much, we do not need your help any more, we are financially independent.' Besides, it might be quite entertaining, after all. They all sound so mad."

"You don't really want to go. You can't want to go."

"But I do. I do, Nan. It's an adventure. A strange land —and stranger people. I told you, did I not, that his lordship crops his hair like a farmer's boy, and does not even wear a peruke."

"But he's a gentleman," protested Nan; she was a conventional child.

"Is he? Well, I suppose one can be a gentleman without a wig. Though I doubt if Ventnor would be a gentleman if he wore three, each on top of each other."

"Shall you call him Ventnor?"

"I should hope not, indeed. I trust I know my place,"

said Mary in a genteel voice that made her sister giggle.
"Maybe behind his back I'll call him a deal of things. But
to his face he shall be my lord, my lord, and again my
lord—— Nan! Stop giggling. It ain't so droll, after all.
Not if I believe half the things Aunt Briarcliffe has been
telling me. Every time she comes down she relates some
fresh horror. I think she must spend all her time with the
Ventnor family archives. Though, indeed, I cannot believe
that one tenth of her stories are true——"

"What, what? Oh, tell me!"

Mary, glancing at her small sister's flushed face, paused.
Most of Aunt Briarcliffe's stories were quite unsuitable for
Nan's ears. They would frighten her; besides she might repeat them to papa, and that would not do, at all. "He is a
wicked man," her aunt had announced in a sepulchral
whisper; most of her vituperation, Mary noticed, was reserved for the elder son, though from all accounts, a deal
of it might have been spared for the stepmother. But
then depravity in a six-foot pirate would be more stimulat-
ing than in the guise of an old lady. Aunt Briarcliffe went
on to talk of murder and worse; there was no doubt that
she greatly enjoyed herself. Mary, who had not enjoyed it
quite so much, said to Nan, "Oh, she talks nonsense as
usual. About the stepmother—— They say of her that she
tormented the guts out of her stepson when he was a little
boy, and he has never forgiven her and hates her like
poison. Her own son, Nicholas, is ten years younger than
Ventnor; they hate each other too. You will see, my dear
Nan, that it is an excessively merry household. No doubt
on the Sabbath we'll all rise up on our broomsticks and
celebrate some saturnalia on the moor."

"If they all hate each other so much," said Nan, "why
do they all live together?"

"Ah, don't ask me," returned her sister sharply. "Who
am I to answer for the quality's actions? I am only a
clergyman's daughter, after all. Probably because they are
all so detestable that no one else will live with them. But
I expect this is all Aunt Briarcliffe's nonsense. One could
scarce live permanently with Uncle George, without an
outburst of fantasy now and then. Life with the Ventnors
will, I suspect, prove tedious and dull. I shall converse

with her ladyship, do the sewing and read to her out of some pretty book. I shall yawn my head off."

"And then his lordship will fall in love with you," suggested Nan.

"Ha!" said Mary, in a most ungenteel fashion. "You have been reading novels again, my girl. No. The Ventnors may be mad, but I'll lay they ain't as mad as that."

"Well, I don't see why he shouldn't. You can be quite handsome when you choose."

"And you are a pert little baggage, whether you choose or not. But I will inform you how our romance progresses from the first enflamed glance to the final passionate kiss."

"Perhaps you'll see the Chevalier. They say he is marvelous handsome."

"Stuff! The Pretender's son—and I wish you will not call him the Chevalier—will never get near Derby. What do you think the Duke of Cumberland is there for?"

"He is just on the Border. His precious Highness don't seem to be stopping him."

"You little Jacobite! You'd best go as companion instead of me."

Nan suddenly clung to her. "You will write? You must—— Don't let them harm you. If they're horrid, come home."

"Ah, my darling, don't be silly. They'll not be horrid. After all, they are human beings like everyone else."

But, on the long journey, she wondered in her heart if they were. The tales were so ugly. And Nan was right: it was unpardonable that people should live together in hate. In her home there had always been love and peace. Catastrophe had threatened the peace, but it could not destroy the love. The unease did not show in her pale, composed face, but it stirred within her like the toothache. She was not afraid of the old lady, whom she visualized as some apple-cheeked countrywoman, nor of Nicholas who seemed to be a nonentity, but the thought of Ventnor disturbed her to the point of fear. She had made a great many inquiries on her own. He had been in Derby on that dreadful day, he had stayed near their house, he was suspected of sending out money to the rebel forces. A man of his character would not hesitate to save himself by ruining an inconsiderable old clergyman. She set her mouth. She remembered again that day when they had brought her father back, a white, shriveled old man with the bloody rents in his ears. In normal circumstances *he* would have been safe enough. Money could buy safety. Even when they flogged a gentleman, the executioner said "sir" before he used his lash. They did not put lords in the pillory. But they put their heads on the block, sometimes, and these times were not normal, and perhaps Ventnor had found himself in danger of something worse than having his ears nailed down. Perhaps he had chosen to escape the law by setting the blame on someone else. But, if he were guilty, he should not escape her. A passionate feeling of protectiveness for her father, combined with wild anger, warmed her despite the increasing cold. In her life she had never harmed so much as a mouse, but so resolved was she now of Ventnor's guilt that she could only visualize him on the gallows.

The stagecoach traveled north to a part of Derbyshire that she did not know. Past Matlock they went, and along to Bakewell where they put up for the night and changed horses. The snow was falling fast now; the wind blew bitter cold. The dales, which they crossed the next morning, must be magnificent in the spring, but now they were black and bleak. They suited Mary's mood, and she stared at them from the window frosted with her breath; she could understand why the Ventnors chose to live as they did, why they seldom came up to town.

The other passengers were talking eagerly of the rebel army, in between grumbling at the weather, for the coach had to stop several times for the wheels to be unclogged. It seemed that Charles was at Kelso, near the Border now, with one foot poised to step into England. And once across the Border, what was there to stop him? David was advancing, and Goliath, it seemed, many leagues behind. Mary barely listened. She was near her journey's end. For the first time a violent panic caught at her. Ventnor loomed in her mind as vast and impregnable as Kinder

Scout, whose bulk she could see grimly lowering in the distance. He was the mountain, and she the mouse. Unconsciously her hand felt for the pistol in her reticule; her heart and breathing were both out of control.

The "Derby Dilly" jolted to a standstill. She saw that they had arrived at the coaching inn where, according to her new employer's abrupt instructions, she was to be met. Abrupt indeed was the word. "You will alight," he had written, "at the *Jacob's Ladder*. You will be fetched. You will please to wait in the yard."

Mary, stepping out into the slushy snow, lifting up her petticoats as she did so, to the interest of a youthful loiterer, grimaced. So she would please to wait in the yard. It was, after all, November. Perhaps he had not realized that the snow would be lying thick, but a simple exercise of imagination might have suggested that it would be more agreeable for a young girl to wait in the inn parlor by the fire. However, she had a strong impression that if she were not in the yard as instructed, she would not be escorted at all, so, wrapping her cloak about her, she stood there, her portmanteau at her feet, with its label inscribed in Nan's childish pot-hooks, Miss Vernon, Wardwick Hall.

She averted her eyes from this. Instead, she turned her gaze on the moors, for the *Jacob's Ladder* was like some toy inn that man had defiantly planted in the midst of the wildest scenery that nature could contrive. She stared at the plateau before her, desolate in the cruel cold. Snow-white, it stretched as far as her town eyes could see, with not a tree, not a house, to break its ruthless, primeval barrenness. Her father's words came back to her mind. Saxon eyes had looked on this. Roman centurions had dented this surface with their sandaled feet, and the snow had swept down to blot them out; here man was of less significance than the smallest fly. The wind blew across it, its force unchecked by human barrier, howling like a wolf after its prey.

She pulled up her hood, and began to pace up and down the yard. Obviously it was natural to a noble family to keep a mere companion waiting. Her fingers and toes were pricking with the cold. To add to her discomfort, the *Jacob's Ladder* did not appear to be an inn of a superior kind. No doubt it was all that was to be found in the district. The men going in and out seemed mostly to be farmers. They scarcely glanced at her, and talked, in their strong accent, of sheep foundered in the drifts, and the new murrain that had descended on the cattle. There were also one or two officers from a neighboring garrison town. These did look at her, and in a way she did not like. She wrapped her cloak more closely about her, and kept her gaze steadily fixed in the direction from which her employer's carriage must come.

When one gentleman had the effrontery to reach out his hand and twitch aside her hood, she swung round, furious, to meet a young and tipsy face grinning down at her.

She cried out, in her most forbidding tones, "How dare you! Please go away at once."

"Why," cried the young man in the betraying accents of the gay and elevated, "it's a pretty young girl. We don't have enough young girls in these parts. I think—I cannot see you very plain, ma'am—but I think you must be quite handsome. Remarkably trim waist, damn it, remarkably trim waist. I hope you will d-do me the pleasure, ma'am, of p-partaking of a glash—pardon me—a glass of wine and——"

"I will do nothing of the kind," said Mary coldly, "and you will please to leave me in peace, sir." And saying this, she turned her shoulder on him, and gazed once more at the moors.

"Oh, what a hard-hearted girl," cried the young man. Really, thought Mary, his mama should not permit him to drink so much—— "But I'll not be refused, damme, ma'am. A small glass of ratafia, now. Come, I must insist. Your arm, my dear. It will serve to keep out the cold—oh, good God!"

And, before she could wither him with her ladylike scorn, before she could even begin to express her opinion of the gross impropriety of his conduct, the young man, with a quite startling celerity, had leapt from her as if she were an adder, and sped into the inn as fast as his drunken legs could carry him.

She was so astonished that she could only stare, her mouth fallen a little open. She was accustomed to think of herself as a plain girl, but, nonetheless, young men did not usually run from her. When a deep voice said at her elbow, "I gather that you are the young woman I am to bring back for slaughter," it seemed an ideal lunatic conclusion to the insanity that surrounded her. She turned to meet its owner, very flushed about the cheeks, but otherwise almost resigned to whatever new shock would descend on her.

She could not, however, pretend to make the efficient, sedate impression she had planned. The icy wind from the moor blew back her hood again, and seizing her hair in rough fingers, twisted and tangled it so that she was half-blinded. She flung up her hand to push it back, and so stared into dark, considering eyes more than a head above her own.

She knew at once that she had met her enemy. She had thought they would send a coachman for her, but this was no coachman though, God knows, he was dressed like any roaring boy from the city alleys, with rough riding clothes, high boots, shirt unfastened at the throat; his cropped black hair was wild, and there was nothing more lordly in his hand than a riding whip.

Her enemy. The pirate. For the moment she forgot how sadly she was at a disadvantage, caught in a situation of unmistakable absurdity. She forgot that she was a young girl of eighteen, many miles from home, alone in a wild countryside that was strange to her. So this, this was Ventnor. Her first thought was: But how enormous——— And then: How black! Black hair, black clothes, dark eyes, face arrogantly boned and burnt to a dark brown by sun and wind. This then was the six-foot pirate who ruled his moorland province; the devil who had perhaps set her father in the pillory, and who, if gossip were to be believed, had sullied his reputation with enough brutality to make him an outlaw.

Her enemy. But also her employer. His formidable

magnificence—her feminine eye could not but notice this
—crushed within her the hope that this might be an easy
victory. Victory, if victory there could be, would be won
at the sword's point. This Goliath would take a deal of
beating. There was intelligence in the high forehead and
great, dark eyes, and even—she saw this with discomfort
—a suggestion of humor. This angered her. It was almost
as if he were laughing at her. She had already envisaged
a total lack of amiability; she refused to allow him the
smallest saving grace. However, his next remark proved
satisfactorily that there was little enough amiability in
him; she was blown, it might be said, from a ten-pounder
straight on to the battlefield.

He said, in a voice plainly created for calling men to
battle from across the Border, "I see there is no occasion
to apologize for keeping you waiting. You have obviously
been able to occupy your time."

If Mary had been momentarily seduced by a magnificent head, and a vast pair of shoulders, she found this
the most efficient antidote. She was not often bereft of
speech, but now she was so angry that she could think of
nothing to say that was in any degree sayable. She glared
at him. She could not but see that the first round was not
in her favor. She was too proud to excuse herself, but
stare she could and, if there were a certain stir (as rep-
rehensible as it was feminine) within her that the face
confronting hers was so worth staring at, this only increased her mounting fury.

He waited for her reply. As there was none, he said
impatiently, "Well? Shall we go? You are late. I called
here an hour back. Do you ride? I suppose not. You look
the prim little town miss to the life, though——" Here he
checked himself, but the flicker of humor that Mary had
already remarked appeared again in his eyes.

She said, stiff-lipped, "I am afraid I do not ride. I am
—sorry you have had to wait, but we were delayed by
the weather. The roadway is deep in snow. Four times
we had to get out while they lifted the wheels up again.
Besides, there is a rumor of the Pretender's son's arrival
at the Border, and this occasioned delay at Bakewell."

"The Pretender's son!" She could not miss the mockery in his voice. "You'd best not speak so to her ladyship. A staunch Hanoverian I see:

> *"The Stuarts' ancient, free-born race*
> *Now must we all give over;*
> *And we must take into their place*
> *The bastards of Hanover."*

Then, ignoring her look of affront, he continued, "But loyalty undoubtedly pays."

"Not always," she said, her voice shaking.

"What? What the devil are you talking about? Come. I've no time to waste. Do you wish to take farewell of your cavalier?"

This was more than flesh and blood could stand. Mary cried, with some sharpness, "If you are referring to that drunken soldier, I should like to point out to—to——"

He misunderstood her hesitation. He said abruptly, "Ventnor. I am the elder son. There is also my stepmother and my half brother, Nicholas. He is twenty. It is no use your setting your cap at him, neither, for if you do, I'll have you sent straight home, with a good piece of my mind to speed your departure. We have had enough mismarriages in the family."

This was so outrageous and unwarranted that for the second time she was robbed of speech. But he only went on, "This way. You'd best give me your portmanteau. You will have to ride on my horse. I suppose you can contrive not to fall off. You were wishing, I believe, to point something out to me?"

She found to her dismay that the tears were insidiously creeping into her eyes. This was a poor beginning for battle. But she was tired and cold and hungry; she would have given the world to be home again, with Nan to cosset her, and her father to make her some ironic little discourse. His lordship seemed as rough and monstrous as the moors that encircled him. She choked a little, then said in a muffled voice, "I merely wished to point out, my lord, that the gentleman you refer to is quite unknown to me. I am not," she added in sudden rage, "in the habit of speaking to strange men in inn yards. He was drunk."

"I know the fellow well enough," returned Ventnor indifferently—he was making no effort to steer her across the slippery, snow-trodden yard. "If he has insulted you, I will see that he is reported to his commanding officer, tomorrow."

She was quite horrified. She began, "I did not mean——"

But he had already gone ahead to lead his horse up to the gates. The half-sentence was blown from her lips by the wind from the darkening moors. She could only stand there, folding her arms across her breast. She said aloud, "Detestable!" For the moment she forgot her desire for vengeance, and longed with all her heart and soul for Derby, that pleasant little country town with its abundant trees and fine arches, and the silk mills to give employment to poor and rich alike. Then, alas for valor, the tears would no longer be restrained. They began to rain down her cheeks. There was nothing round her but this old, cold, black, barren waste of land. She was momentarily deafened and blinded by her misery, and she started as a hand came down on her arm.

"I know," he said in a voice that held a surprising hint of laughter, "that I am detestable, but you really must not stand there sniveling. I gather that you passionately desire to run home to your mama."

"I do not," said Mary, stung back to self-control. "And I am not sniveling. I—I have the headache." Then the full impact of his words struck her. She looked wildly around her, thankful that the darkness hid her blushes.

"It is a traitorous wind," said Ventnor gravely. "And yet," he added, "on the whole I am less detestable than my stepmother, and I feel at this point that you should compose yourself and make up your mind. If you cannot endure me, you will certainly not be able to endure her. You are, after all, extremely—I would almost say, excessively—young."

"One can at a pinch," she said, recovering herself, "endure anything. Did you say I had to ride?"

He looked down at her. It was too dark for her to see his expression, yet she sensed it was not unkindly. Then, without a word, he lifted her up as if she were no heavier than her little sister, Nan, and put her sidesaddle across his horse. Then he mounted behind her, and placed his arm about her waist.

He said abruptly, "You'd best hold on. The path is treacherous."

It was snowing again. She was compelled, much against her will, to clasp him as if they were lovers. It was disconcerting, yet it made her smile that, sworn enemies as they might prove to be, they should be so entwined. She found the proximity disturbing, but dared not let go. She could feel the steady beating of his heart. How enchanted Nan would be!

He said, with a sudden harshness, "Who are you? Oh, I have read your references. I know you are a clergyman's daughter. I know you are a young woman of unblemished reputation, brilliant intellect and of a sweet and patient disposition. Not that I have remarked an excessive sweetness up to date—— A vicar spoke for you, did he not? And Mr. Franceys. I have not a great acquaintanceship in Derby, but I believe he is the sole apotheary who is allowed to attend the Assemblies. Physic is, after all, a great class-leveler. But all that means nothing. I wish to know more about you. The worst cheats have the best references—— Are you laughing at me?"

He must have felt her tremble; he would know it was not fear.

She said steadily, "You'll not let me snivel, and now I must not laugh, neither. But I will answer you. My father is a clergyman no longer. He was impeached of Jacobitism in March of this year. Letters were found in his possession, addressed to 'V'. Our name, as you know, is Vernon. As yours is Ventnor. All the evidence was against him. He might have been hanged. But they set him in the pillory, in the market square. For two days. He is sixty. They—they nailed his ears to the pillory. I am sure you are interested to know this. Perhaps this time it is you who will laugh."

He said, "Naturally. Naturally to me the barbaric laws of our land provide an endless store of merriment. For if one is not laughing at the pillory, one is laughing at the stake, and so by mathematical progress to the gallows where one laughs till one chokes. So you are the daughter of an impeached Jacobite?"

"No," she answered, "I am the daughter of a good man who could never even dream of treachery, who is so gentle and kind that even now he does not consider vengeance. But I am neither kind nor gentle, and I think of vengeance a great deal."

"Why," he said, "I have misjudged you. You and my stepmother should get on marvelous well. And now you shall hear about us, for I am a fair-minded man in my destestable way. For myself—why, doubtless you have already judged me, and condemned me, too. My stepmother is an old witch whose sole love is the handsome Chevalier, him whom you call the Pretender's son. She is the most detested woman in the county. She likes a mouse to play with. But she has tired of me, for she dare not strike me now, and her words no longer touch me. And my half brother is a mild-seeming boy who cringes too easily for the both of us. She wants a new victim. She has decided on a companion. An all-male household proves tedious. Besides, she likes to talk, and we are not paid to listen to her. You are. You will listen, Miss Mary, to her words and her laughter. For, like many who are devoid of humor, she laughs interminably."

"You speak so of your own mother!"

"My stepmother, I beg of you. She is no blood relative of mine. We have always detested each other. I was eight when she married my father. She never gave me one word of kindness. Perhaps I did not deserve it, yet at that age one craves occasionally for some pretence of gentleness. But do not let this disturb you. My half brother will comfort you. He is politer than I am. Are you laughing again? What the devil ails you?"

"You paint so charming a picture. You are trying to frighten me," said Mary. "Yet I am not so timid as you think. Sir! There is someone hailing you."

And, as she spoke, a great roar of "Ventnor!" surged upon the air.

(Not "My lord," she noticed—no respect here, no subservience.)

"Why, man," came the roar again, "are you running away? They say the Scottish boy is perilous near us, with his unbreeched banditti armed with claymores, and skirling away at their heathenish pipes."

It was, as far as she could see, a great burly man, with the look of a shepherd; sacking was tied round his head and shoulders.

Ventnor reined in his horse, and bent down, extending his hand. "Why, man," he said in rough imitation, "I've been breeched for many years now. Would you have me swoon before petticoats? Let the bonny Prince come, and we'll guarantee him a bonny welcome. Well, Sam? How does life go with you? How's the wife and family? I've forgot the number. You increase too quick."

"New one on the way, Ventnor," replied the shepherd, unabashed. "New one on the way. You'll have to raise my wages, sithee."

"I could comment on that," said Ventnor, glancing sideways at his companion, "but this young lady is new to us, and would not care, I fancy, for such freedom of speech. This is Miss Mary Vernon. She has come all the way from Derby to teach us gentility. She is to be my stepmother's companion. We are to be whistled to heel."

"Poor lass," said Sam, and tipped his hand to the astounded Mary.

Ventnor righted himself and laughed. "You were always impudent, man," he said, "and so, thank God, am I. We are well-matched. One day soon we'll fight it out between us, and you can see if you can get my head in the sheep-dip—— Poor lass, indeed. She'll find herself the lost ewe presently, if I'm not mistaken."

Sam said, pulling the sacking further over his head, for the snow was now blanketing down, "They say t'neighbor's bitch has gone raving mad, and is killing off the sheep. We're all out for her, to shoot on sight. When a dog gets the taste for blood, it's done for."

Ventnor received this in silence then, urging on his horse so violently that Mary nearly fell off, raised his gloved hand in passing and brought it down with an enormous crack across Sam's shoulders, the sound clapping in the dark like a pistol shot.

Mary was quite appalled, then perceived that this was nothing but a masculine expression of friendliness, for the shepherd broke into a vast laugh, shook his crook at them, and roared, "Man, it'll be the sheep-dip for you—— Wait till you're by again. Give my respects to her ladyship. Tell her not to devour all her sheep."

Ventnor gave a brief laugh, waved his hand, and then they rode on in silence. Mary, seeing at last some kind of building in the distance, said, breathless with the jolting, and discomfited too by the nearness of her enemy who held her pressed against him, his chin just above the top of her head, "Is that—— Is that Wardwick Hall?"

She instantly regretted this, for he at once stopped. It did not seem to enter his head that this was an unusual setting for a *tête-à-tête*, though the dark had now fully descended. They halted there in an elemental night, the snow blown before them, the clouded moon cratering the white-blanketed ground.

She cried out, forgetting her question, "It is like the end of the world."

"But what an ending," he said. His body stirred a little. "Do you know," he said, "I once went up to London, when I was a young boy. Oh, some cousins of mine thought to do me a good turn, to show me the glories and gaieties of town life. I stayed there three days. I was taken to White's, where I won a great deal of money. They said it was beginner's luck, and smiled on me. When I walked out with my winnings they said I was a country bumpkin and smiled no longer——"

"Did you wear a peruke?" asked Mary. Then she was appalled at herself; so might she have spoken to Horace, but this was not Horace, this was a stranger, her employer and her enemy.

"I think," he said, in a voice that bore out all her misgivings, "you are the sauciest young woman I have ever met. Did I wear a peruke! Yes, ma'am, I did. Society would never have countenanced me, if I had not done so. But it is no concern of yours. How dare you be so impudent to me?"

"I am not well schooled in servility," said Mary, turning her head towards him defiantly, though, what with the darkness and the falling snow, she could not make out his features. She added, "Any more than you are in courtesy, my lord. But will you not continue with your story? For I am very cold."

"Have you ever been out as companion before?"

"No, my lord. But I am used to dealing with school children, and that is a most efficient training."

"Then why, schoolmarm, am I so unschooled in courtesy? I feel that at the moment I am being quite unnaturally polite. You had best beware lest the schooling is not so one-sided. Well? Answer my question, please."

"You made me wait in the inn yard!"

"I have already explained——"

"When it would have been more suitable to stay in the parlor. You also accused me of making the acquaintance of a drunken soldier, when you must have known that I should never dream of doing such a thing. But if I have been impudent, I apologize, for indeed I did not mean it. However, I daresay you did not mean it, neither, for I understand you have no sister, so perhaps you do not understand women very well."

He said after a pause, "Have you done?"

"Yes," said Mary in a small voice, and wondered privately how it was that she had permitted her tongue so to run away with her. If the adventurer within her was secretly delighted and entertained, this was not entirely without apprehension. But at this moment her hand touched the pistol inside her reticule, and she remembered that this man might be the enemy she was out to destroy; her fear intermixed with an angry defiance. However, her new employer's continued silence and immobility—as if, for all the world, she thought, the sun were in the sky, and it were midday—impressed themselves unpleasantly upon her attention. She said, determined not to be terrorized, though her voice shook a little, "Will you not conclude your story, my lord?"

He still said nothing, and at last she could not endure it. "Oh!" she cried, clasping her hands together, and nearly falling off as she did so. "This is absurd! I think, indeed, I have come to a mad house. My lord. It must be all of nine o'clock. It is November, and the temperature surely below zero. I know you are angered with me, but I cannot believe it is your intention to freeze me to death. Will you not please tell your tale, and then perhaps we may go on, for surely your stepmother will be wondering what has happened to us."

Ventnor said, "It seems you must do the talking for both of us. And the story now lacks point. It was indeed only started to exemplify how ill I suited the town life, and how far more at home I am in this wilderness. But whether you will be at home here, I am beginning to doubt." A roughness crept into his voice. His hand came down on her shoulder and gripped it. "Are you normally so free of speech?"

Mary raised her chin. "I have always lived," she said, "in a home where one could speak one's mind without fear or favor. But I will try to cultivate meekness, if my outspokenness displease you."

"I think," he said, "you would find it advisable. Upon my soul, I do not know if I should not take you back at once to the *Jacob's Ladder* and leave you there—by the parlor fire, of course to find your way back to Derby as well as you may. I had not thought I was bringing a vixen into the chicken house." The hand on her shoulder tightened so that she almost cried out. He exclaimed, "The damned bitch!"

"My lord!"

He gave a half-laugh. "Did you think I was speaking of you? I might well have been. But I suppose if I did so, I'd only receive another lecture, and I doubt my temper would stand the strain—— Look!"

He moved his gloved hand up to her cheek, and pushed her head so that she was forced to turn. "Look!" he said again, then angrily, "Good God, you town misses can only use your eyes for ogling. Can you not see?"

The moon for an instant shone clear out of the clouds. The whiteness of the snow dazzled her. Yet she thought she could perceive the faintest speck moving across the surface. She stared, but after a second it disappeared.

He muttered, "If only I had brought my gun——"

"Was that the killer dog?"

"That, my dear, is the killer. That signifies another dead sheep or so with its throat plucked out, another trail of blood upon the snow. Oh, God," he cried in a kind of exasperated roar, "that I should be unarmed—"

Mary said in a clear voice, "I havé a pistol, my lord, if that will be of use to you."

"Ah, it's too late now. She's back to her brood with—— *What* did you say?"

"I said that I have a pistol." She had been pleased with this. It would warn him she was not to be trifled with. But his reaction was not what she expected; he burst out laughing.

"Good God!" he said. "Good God! This is not a vixen I am bringing home, but a highwayman. Though I seem to remember that your sex has taken to the road, these days—— Do companions always go armed?"

She did not answer. She was afraid; she saw that her admission had not been a fortunate one.

He said more quietly, but with an underlying grimness to his words, "You are very foolish." His hand descended on hers, pulled it away from the reticule, then lightly brushed against the hard bulk of the pistol. The clouds had scurried across the moon again so that she could not see him clearly, but she was aware that he was staring at her. He said, almost as if he were speaking to himself, "I don't know if—— Oh, well. You shall keep your little toy. I am sure you are an excellent shot. Come—— We'll go. And that building, God save us all, is not Wardwick Hall. Do you think we live in a rabbit hutch? That is a derelict cottage with its shippon attached."

"Its——?" repeated Mary faintly. The elation had died in her; she was tired and chilled to the bone, though they were now galloping along.

"And you a Derbyshire girl! Do you not know what a shippon is? Ah, but I'd forgot—you come from the town. It's a cow-byre. It is no longer used, and the cottage is uninhabited, save by a ghost and an echo."

"A ghost!"

"Does that frighten you? But it need not. It's a poor thing. A child, so they say—a little boy frighted out of half his wits, and angered out of the other half. A wretched puling brat, who once spent half his days there. He is not even worth your shooting down. He is gone, long ago. Fear destroys, and anger too. But the echo survives. You must meet it one day. It will match you in talking, word for word, so even you will be outdone. You see, Miss Mary, we provide you with everything here, even with ghosts. What tales you will tell your grandchildren! But we are nearly there. Do you not see?"

Wardwick Hall was, after all, no witch's den. The Ventnors were undoubtedly mad, but they wore their insanity in comfort. Mary, expecting some black, Gothic ruin, was amazed to see the Hall sprawling comfortably, in surprising elegance, across the moor, with its vast farm lands behind it; lights shone from all the windows.

"Oh," said Ventnor indifferently, "we light the lamps, but not for company. My stepmama is seized by the fever of entertaining from time to time, but our nearest neighbors live some ten miles away, and we are not, for some reason or other, the most popular of hosts." She could see him clearly now in the light from the house; there was a gleam of derision in his eye. "Do not imagine, Miss Mary, that this is a gay house filled with dancing and laughter." As he spoke, he lifted her down. "If that is what you expect, you had best let me book your seat on the 'Derby Dilly' for its return journey. There was once laughter in this house, and happiness too, but that is over. And indeed I believe I have come to prefer it so. I am no boy of quality to think the rattle of dice and the giggling of silly women anything desirable. The silence of the moors is for me my true background. Will you go in, please, while I stable my horse? You will find the door unlatched. Walk straight in as if you own the place." Then before she knew what he was about, he had seized her reticule from her, and pulled out the pistol. He held it in the palm of his hand. It was a beautifully shaped hand, as she could not help but see. Then he held the weapon out to her. "There," he said. "It's cocked, ready for use. You do know how to use it, don't you?" But her instinctive recoil answered for her, and he began to laugh again. "My dear young lady, you must learn. You hold it—so.

You press this—— Even the mad Ventnors will succumb to its charms." Then he said angrily, "Here. Take it. Put it away. And I suggest you do not let my family see it."

Mary was left standing outside the main entrance. She could hear a faint sound of music. She hesitated. She could scarcely look on Ventnor as a comforter, yet it would have been easier to introduce herself if he had been at her side. She glanced back over her shoulder at the snow-blurred outlines of Mam Tor and Bleaklow Hill, with the plateau of Kinder Scout merging into the clouds. It all looked dreadfully wild and cruel, but its very savagery seemed a reproach to her cowardice, and put her on her mettle.

She pulled off her mittens with a gesture as of a declaration of war, pushed open the door and stepped inside.

The hall was a blaze of light. It was a beautiful house, but her feminine eye at once perceived that it was very much a man's house. It seemed that Lady Ventnor was not of the housewifely kind. The pictures—mostly portraits of piratical Ventnors—hung crooked, frames undusted, the oils so black as in some cases to be indistinguishable. The stair carpet must have been priceless, but was wearing sadly in places as if hobnailed boots had torn it down. Plaster flaked down from the high ceiling, there were cobwebs in the corners, and a thin salting of dust on polished surfaces. Yet the atmosphere was neither gloomy nor evil. The house's beauty had survived its neglect like that of a woman who only needed attention to set herself to rights again.

The wind from the moors streamed in at the open landing window, blowing a thin powder of snow before it. Mary instinctively put out her hand to close it, then reflected that this was not yet her business; if the Ventnors liked snow on their carpets, it was no concern of hers.

She walked up the stairs, in pursuit of the sound of music, then, on the first landing, turned the handle of the door opposite and came inside.

Her entrance was too quiet to be at once noticed, so she stood there, her hands folded in front of her, a small, insignificant figure looking about her with a seeming composure that disguised the swift-beating heart and breath grown uneven.

It was a vast room which, like the house, must once have been magnificent. There were only two people there. One of them, a young man, sat at the harpsichord, strumming at it in a vague and desultory fashion. Hovering at his side was an old woman whom she assumed to be the housekeeper—a squat, savage-looking old lady with snapping black eyes, overhigh color, grizzled hair that was half away from its pins, and a torn, black gown covered in snuff and stains. Mary looked at her in some dismay; Hannah would have called her a "slummock." She disliked at once the greedy, stupid face and the enormous peasant hands that from time to time rubbed at her skirts as if to remove the dirt. She hoped that her work would not bring her overmuch into this person's company. There was a grossness to her, a vulgarity and brutality that was distasteful. It was strange that the Ventnors should employ such a person. His lordship, for all she disliked him, was plainly not devoid of sensibility in his own way; a man who had such a passion for the scoured wildness of the moors must surely wince from this ill-bred, unkempt creature. However, it was no doubt difficult to find servants for so out of the way a place, and the family, perhaps, had to put up with what they could find.

Her gaze came back to the young man and, as she looked at him, he slowly turned his head so that his eyes met hers. This, of course, was Nicholas. He was quiet unlike his formidable stepbrother—tall, too, but not so tall; slighter of build, fairer of hair, with mournful gray eyes, and a face that was a monk's face, sad, withdrawn, vulnerable in its youth and beauty.

He rose to his feet and came towards her. He looked exceedingly young. As he came up to her, he smiled. It was a generous yet deprecatory smile, and Mary's heart warmed towards him. She thought, this is someone whom I can like—then, meeting the frank admiration in his eyes, remembered with some dismay that she was, after all, only the paid companion, and that too much friendship would not be seemly.

(He had said, "It's no use your setting your cap at him——")

She flushed at the memory, then smiled back, dropping a curtsey as she did so.

He said—his voice was like himself gentle and pleasing—"You are Miss Mary Vernon. What ails my brother that he does not escort you in? You must be nearly froze to death. Come by the fire."

Ventnor's voice came from the doorway, so roughly that she started. "Your brother, Nick, finds his horse as worthy of attention as a young lady. There are, after all, plenty of young ladies, but few mounts as good as mine. But you can always erase any bad impression that I may have made, for you are as always the little gentleman. Take her to the fire, for God's sake, give her wine or whatever else she asks for, and stop playing the gentle martyr, for I suspect this young woman is shrewd enough to strip us of our fancy trimmings. Do you keep a diary, schoolmarm?"

Mary flushed again. It seemed to her that his lordship had a disastrous flair for asking the wrong kind of question. But she was not allowed to reply, and neither was Nicholas. All further speech was drowned in a crackling gale of merriment from the vulgar person in the black dress who shrilled out, "A fine little miss from the city! Is this all you could lay your hands on, Ventnor? Why, 'faith, she looks as if the winter winds'd blow her away. Come here, girl. Let's have a look at you. Don't pay no attention to Nicholas—he's a fool, and don't pay no attention to Ventnor, neither—he ain't a fool, but he ain't the master of this house, not by a long chalk he ain't. I'm master here, and you'll come and make your pretty speeches to me, and if you ain't the sort of piece I want, you can go home instanter, and that's all there is to it."

Mary thought she heard Ventnor laugh. She was, however, too confused by her appalling error of judgment to be sure. This disgusting woman who looked so dirty and so ill-bred, whose laughter was still pealing on, was no housekeeper but her new employer. She came up to her ladyship—it was hard to think of her as such, and harder to believe that the old Ventnor could have married her, despite her good cooking. Perhaps in her youth she had been comely, but now, God knows, she was dreadful, and that laugh! Does she laugh like this all the time, thought Mary, and at nothing at all?—for indeed, if she does, I shall end by being as mad as the Ventnors, themselves. She stood there, as the old lady looked her up and down in a most insolent fashion, then said grudgingly, "Oh well, I suppose you'll have to do, but I never saw such a skinny bit of goods in my life. Couldn't get yourself a man, I suppose, so you're out a-hunting. You'll not find any men here, dearie. Nick ain't a man, at least not when mama's looking—and as for Ventnor, you can have him with pleasure, but I'd as soon take a Derby ram, myself."

How they harp on marriage, thought Mary, but she said as composedly as she could, "I have not come here to marry, ma'am. I have come to work. Marriage these days has become a business proposition which is best arranged at home. I am sorry to be so late, but the coach was delayed by the weather. I should be glad if your ladyship would have me shown to my room, for the journey has been a long one, and I should like to unpack my things. Unless of course you wish me to start my duties now——"

The old lady was still eyeing her, as if she were some creature at a fair. The laughter was tittering forth again, but the black eyes were as hard and cold as pebbles. "Duties!" she said. "Duties! I wont to be looked after——"

"I will endeavor to do so, ma'am."

"Endeavor! Speaks as if she's a mouthful of pins, don't she? We ain't so genteel here, miss. We don't want none of your high-and-mighty town ways. I want to be talked to. And read to. I'm a poor, lonely old woman. I need a bit of cosseting at my time of life, and precious little I get from these two boys who think of mama as a piece of dirt and would as soon kick her out of the way——" Her voice rose to a screech. "Nicholas! God damn you, Nicholas!"

"Yes, mama," said Nicholas, quickly stepping forward.

Mary heard Ventnor murmur, in a mocking voice, "Yes, mama——" but Nicholas seemed unaware of the taunting mimicry. He stood there in an attitude of such humility that it hurt Mary to see him. She turned away, thinking, I must go home, I cannot stay here, I told Nan they were human, but they are not, they are not—— Then for the second time she met Nicholas's eyes. There was in them a most desperate look of entreaty. It was not in Mary to refuse such an appeal. All her life she had been urged on by a passionate protectiveness—for Nan, when their mother had died, for her father, for so many who had asked for her help. It glowed now within her. At that moment nothing would have driven her away from Wardwick Hall. She dared give him only the briefest of looks, but it said as plainly as words, Don't worry, I'll not go.

The old lady, ignoring her, was in the midst of some long complaining speech, then suddenly burst out, "Sing us a song, Nicholas. Sing us a pretty song. I'm sure the young lady would enjoy it. It's the only thing you can do, ain't it?—a milksop like you. You bore me, Nicholas. Ventnor don't bore me, but I'll cut his throat one of these days—— Go on! What are you waiting for? I said, 'Sing,' didn't I?"

Nicholas, without a word, went back to the harpsichord. He played a few chords, then began in a subdued but pleasing tenor,

> "Come o'er the stream, Charlie, dear Charlie, brave Charlie,
> Come o'er the stream, Charlie, and dine wi' Maclean——"

Mary, still standing, for no one so far had thought to offer her a chair, lowered her eyes. A fine nest of Jacobites I have fallen into, she thought, then jumped as that astonishing laugh burst out again, smothering the final cadence of the song.

The old lady was crying out, rubbing her hands with glee, "He's come o'er the stream, oh, he's come o'er the stream—— We'll see what'll happen now. His bloody

Highness waiting for him with his lovely army and all, and can't do a thing about it—he'll be running like Johnny Cope yet, and serve him right——"

Mary saw Ventnor look as black as thunder, saw Nicholas's face tighten up. Then Ventnor went over to the harpsichord, pushed his brother away, and shut down the lid. He swung round on Mary. He said, "We've had quite enough of this. You'd best go to your room, schoolmarm."

The old lady began—she was not laughing now—"So you didn't like that song, Ventnor? So it wasn't good enough for you? You think you can order people around in my house——"

He interrupted. "It is not your house, madam. It never was. It is my house and, if I cannot have order in it, I will at least have a little discretion." He held out his hand to Mary. "Come," he said. It was unmistakably an order. "I will show you to your room and have supper sent up to you."

Nicholas at this stepped forward. He said in a shaking voice, "I could take Miss—Miss Mary upstairs."

"Oh, I daresay you could," replied his brother, "but these are early days yet, and instead you can give your mother some of the attention she so urgently requires, and try to check her from crying treason to the world and its companions."

Mary followed him out. Walking up to the next floor, he said briefly, "My stepmother's rooms are on the ground floor, together with the dining room. The library faces the drawing room. You may use it if you wish. Do you read?"

"I can piece words together here and there," replied Mary. As he did not answer, but continued on his way, she said with less assurance, "I am taking you away from your family, my lord. Can the servants not show me where my room is?"

"Servants?" he repeated. He swung round to face her. Standing some three steps above her, he seemed enormous, so that her hand instinctively gripped the banister. "Servants, indeed! We have no resident servants, ma'am. We are too agreeable a family to keep them. They do not care for my stepmother's incessant cascade of mirth; my own temper is not of the most reliable, and my young brother— Oh, we all have our oddities, and they are not of the kind to make a stable household. Our servants come in the daytime, and leave at nightfall. The only one who lives here is old Betty, and she has known us from the moment of conception and is inured to anything. She is hard of hearing. It helps." He turned round again. "Your room is on this floor. My brother and I have rooms across the corridor."

"I see there is one more floor," said Mary, staring up the well of the staircase. "Is that where Betty lives?"

They were facing each other on the second floor now. He said softly, "You are very inquisitive, Miss Mary."

She opened her eyes wide at this. "Am I? I'm sorry. I thought it was necessary for me to know where everything was."

He said, after a pause, "There is nothing up there which need concern you. Nothing. Do you understand?"

"Perfectly," said Mary, filled now with a firm decision to explore the top floor at the earliest opportunity, though her voice could not have been meeker, and her eyes were demurely lowered.

He said, almost unwillingly, "If you really wish to know, there is nothing there but storerooms, and an old attic where we used to play as children. It is never used now. Betty sleeps down in the basement, and seldom comes upstairs, only cooks for us, and reminds us from time to time of a youth we would prefer to have forgotten. This is your room." He added, in a burst of annoyance: "They have not even lit the fire. But I see your supper is waiting for you. One moment——"

He stepped in before her. It showed some lack of propriety, she thought, that he should come into her room, but probably in so mad a household such a thought would never cross his mind. Kneeling before the fire he struck his tinder and lit it. For a while he stayed there, watching the flames flicker up, while Mary, overcome now with fatigue, and wishing he would go, stood behind him. Then he slowly rose to his feet. "It will burn," he said. "The wood is very dry." He strode back

towards the door. There he paused and, to her surprise,
smiled at her. "I do not believe you are a timid girl,"
he said. "Do you think you know how to deal with us?"

Mary returned the smile. "I told you," she said, "that
I am a clergyman's daughter. It is sometimes imagined
that a clergyman's daughter leads a sheltered life. That
is not so, my lord, believe me. One learns to deal with
difficult parishioners and unwilling children, and one is
always on a tight rope, for the clergyman's daughter is in
the limelight and, if she goes against convention, at
once has the parish against her. I believe, then, I shall
be very much at home here, and I hope I shall give satisfaction."

He repeated in derision, "You hope you will give
satisfaction!" Then he laughed. "Why, I hope so too. For
your own sake. Well, Miss Mary, I will wish you good
night. Is there anything more you require?"

"Yes!" She moved quickly up to him. Her face was
eager and young, its caution dropped. "You can tell me
where to take my letters. My father will wish to know
that I have arrived, and my little sister—she is only
twelve, my lord—will be anxious for my news."

"Are you proposing to go out tonight to post your
letters?"

"Why, yes."

"You would have to walk twenty miles, my dear. The
snow is lying thick, and a Highlander might leap out of a
drift at you."

For the first time she was not only disconcerted but
genuinely distressed. He saw this, and said more gently,
"I will take your letters for you, tomorrow. Your little
sister will only have to wait one day more, after all. I'll
see that she is not disappointed."

"Thank you," she said in a flat voice, then, "Good
night."

When he had gone, she threw her cloak on the bed,
and knelt before the fire. This meant that she could only
send the briefest letters home. She would trust none of
them; she dared not write down half the things she
wished to say. She had forgotten that Wardwick Hall
was in the wilderness, how completely she was cut off

from the outside world. A cold depression descended on her, despite the heat from the fire. She stared round the room in fatigued despair; there was little to comfort her. It was small and bare, sparsely furnished, with not one feminine touch to relieve it, not even a picture on the wall. Then she thought of Nicholas, and her courage began to return to her. Here was someone who needed her help, and this was a challenge she could never resist. Poor boy! With such a mother, and this stepbrother who bullied him, he was far more in need of friendship than she was, with her father and Nan back in Derby, and the faithful Horace, too. She began to eat her supper with a good appetite and after this was so restored that she thought she might go down to the library, to look for a book.

She hesitated a little, but after all it was a perfectly reasonable thing to do; not even Ventnor could object. She lit her candle—it was wax, she noted, not tallow— and stole softly down to the first floor again. She heard the faint sounds of the harpsichord, and a faint giggling laugh that even at this distance could send shudders down her spine. She closed the library door behind her. The only light was her candle flame. Before the windows stretched the moors, with the wind howling across them. She stared out, fascinated by the beauty and savagery of the scene, scarcely glancing at the bookcases that lined the wall, though she could see that the library was a well-stocked one; the Ventnors were at least not illiterate. She could not take her eyes off this white expanse, with the flurrying snow blown across it; she exclaimed aloud, "Oh, God, how beautiful it is."

A voice replied, "If you knew how weary one grew of it— How one longs for the ordinary sights and smells and sounds of town——"

She whirled round, unreasonably disconcerted; she had fancied herself alone. But she knew at once who it was, from the low, unhappy voice. She leant back against the window ledge to stare up at Nicholas; she could scarcely discern his face.

"Did I frighten you?" he asked. "I did not mean to. I

came in here for a moment because—— Oh, but now you know how it is with us. You cannot have a good impression of any of us. I wished for a space of peace. Books do not dispute with you, nor do they indulge in fits of temper. But you are not here to receive our confidences. You wish to be alone—— Would you not prefer me to go?"

"No," said Mary. "You can help me to choose a book, if you will. That is all I came down for. But I had not realized how magnificent the moors could be, and I could not take my eyes off them."

He said suddenly, "Are you a Jacobite?"

"I am beginning," returned Mary with temper, "to hate the very word. No, sir. I am not. But I see it is a subject on which I had best hold my peace. My position, after all, is surely not a political one."

Nicholas said dryly, "We hold violent beliefs here."

"Which extend, I understand, to Derby. Do you often go to my home town?"

"I? No. I am the little boy here, Miss Mary. I do what I am told. I am a very good little boy. I would never dare to assert myself." She could not miss the bitterness in his voice, and half-held out her hand. But he went on coolly, "And like all good little boys I stay mostly at home, while my big brother amuses himself elsewhere. He is often in Derby. He was there a few weeks ago."

"In March, I believe?" said Mary, adding untruthfully, "I believe I saw him in the streets. He is not easy to forget."

"No. He is not. But I believe he was in Derby then. And in September, too. He often goes. I do not ask why. In this household it is best not to ask questions. Tell me something of yourself. How many are you at home? Do you have brothers? Do young men kill each other for love of you? After all, we have been thrown into acquaintance with a pitchfork; we must know something of each other."

She was pleased to talk of Derby. It shifted a little of her homesickness. She did not speak much of her father, but told him a great deal about Nan, and mentioned her disappointment in not being able to post her letters.

Nicholas cried out, "I will always post them for you. It would be a privilege and a pleasure." His voice altered. "Has my brother offered to do so?"

"Yes."

"Then—will you forgive my saying this?—will you please be very careful? I think perhaps it would be better if you gave your letters to me. I must go now. They will be wondering where I am. I have not found you a book, I'm afraid, but if you wish for a light romance, there are some novels on the bottom shelf. I hope you sleep well." He added below his breath, "Don't be afraid. Whatever happens, don't be afraid."

Mary saw him hesitate by the door, a shadow in the dim-lit light. The next instant he was gone. She heard the sudden loudness of voices as he opened the drawing room door.

She still remained there, staring out at the moors. She was very tired, but so confused were her thoughts that she was almost unaware of it. When at last she stepped over to the bookshelves, she thought how strange it was that though she had been in Wardwick Hall for barely three hours, she should now find the life at Derby with papa and Nan—dead Nan, probably now crying into her pillow—a hundred years away.

She took out at random a couple of books—some poetry and a volume of essays; neither particularly suited her mood, but she felt she must have some reason for coming downstairs at so late an hour. She came back into her room and, throwing more logs on to the fire which was now blazing high, sat down at her table and began to write to Nan and her father. She had intended to pour out all that had happened, but now she hesitated, the quill poised in her hand. That Nicholas was willing to help, she did not doubt, but he was so pitifully under his brother's thumb; besides, if she refused Ventnor's offer, he might grow suspicious. In the end she wrote briefly, describing her journey at some length, but only saying of Wardwick Hall that it was a most beautiful

house, and that her new employers were being very kind
to her.

Then she took her diary out of the portmanteau, and
began to write in it as if she were talking to Nan.

> *"I will admit,"* she wrote, *"that his Lordship is
> handsome in his own Way, tho' for my Part I would
> prefer a Barbary Pirate.* YOU, *my romantic Fool, would
> be enraptured with a Pair of magnificent dark Eyes, a
> fine, arrogant Profile, a Chin as stubborn as Kinder
> Grit-stone, and Cheekbones that would do well modeled
> in Bronze. There! Are you not already swooning?
> And in Addition, my Doll-sister, not only is he a Lord,
> but he is even a six-foot Lord, or perhaps more, as
> well as my Eye can judge, and even his Voice is grand
> and deep, and he speaks like the Mighty who own the
> Earth. But oh dearest Nan, it only proves what I
> have often preached to you, that Looks are not every-
> thing. I have never so instantly taken a Dislike to
> Anyone. I have indeed never met Anyone so* EXCES-
> SIVELY *disagreeable. It seems as if my Lord were
> given such Looks to compensate for the most shock-
> ing Disposition———"*

There was a warm color in Mary's cheeks as she wrote
this. When she had penned the word "disposition," she
laid her quill down. There was no denying that his lordship was disagreeable, but there was no denying, neither,
that such looks were not to be met with amongst her
father's parishioners. Her preaching to Nan, therefore,
was intended rather for herself; she grew angry as she
realized that the thought of seeing this shocking gentleman tomorrow had aroused in her a certain pleasurable
excitement.

She slammed her diary shut, and put it carefully
away. And then for a while she rested her forehead on
her arms.

Outside on the snow-covered moor, a bony, gray-white
thing slunk out of sight among the hummocks, leaving a
red-dotted trail behind it.

III The Elder Son

Mary found that, as the week went by, her duties, though not arduous, took up all her time. She had the impression that by deliberate intent she was never alone. She did not see her watcher, but instinct warned her that he was there. It was certainly not the old lady, who kept mostly to the ground floor; she was crippled with rheumatism and seldom came upstairs. Nor was it Betty, a harmless old body who lived in her kitchens, who spoke lovingly of "my boys," and to whom even Ventnor was surprisingly charming.

Naturally she met the young men at every odd hour of the day. They both worked in the farm lands attached to the back of the Hall, but they strode in and out of the house continually, leaving great marks of slushy mud upon the carpets, and Mary could not believe that it was entirely by chance that every time her eye glanced up the attic stair, Ventnor seemed to materialize at her elbow, and when she looked longingly at the great writing desk in the library, Nicholas should at once engage her on a somewhat aimless conversation about her favorite authors. Both brothers seemed determined to guard her, either for her protection, or theirs.

She could not really complain. Ventnor was not a man much addicted to courtesy, but he spoke fairly enough to her, and—she could not help marking this to his credit—always as if she were an equal. At least, she thought, when he discarded his peruke, he discarded his lordly airs as well. And so she waited, though the waiting was hard, and the letters she received from Nan and her father so gay and amusing that they nearly broke her heart. Winter had come to Derby, too, it seemed, and her father was old and in ill-health. There was a guarded reference to a cold—"nothing serious, of course," wrote Nan, who sent the most delightful letters, illustrated in the margin; a brief mention of Aunt Briarcliffe "who nags at me like an old Hen-wife, and swears we neglect ourselves, and seems to think, darling Mary, that you are now buried in a Snowdrift, with his Lordship's Perouk on top as a Headstone." There was little mention of visitors and friends, though Nan wrote in her second letter that Horace had been down to see them, looking "like a sick Dog, I vow he is mad for Love of you, and he will go for long Walks by himself, perhaps to swim in the Derwent to remind him of old Times." Mary giggled at this, then suddenly had to blow her nose, at which Ventnor, who had just come in from some excursion which seemed to warrant bringing half the moorside with him, looked at her sharply.

"Well?" he said, coming to stand over her. "Are you still sniveling for papa? Shall I play the paternal role, and take you on my knee to comfort you?"

She said coldly, "I never snivel," then with a suppressed sob, "Except when Nan writes to me. She is such a good child, and I love her dearly."

"And how is the little sister?"

"Oh, well, I think. Only my father ails always in this weather. He cannot really stand the cold."

"Then he must do as my mother does," said Nicholas who had followed his brother in. "Bank up an enormous fire, shut the doors and windows, and stay there till the Spring comes."

Mary said rather bitterly, "Wood costs money, sir." She rose to her feet, adding as she did so, "You would both like Nan. She is a violent admirer of the Pretender's son."

"We must fetch her down," said Ventnor, eyeing her; Nicholas was silent.

"Oh, I think you would get on famously. She would put up with no nonsense from you at all. She is a child of spirit."

"I see," he said, "there is a marked family resemblance."

She saw no reason to answer this, but she wondered if

it were true. She was sure that Nan, in her circumstances, would have contrived long ago to search the attic, and would probably in a few days have learnt more about the Ventnors than they knew themselves. She wondered, too, if Nan would ever endure the old lady, with her hysteric laugh.

One would not grudge her laughing," she wrote in her diary-letter, *"but what she says is always insolent and never amusing. And once she starts, she will not stop. Oh, and the things she says! But indeed they are not suitable for you or anyone to hear. Not even my Diary can receive such confidences."*

A bawdy tongue, a talent for detecting the soft places in one's armor, a passion for sweetmeats with which she continually fed herself—— The old lady sat in her sitting room, with windows tight shut, and a fire that burned night and day, so that Mary, coming in to read to her, sometimes thought she would faint for lack of air. She said nothing, but the stepson was not so restrained; he scarcely even came in, but, when he did, would exclaim in disgust, "This stinks like a fox's hole! In God's name, ma'am, why don't you let in a little fresh air? You'll stifle the town miss to death. She's already the color of whey."

The old lady would swear back at him, while Nicholas who, it seemed, was compelled to endure the readings with her, would sit there in silence, and Mary would stare into the fire and wish within the fastness of her rebellious heart that mother and stepson could draw their swords and kill each other off. How they roar, she thought—it is like the wild beasts in the jungle. The old lady had a fine flow of obscenity at her disposal, and would hurl gobbets of this at Ventnor who would drown her crackling with his stentorian roar. Once, in the midst of a brawl of this kind, he caught Mary's eye and burst, much to her annoyance, into a great shout of laughter, swinging round on her as he did so.

"How you look!" he said. "How you look! Oh, God, such propriety to each eyelash, such vituperation to the tilt of the nose, a challenge in every turn of the head. Do you find us overloud, Miss Mary? Do we shock your

gentility? Do we offend you by our coarseness of speech?
One day, you shall speak your mind, as man to man,
and then I believe we will all wilt before you. Did I not
ask you if you kept a diary? I swear you do, and I swear
there's such damnation in it as would blow the Highlanders over the Border again, their kilts flapping in the
breeze." He saw the color creep into her face, and
grinned triumphantly. "You do keep a diary. Confess it
now. Will you not read it out to us? It would give her
ladyship relief from all the romantic nonsense she stuffs
herself with. Indeed, I suspect it would give us all a
bellyache from which we'd none of us recover."

And that is true enough, thought Mary, refusing to
reply, but unhappily aware of the old lady's sudden
interest, and the way in which the cruel black eyes were
surveying her. She was relieved, though apprehensive,
when Nicholas said mildly, "Miss Mary is surely entitled to her privacy. What she writes in her diary is no
concern of ours."

His brother stepped up to him, saying in that soft
voice of his that frightened Mary far more than his
roaring, "Have you been looking at it, Nicholas? What
does it say? Are there perhaps some pretty tributes to
you in it?"

Nicholas had risen to his feet. He was very pale.
There was a look upon him that Mary had never seen
before. He said, "I do not spy on people. I do not follow
them round and remove them if they cross my path. But
then you see, brother, I do not have illusions as to my
own grandeur. I am content to live peacefully, and let
other people do so, too. I think perhaps it is safer."

And with this he left the room. Mary could not but
notice that he did so rather quickly. When she saw
Ventnor follow him, to the accompaniment of a delighted shriek from the old lady, she momentarily closed
her eyes.

"Well, miss?" shrilled the old lady, "Well? Where's
my novel? I want to know what happens. You're paid
to read to me, ain't you? You're paid to do what I tells
you, not sit there all pale and genteel as if you was the
lady, not me——"

Mary began hastily to read again. The old lady had a passion for romantic three-volume novels of the most tedious kind. Mary did not know which she disliked more, these or the indecent tales that were the alternative. She had not received a conventional upbringing, and her father had encouraged her to read what she chose, but the dirty, sniggering stories offended her dreadfully, especially when they had to be read in Nicholas's presence.

Nicholas distressed her more and more. Herself a determined character who had always stood up to her enemies, she could not understand why he was so afraid of his half brother who ordered him about, threatened him, snubbed him, until Mary could only dig her nails into the palms of her hands to keep silent. Why should an able-bodied young man of twenty endure such treatment? He could surely at last leave home——

She could understand Ventnor's attitude even less. She saw a great deal of him and found to her dismay that she could not hate him as she intended. She began to wonder if her suspicions were unfounded. They had, after all, been pure hypothesis. Every time she tried to refuel her dislike, she found him at his most disarming.

He remembered, it seemed, her tears over Nan's letter. This homesickness did not entirely leave her and once, when it was unendurable, she had gone up to her room and wept, not coming down again until she was certain all traces of tears were gone.

She went into the library, to find Ventnor there, in his disreputable riding clothes and with his hair wild, crouched before a cupboard that ran the length of the wall beneath the bookcase. She wished to leave, but he glanced over his shoulder at her and said, "Wait!" Then: "Your sister. How old is she?"

"Nan?" said Mary in some surprise. "Why, twelve."

"Then I have something here that you might care to send her." His eyes roamed over her face as he spoke. "You have been crying." As he said this he came up to her, putting his hands on her shoulders, which astonished her very much.

She nodded, trying to smile. It was not much of a

smile. She said, "It is foolish of me. But sometimes I think of my father, and then I suppose I grow sorry for myself. It is not important. It does not occur often. It is one of the privileges of our sex, after all, though not one I usually profit by. If a woman weeps, the world is sorry for her. If a man weeps, the world despises him. Why, even you are sorry for me, my lord."

"Even I!" He smiled down at her, a little derisively. "But weeping is not the prerogative of women, after all, though men may tell them so. Why have you been crying? I do not believe it is just homesickness. Are you unhappy with us? It is not the gayest of households for a girl, though I cannot believe the world did not warn you before you came. We are well known. Has my stepmother ill-used you?"

"No, of course not. Her ladyship——"

"——Is the most consummate old bitch," said Ventnor, "as well I know. If she dares to raise a hand to you, you will tell me immediately. It will never occur again."

"I did not know," said Mary, "that there was so much danger involved in being a companion."

"These are hazards in every profession. Has no one —no one—harmed you or threatened you?"

"No!" Then she laughed. "What could happen to me here?"

"Have I—have I hurt your feelings in any way? I have a rough tongue, but I mean you no harm. Well? What have I said? I cannot apologize, you know, if I do not know what I am apologizing for."

She was quite bewildered, and moved too, though against her will. She said weakly, "You have said nothing. It is a fit of the vapors. You make me feel ashamed of myself. Tell me what you have for Nan. To receive something from you will swell her head to such an extent that there'll be no talking to her when I come home."

And at this point she had the most extraordinary conviction that he was on the verge of kissing her. There was no movement on his part, no perceptible change of expression, yet the atmosphere between them snapped and flickered in a way that stirred her, left her feeling weak and bewildered. However, he did not do so. Perhaps he saw the incredulity in her eyes. She decided the next instant that it was purely imagination on her part, for he moved a little away from her, and said calmly, "You shall send her this. You shall tell her it is from the mad Ventnor who devours little girls for his supper. I will have it parceled up for you, and sent by carrier before the snow becomes too heavy to get through. It belonged to my mother. No! I do not mean that cackling old she-devil downstairs. She is nothing to do with me. An ill wind blew her here, and she is like a poisonous plant that takes root and spreads over healthy foliage. This is something from the old days when this was a happy house, and a healthy one. And," he added, his brows meeting, "I beg of you not to look at me in that missish fashion, Miss Mary. If a man has not the right to revile his own stepmother, then a companion has not the right to tell him so. This, I repeat, was my mother's. She died when I was eight. I am sure Nan will take care of it."

Mary exclaimed in pleasure. It was a small workbox that would delight Nan's housewifely soul, especially now that she was looking after papa in so matronly a fashion; it was stocked with every kind of silk and ribbon, with a pair of gold scissors attached to the lid by a cord.

She looked up at Ventnor. She forgot entirely that he was her enemy. She cried out, "How very kind you are. This will please her so much. I have always been a little sad that I could not give her half the things she deserves. Will you really send it off to her?"

"Today."

"How can I thank you?" she began, and was startled when he interrupted, "By keeping an open mind, my dear, by curbing your tongue, and by exercising a little more cleverly your powers of observation."

He left her standing there. It seemed to be his custom to break off a conversation in this abrupt manner. She stared after him. She put a hand up to her cheek. She felt indeed so confused that she decided to take a walk in the snow so that the cold air might clear her mind.

The old lady always slept after her midday meal. It was one of Mary's few periods of respite. The Ventnors kept a good kitchen and a good cellar; the old woman would stuff herself with food and drink, grumbling at its quality, yet swallowing enormous quantities. After the meal she would be too torpid even to laugh, and so she slept for two to three hours, leaving the household to its own devices.

Mary was relieved to set foot on the moor. It was a magnificent day. The snow lay thick on the ground, but the sky was the brightest blue, and the hills that encircled Wardwick Hall stretched pure and clean to the heavens, each outline etched in dazzling clarity. She walked across the crisp, hard ground, then, a little way away, saw Sam standing there.

She made towards him. She had liked the look of him from the first moment. Here, she thought, was an ally if she ever needed one. He had the look of calm, imperturbable strength that sometimes comes to a man who spends all his life in the open air, dealing with life at its most elemental; the far-sighted eyes, too, of one always scanning the horizon.

"Well, lass?" he said. "How are you faring with us? You've not run home yet to Derby, I see."

"I have no intention of running home." She smiled at him. "I'm not a little girl, Sam. I'm a young woman. I am capable, I think, of looking after myself."

"Ay," he said, and fell into the easy silence of one to whom silence was most natural; it was companionable, and Mary, standing beside him, was silent too.

He said unexpectedly, "She's an old werewolf. Don't let her eat you alive. She's tried to eat *him* alive, these many years. He was a fine little lad, with all the guts in the world. And now—— Why, she's made him as he is. To live with her and that brother of his——"

Mary forgot that a minute ago she had been on the verge of embracing her enemy. She was suddenly swept with anger. She thought of Nicholas, with his gentle smile, and the humility that made him endure so much that was not endurable. She cried out, "What have they done to him? What right have they?"

"Ah," said Sam. "Right! We makes our own right here, girl. And he, he's bad all through. He can talk pretty. He can cozen the soul out of you if he wills——"

"Yes," she whispered.

"——So that you could weep for him, so that you'd think he was the most ill-done by lad in the world. But thwart him, thwart him once, and you'll see his teeth, and if you're not on the lookout, those teeth will be in your throat. I'd not let no daughter of mine near him. That lass that worked here before you—— She doesn't come no more."

"What do you mean, Sam?"

"Oh, we gets to know these things. I shouldn't talk to you of them. Maybe she laughed at him once too often. Maybe she found out summat she shouldn't. And for once his brother wasn't looking out for him. He watches him like a kestrel. You must have seen. He knows. He has always known. She knew too late, poor lass."

Mary, staring at him, sickened, thought how nearly she too had been deceived. She remembered now that Ventnor and Nicholas were seldom apart. Despite his brother's mockery and rough bullying, Nicholas was nearly always at his side. She thought how she had called him coward, and muttered, half to herself, "What a fool I've been. Yet he can seem so kind."

"It's easy to seem kind," said Sam. Then to her great astonishment he spat in the snow. "Don't trust him, girl. Don't trust him. We all knows him here. There's dogs like him. They fawn over you, lick your hand, look soft at you all whimpering-like, but when your back's turned—— There's one out now. There was two bloody carcases on Kinder's slopes at dawn. But she's white, the damn bitch, the snow hides her. We'll get her when it melts. As we'll get the popish boy, too. They say he's at Manchester. Did you know?"

"Manchester! That's near enough."

"Ay. Warrington Bridge has been pulled down, and perhaps Stockport'll go too. My mother came from Stockport way—— They say the Highland army's swarming in like bees. There's three thousand in the town already. His Grace has sent out notices to Scarsdale and the Peak and Chesterfield and Matlock. But never mind the boy from across the water. It's the boy here that mat-

ters; he worships no God but himself. Leave him be.
He's dangerous. And when he talks soft, he is most dangerous of all."

Mary did not see Ventnor for the rest of the day. He
and his brother were out on one of their expeditions;
what they did she did not know, but all the countryside
around was their property, and both men worked as hard
as their own farmers and herdsmen.

But she met him at breakfast the next day, and looking
on his grim, blackavised face, wondered how this pirate
could ever have cozened her. As indeed he had
done—— A bitter shame came upon her. She loved her
father, but what kind of love was this that could lose its
purpose before a handsome face, kindly words, hands on
her shoulders? She could feel those hands, even now. A
shiver went through her. She could see that formidable
face inclining towards her, as if in tenderness. Perhaps it
had so inclined towards that other young woman whose
fate she still did not know, but who apparently would
never go anywhere again. Mary vowed within herself
that before the week was out, she would have explored
every corner and cranny of Wardwick Hall. If Charles
were at Manchester, the danger was desperately near.
There was no more time to waste. No time for talks
about Nan—— No time for hands to descend on her
shoulders. She raised her head and met his gaze direct.

He must have read something of what was in her
heart. He was, she realized with a prick of fear, quick to
sense other people's reactions. But she returned his stare
proudly enough. He was her enemy. And she saw, almost with pleasure, that he knew it; the mask slipped
down across his features. Then his mouth tightened into
an ugly smile. It was as if he had drawn his sword half
out of his sheath, though indeed he wore no weapon. But
with those powerful hands he would have no need. Then
she looked away. She was human after all, and young
and frail. He could have picked her up and thrown her
down again as if she were one of his lambs. She had
nothing to pit against him but her wits, and his were not
negligible. She wondered secretly if by the end of the
week she would still be alive. Then her courage reas-

serted itself. She was not, after all, completely alone.
There was always Sam—— And Nicholas. She sat down
at the breakfast table, trying to avoid his eyes which
were fixed on her, terrified lest he might read her entire
purpose. She could not doubt his rage. She had never
seen him in such a temper. There was no fawning now,
no speaking soft. She wondered that the old lady was
not afraid of him.

The old lady seemed, however, to be afraid of nothing.
Mary could see plainly now that once she would have
been a bold, handsome girl, but all that now remained of
her looks were the startling black eyes that flickered
amusement and derision from her bloated, fleshy face.

"I don't wear corsets," she remarked to Mary—she
was given to these personal irrelevancies—"I like to eat,
and I can't eat with those damned bones clamping my
belly down. You fine young misses pin yourselves in, no
doubt, so that a man don't know if he's hugging a girl or
a wire basket. A man likes to feel what he's handling.
Don't he, Ventnor? Don't he?" And out came the great
laugh, soaring up and up till its hysteria shrieked across
the moorland.

Ventnor gave her one look, then lowered his eyes to
the *Derby Mercury*.

Her ladyship, as Mary had already noticed, could not
bear to be ignored. She said in a slow, spiteful voice,
"But Ventnor don't hug the girls. Oh, no! Ventnor don't
go to Derby without telling his fond mama where he's
going. What was you doing, Ventnor? We'd all like to
know, wouldn't we, Mary? Why don't you answer me,
Ventnor? Why don't you tell us why you're always at
home these days, Ventnor?"

The hammer-blows of his name must be driving him
crazy, thought Mary; though she hated him, she could
not but sympathize. But he seemed impervious to them;
he still did not answer.

"We ain't seen him so much for years and years,"
persisted the old lady, then she began to giggle again,
and the giggle grew until once more her laugh pealed
forth. "Out on the hunt, Ventnor? You can't say I ain't a
good stepmama. I bring you a fine, nice girl all the way

from Derby, a little brown-eyed ewe, ready for the tup-
ping—— But he won't answer me. He was like that as a
boy, Mary. A fine, saucy boy who thought he'd be pert
to his new stepmama. But he learnt different. Indeed he
did. He wasn't so saucy when I'd finished with him."

He did stare up at that, with such a look to him that
her laughter checked. "It's a pity," she said, "that he's
too old to whip, now. You bring your children up proper,
Mary. Didn't your father correct you? I warrant he
should have done. He's a Jacobite, ain't he? They put
him in the pillory. I remember seeing it in the paper.
Nailed his ears down. I vow he was lucky not to catch the
Tyburn ague."

"There'll be many catching the Tyburn ague yet,
ma'am," said Ventnor suddenly, laying his newspaper
flat on his knee; his words miraculously saved Mary
from bursting into frantic, furious retort.

"Oh, will there indeed?" shrieked his stepmother,
flaring into rage. "Be careful you ain't one of 'em. It'll be
a fine day when I see you dancing on high before all the
roaring boys of London town. You think the Chevalier
won't win, do you? They're at Manchester, ain't they?
They took it with two and a half men, so the paper tells
me. But maybe the paper's wrong. Maybe I'm wrong.
You must always know better than everyone else. It ain't
true, of course, that the mobile appeared publicly for the
Prince, that all the lords and them as matters came to
kiss his hand, that the town assembled there to watch him
sup. Oh, no. That ain't true, of course it ain't. Ventnor
says so. The lord high and mighty says so. Why don't you
go to fight for king and country, then? Why don't you go
a-bowing and a-becking at the George Inn, where all the
noble lords is rubbing their noses in the muck, while our
gallant Lord Lieutenant of the county of Derby, the
Duke of Devonshire, is spewing out stuff about this most
wicked and unnatural rebellion. Read it out to me,
Ventnor. And Nicholas should hear it too. Where is the
boy? Nicholas! Nicholas, damn your eyes, where've you
got to?"

"I'm here, mama," said Nicholas, appearing in the
doorway.

"Certainly I will read it out," said Ventnor, and proceeded to do so in his most sonorous voice. " 'We, his Majesty's most loyal subjects, hereby declare our utmost abhorrence of so wicked an attempt, and in the most solemn manner engage that we will, at the hazard of our lives and fortunes, support and defend our excellent institution in Church and State, and oppose all attempts against his Majesty's person and government, particularly the Rebellion now carried out in favor of a popish, abjured Pretender——' "

She let out a great screech. She sprang up with an extraordinary agility, considering her size; snatched the paper from him, and began savagely to rip it through and through. She said in a hoarse, heavy-breathing whisper, "So you'll insult your mama, will you? You think you're big enough to do it, I warrant—but you ain't, you ain't——" And here she raised her great hand, a peasant's hand with broad palm and square nails, and would have clouted her stepson across the head, had he not seized her wrist and forced it down. At this, she broke again into peal after peal of laughter. "That scared you, didn't it?" she cried. "That'll learn you. That'll learn you, my bully——"

Ventnor rose slowly to his feet. He said, "You damned old beldame, sit down. And you——" Here he turned on Mary, who had also sprung up, trembling and pale. "Get out," he said. "Get out! This is an intimate family scene. Do you not understand that sometimes my stepmother and I wish to be left alone? Will you never permit us to indulge in tender family intimacies without your prying, prudish eyes following us? Leave us to our happiness, for God's sake. I can no longer endure to watch you."

Mary, the tears beginning to fall, turned towards the door without a word. She heard the laughter stop suddenly, as if a hand had been clapped over the mouth. She fled up to the library, and stood there in the middle of the floor, shaking and shivering. The sweat was trickling down her. Her heart was thudding fit to choke. "I cannot bear it," she whispered, "I cannot bear it. They are not civilized."

"I am afraid we are not," said Nicholas's quiet voice, and at this she swung round, scarlet with shame. But he came up to her and touched her gently on the arm.

"You must not mind my mother," he said. "She does not always mean what she says. And Ventnor——"

Mary cried suddenly, "You call him Ventnor, all of you. Has he no other name?"

"Why," said Nicholas, a bitter humor in his voice, "he was baptized like any other Christian. He was named Robert. My father called him Robin. But we—we are not on very brotherly terms. He is always known as Ventnor. It gives perhaps the true disciplinary touch."

"Why do you put up with him?" asked Mary directly, then. "I know it is none of my business. You may tell me so, if you wish. But you are a young man, and he treats you as if he were a schoolmaster and you his worst pupil. If I were a man," she added, drawing herself up to her full five foot, "I'd not endure such treatment. Are you angry that I speak like this?"

He answered with a wry enough smile, "The luxury of anger is not for such as me." He looked down at her. "I could never be angry with you. Do you not know what a difference your being here has made to me? Are you so unaware of the pleasure and happiness you have given me?"

She said weakly, "You should not say such things," yet hoped he would continue to do so, for the candid admiration in his eyes was most comforting and agreeable.

He said, "I am afraid you are badly shocked by what you have just witnessed. It has happened so many times before. And, believe me, it is not all my mother's fault."

"Was she really so brutal to him as a child?"

He shrugged. "I doubt it. She was always kind to me. But how can I know? He was ten when I was born. At least he has compensated for it in his treatment of me. If I told you—— But, forgive me. It is a long time ago. It is not worth mentioning now."

"But it is," she protested, "Oh, it is. I still do not understand how you endure it."

He cried in sudden anger, "Miss Mary, I am only

twenty. I have nothing in the world. In my father's will, it is stated that my brother is my legal guardian, till I attain my majority. Do you think I would stay here, otherwise? Oh, I am the little boy here. I am to receive his insults, cuffs and kicks. I am not expected to speak. I must watch and keep silent, while he and my mother dispute day in, day out, and when they are not disputing, talk treason. And now the invasion is upon us, and we wait for God knows what. Perhaps we shall all end on the gallows. They have been dangling for my dear step-brother, for a long, long time."

"They say," said Mary, looking at him steadily, "that there is a killer loose on the moors."

Nicholas broke into a sudden harsh laugh. "Ay! A killer, with its muzzle slobbered in blood. I have seen it. A gray-white, slinking thing that lopes along as its ancestors did, a thousand years ago. Would you have me shoot it down? While Ventnor rides the moors? Let it have its fill of massacre. Its life will be short enough. It is not the only killer here."

She whispered, "What do you mean?"

He looked aside. "I should not speak to you so. But treason is a dangerous profession. And those who oppose it are safest dead—whether they are shepherd or soldier, or perhaps old clergymen to whom the word is an unknown quantity. We must talk together, you and I. But not now. I hear my brother's footsteps. To have someone to talk to, at last——"

"At least," said Mary, "it gives me some purpose in being here." She moved back as she spoke, and picked up a book from the table, for she too had heard the footsteps in the passageway. "Indeed there seems to be nothing whatsoever for me to do, save managing the servants who know their business infinitely better than I, sewing a little which I do badly, reading novels and listening to your mother's confidences."

"And what could be more useful?" said Ventnor. He stood in the doorway, his cropped hair almost touching the lintel. But his eyes were on Nicholas, not on Mary, and she saw to her anger and distress that the young man had grown small before his brother's gaze, that the flame within him had instantly died.

He said again, "We have spent our lives listening to our mother's confidences, have we not, Nicholas? You, Miss Mary, are the new victim. I see that you are receiving confidences of another kind. Is Nicholas also unburdening his soul to you? We shall have to double your salary."

Mary saw Nicholas flush deeply. She wished with all her heart that she could speak for him, but realized to do so would only make matters worse. Why, she thought —why does he not answer as he should answer? Why does he not tell his brother to go to the devil, and never mind the money? He is not a child any longer. He cannot be afraid of physical violence, and the tongue can be answered with the tongue——

But Nicholas showed no disposition to answer. He said in a low, dull voice, "You will excuse me——" And, with only a perfunctory bow to Mary, pushed his way past his brother and out of the room.

She could not but see that she was being abandoned to the lion's jaws. Something of this showed in her face, and Ventnor, perceiving it, laughed.

"The age of chivalry," he said, "was over some five hundred years ago. What can you expect? Ladies who descend from their ivory towers must expect to find their *preux chevaliers* a little tarnished. I believe, Miss Mary, you are about to presume, and in an unmistakable manner. I can see the flush mounting your cheek, the defiance glittering in your eyes. You look like a child who says, I *will* be naughty, I *will* say what I should not, I *will* defy papa—— Well? I do not answer for the consequences, but—— Well? What has Nicholas been saying to you that has provoked this militant presumption? Though God knows, I know, I know—— You are sorry for him. Filled with pity. He has aroused your maternal feelings. Or are they not so maternal? You wish to rate me. You would use your ferrule, schoolmarm, if you could—would you not? Come. I give you full permission. Call me what you will. I'll answer you."

"In this house," said Mary, trembling, "you are so fond

of brawling that everything becomes an occasion for blows and insults. I have not been brought up that way, my lord. I have not been brought up that way."

"No," he said meditatively, "I can see that you have not." He sat down on the edge of the library table, picking up the volume that Mary had handled, turning it over and over. "No. I see you have always been grossly indulged. Perhaps that is not such a bad thing. But it seems to me that you take very kindly to brawling, for you are challenging me now, the only difference being that you are a woman and half my size, so you cannot take your fists to me. I do not see that shows any particular self-control; it is pure necessity. But never mind. Speak as you wish. But you must not reproach me if I reply as I wish. As you say, I have been brought up to brawl. Well? I am waiting."

"Very well," said Mary. Her heart was nearly choking her, but by clasping her hands together, she managed to preserve an appearance of calm. "I'll ask you this, then. I know it is none of my business——"

"Ha!"

"You choose to jeer at me, my lord——"

"I note that you always call me 'my lord' when you are being entirely impertinent. Come, Mary. This is a democratic age. The Pretender's son sleeps by the side of his Highlanders; besides, in time of war, all men are brothers. We'll be democratic, you and I. And I believe—will you not give me my due?—that I am not one to insist on such formalities."

"That is true."

"A hanging judge, but a just one—— Call me Ventnor and be damned to you. You see. I am treating you as an equal, in sex as well as rank. I am even swearing at you. Could you ask for a greater compliment? Now tell me what you are thinking."

"I am thinking," said Mary, before she could stop herself, "that you are laughing at me."

He looked suddenly so grim that she backed. "No," he said, "I find remarkably little to laugh at. And before you deliver your broadside, my girl, and make me so angry that I shall quite forget myself, I am going to say this:

When you came—— Be quiet! I wish to speak, and you shall not interrupt me till I have finished——"

For, amazed by his violence and the color that had darkened his face, she had opened her mouth to protest.

"You shall not interrupt," he repeated in what seemed to Mary a veritable roar. "Whether I am a lord or not is immaterial, but I unquestionably have the louder voice."

"That I would never deny," said Mary.

"And I will say this: When you came, I thought I liked you. You had spirit. You stood up to me. That is a quality I admire and respect. I knew our life here would prove difficult for you, and I was prepared to smooth it over for you to the best of my ability. Do you dare deny that? Do you? Do you?"

"Oh, no," said Mary in a stifled voice, "you were very condescending, my lord. But then I suppose one should take a certain interest in one's dependants."

He did not at once reply to this, only looked at her. She met the look as well as she could. Then he said, in a voice as chill as the wind that streamed across the moor, "Why do you speak like that to me?"

Mary, in the confusion of emotions that filled her—compounded of fear, anger and a certain unwilling respect for this extraordinary man who was now staring at her as if she were his mortal enemy—stammered, "I hate you. I hate everything about you. I hate the way you treat your unhappy brother. I hate your belief that you own these moors and everything that lives thereon. I believe you are mad, and I should pity you, but I find you overbearing and cruel and proud——" Then, as her own appalling words crashed round her ears, she said in a frantic whisper, "I'm sorry. I should not have said that."

He said calmly, "Why not? I invited you to be candid. And now we know exactly where we are. You must let me finish what I was about to say. It is what Mr. Bach would term the contrapuntal theme. Why are you so distressed? You hate me. There is nothing wrong in that. So do a great many other people. Including my half brother."

"Can you blame him!"

"I think we will not discuss that. I might grow angry. It is so much better to hate in cold blood. But what I wished to say was simply this: I tried to be friendly to you. I see now that it was a most ridiculous mistake. You dislike and despise me. You believe everything that is bad of me. You have set out to be my enemy. We will have no more pretense of friendship. You desire my enmity. You shall have it. I am a good enemy. I once imagined I was a good friend, too, but that was doubtless just my arrogant conceit. I cannot be capable of anything good. So now we understand each other. There shall be no quarter between us."

She said, "I much prefer it that way."

He nodded at her. He was smiling. The smile pricked the hair up on her head. He said pleasantly, "So I shall just say this, without further preamble. I believe that in your mind, Mary, there are certain little plans and schemings. You will please forget them. There is enough spying in this house without your adding to it. If I catch you interfering in any way in what does not concern you, prying, creeping or meddling, I shall break your neck. Is that understood?"

This was delivered in the most amiable of tones, but the eyes that looked into hers were not amiable at all. She longed to cry out, No! It is not understood. I shall do what I choose—— But this, as she knew, would be foolish in the extreme. With an effort she managed to hang her head. She said in a stifled voice, "Yes."

"From now on," continued Ventnor, "you will confine your activities to the duties laid down for you. And these do not include little intimate conversations with my stepbrother. You were engaged as a companion, not as Nicholas's wet nurse. I hope this is all quite clear." He looked at her; he noticed her humble attitude, and frowned for a moment. He went on, "Oh, and I think perhaps too much familiarity between us might lead to misconstruction. Besides, we have finished quarreling; have we not? —and when peace comes, democracy is shelved. I think I should like you, in future, to address me by my proper title. You are, after all, a very young girl, and you should learn the necessary respect for your superiors."

"Yes, my lord," said Mary, and permitted herself one glance before lowering her lashes to stare modestly at the floor.

He looked for the moment almost as if he wanted to laugh. But he only said, as he slipped off the table to stand over her, "I think that is all. Unless there is any further point you wish to raise?"

"I don't think so," said Mary. "Have I your permission to go now?"

"Where are you going?" he demanded. His voice had grown strained, as if some strong emotion were struggling to break through.

"To my room," she said. "Or perhaps I should say, to my ivory tower. If I cannot receive chivalry, I can at least seek solitude."

And with this she walked towards the door, very conscious of his eyes still upon her. It was only when she was well out of his sight—he made no attempt to follow— that she ran up the stairs as if the devil were after her, and flung herself down, panting, on her bed. She had never in her life refused a challenge, and this was a challenge after her own heart. She knew she should welcome it, even though it were directing the sword point at her breast. They had declared their enmity now. She need no longer have the mortifying consciousness that she was the traitor in the house, returning evil for kindness. There would be no kindness any more. He had said so plainly enough. He could not have said it more plainly. She knew him now for what he was—the pirate of her imaginings.

Yet her father had brought her up to be honest with herself. Deep in her heart lay two discrepancies that disturbed her. She sensed that behind his words, insulting and violent as they had been, lurked something like pain; she could not account for this, and it angered her; it was inconsistent. And secondly there was a purely personal feeling of dismay that he should be her enemy; despite all the evidence, she could not bring herself completely to believe in his wickedness.

She said furiously to herself. It is only because he is so good-looking. If he were small and stout, I should never hesitate——

She cried aloud, "How stupid I am!" and prepared to go down to read romance to Lady Ventnor. She combed her hair, staring at herself in the mirror—and saw a flushed, soft face, the face of a foolish girl, not that of a stern avenger. She tugged at her hair until it was scraped harshly back, but this, she saw, only accentuated the youthfulness of her countenance, at which she gave it up in despair, and confined herself to fastening on her primmest and stiffest starched collar, walking downstairs with a back as straight as a poker.

She met Ventnor at the foot of the stairs on the first landing. She said nothing, and neither did he, but his stare brought the blood to her cheeks. She felt suddenly small and weak and afraid, wanted quite absurdly to cry out something childish, like: "I did not mean it, let us be friends." She would not consider what prompted this imbecility, but merely continued her progress down the stairs, and, for the first time since her arrival was glad to step into the old lady's hot and stuffy room; Ventnor was unlikely to follow her there, for he avoided his stepmother as much as possible.

The next few days were not as bad as she expected. The weather had grown worse. The brothers spent most of their time rescuing livestock from the snowdrifts, salvaging crops, repairing the damage done to cottages, byres and pens by the blizzard that swept unceasingly across the moors. Amid such catastrophe, the news of the Pretender's son's continued advance seemed unimportant. There were, of course, the perpetual pinpricks. Ventnor spoke little to her, these days, but at meal times she was only too conscious of his staring at her from beneath his lowered brows, and this constant watching made her nervous, despite herself, so that her hands made clumsy gestures, she dropped things and sometimes broke them. When he did speak to her, he baited her. She longed to reply in kind, but knew she must keep up the pretense of meekness if it choked her—and choke her it nearly did, for she had never been the girl to endure insult in silence. But she managed somehow to control herself, answering his taunts and gibes and pricks with a "yes, my lord," and "no, my lord," while the anger drummed in her ears and she could almost have picked up a tableknife and thrust it into him. There was at least no pretense now of pleasantness between them, no references to the little sister—had he sent off the workbox? she wondered, and believed somehow he had, for she did not think he would vent his ill-temper on Nan—no more kindly attempts to salve her homesickness.

In all honesty she had to admit that she deserved this, for she had no more minced her words than he had, but it upset her, all the same, and she began to sleep badly, spending half the nights in wondering how she could get to the attic to look for what she was certain was concealed there. Here everything conspired against her. The brothers slept on the same floor as herself. Twice she tried to creep out in the night and each time heard the door across the landing immediately open. She dared go no further; if she were caught, she would never have the chance again, even if she escaped with her life. And in the daytime the old lady grew more and more exigent, so that she had scarcely any time to herself. She could only wait, and she was growing desperately tired of waiting, and the Pretender's son was advancing, day by day, and her father was in Derby——

She kept her diary during all this time, continuing to write as if to Nan and her father, while she sent them chatty little letters that revealed nothing. Nicholas took them for her now, whenever he had the time and his brother was not by. The diary afforded her a little relief. Here at least she could speak with frankness, though she did not write down her plans, these being too secret even for her diary. "In this age," her father had said, when he presented the volume to her, "we write such interminable journals and letters that future historians will be driven mad by us. You may as well add your quota, Mary. Perhaps one day a student of history will find it and write thereon a minor masterpiece."

She hoped this would not be so. She could not bear the thought of eyes other than hers seeing so intimate and private a document. Sitting in her room, late one evening, she flicked back the pages to see what she had written the night before:

"This seems to me a shocking Household. There was another HORRID Scene at dinner. 'Ventnor,' said the old lady—for she always addresses him so—"Ventnor has not quite made up his Mind which Side to be on, he is like old Simon Lovat, hoping to touch the right Boundary when the Rebellion is over.' Then she says to Nicholas, 'You at least will side with your poor, neglected old Mother, will you not?'—and then she begins her dreadful Laugh again, upon my Soul, one day I hope it will CHOKE her. . . . Ventnor says, 'Nicholas will always side with you, Ma'am, provided you hold the Purse-strings. I'd not give a Fig for your Chances,' he says, 'if you did not, for you'd perhaps be lying on the Moor with your Throat plucked out, as if the Killer had been at you.' And poor Nicholas, he looks up and he says, 'One day, Brother, you may regret having said that.' And the old Lady laughs more and more. I swear she enjoys it. And Ventnor rises to his Feet, and he says, 'Be quiet, you old——' "

Mary paused here. Perhaps she was thinking of the future historian. She contented herself with a long, thickly inked dash. She had added:

"He uses the most SHOCKING and PROFANE Language. And then he reaches out, and he gives his Brother such a Box on the Ear as near knocks him spinning. And he says, 'Leave the Room. And he did so, he did so—it was shameful. . . ."

Mary paused, and gave a sigh that was nearly a sob. She could not expunge from her mind the picture of a tall young man stumbling out, his head bent, the red mark on his cheek. She had always hated injustice. She began to write again, with the utmost rapidity, the ink sputtering from her quill as she did so:

"I do not understand him. I admit he is handsome. He has not been unkind to me, though now he is out to make Life as un-unpleasant as he can. Yet when he chooses to exert his Charm, I can almost forget for the Moment my Purpose in being here, almost forget that he may be the CREATURE *responsible for papa's unhappy State. But when I remember that fully, how gladly could I kill him! He has, it seems to me, no real Virtues. He is proud and vindictive and brutal, with no Love in his Heart for Anyone save himself; he is as wild as the Moors that have bred him, as cruel and as unfathomable. He is a Man, I am sure, who would sink to any Depth of Vengeance. . . . How I hate him——"*

She had not heard the door open. When the squat shadow fell across her page, she turned a startled face on her interrupter, who had never before, to her knowledge, come to her room, and whom she believed to be safely in bed. Then, suddenly remembering what she had been writing, she flung her reticule across the page. But it was too late. The old lady snatched the volume from her, shrieking in appalling, malicious glee.

"Ah!" she cried, her fat body shaking. "So the young miss does keep a diary, after all! All her little outpourings, hopes and dreams, all no doubt of what she thinks of me——"

"Give it back to me!" exclaimed Mary, her voice almost a scream. "Oh, give it back! You have no right——"

"This is my house," said the old lady, "and here I have the right to do what I please." And she began to read out in a high-pitched voice, her black eyes gleaming like elderberries, " 'He had, it seems to me, no virtues——' Now, who could that be?"

Mary, beside herself with shame and humiliation, said in a low, furious voice, "If you do not give it back to me, ma'am, I swear I'll take it from you."

"Why, it's Ventnor! And, upon my soul, the slut admits
he's handsome—— Oh, the sly piece! The saucy faggot!
So you're setting your cap at Ventnor, are you? I must
show him this. He'll enjoy it——"

Mary gave a great cry and, hearing nothing now but
the roaring of her blood, raised her arm. As she did so,
a hand descended on her wrist and jerked her back.
"What the devil is going on here?" demanded Ventnor,
staring down at her. "I heard the screeching a mile off.
Are you presuming to threaten my stepmother, miss?"

"She was about to strike me, Ventnor," screamed the
old lady, convulsed with enjoyment. "Oh, the little dear
—— Will you let her, then? She should be whipped for
it, she should be shut up on bread and water. You'd not
let your poor old mother be so ill-used, would you? But
you ain't heard what she writes about you, Ventnor. You
ain't heard. But you shall——"

"Oh, God!" whispered Mary, and covered her scarlet
face with her hands.

*"He has, it seems to me, no real Virtues. He is
proud and vindictive and brutal, with no Love in his
Heart for Anyone save himself; he is as wild as the
Moors that have bred him, as cruel and as unfathom-
able. He is a Man, I am sure, who would sink to any
Depth of Vengeance. . . . How I hate him——"*

"That will do, ma'am," said Ventnor dryly. "For both
of us." As he said this, he caught Mary's wrists in his
strong fingers and forced her hands down. For a minute
he surveyed her in silence. Then he went on, in the same
dry voice, "I see that you have read my character well.
But I do not recommend that you threaten my stepmother
again. She is a most pernicious old she-devil, but she is
the mistress here, and you are nothing. In any case——"
And here he turned to the old lady, who seemed to
accept his remark as the greatest compliment, and who
was tittering again, rubbing her great, coarse hands against
her thighs, "——all this is now vastly unimportant. We
have news that means more than a silly girl's outpourings,
and an old witch's cackling. The Prince is arrived at

Derby. Yes. The information has just reached us. The rebels' vanguard rode into the town at eleven o'clock this morning, and at three in the afternoon Lord Elcho arrived with the Lifeguards. They have been marching through the town—it seems it's a parcel of shabby, lousy, pitiful-looking fellows, mixed up with old men and boys, dressed in dirty plaids and shirts, and without breeches or shoes. The Pretender's son, so Sam tells me, arrived a couple of hours ago. The common crier has proclaimed him in the market place, and now he's safely lodged at my lord Exeter's. Every house in town has had to take them. It seems, ma'am, that your gallant Highlanders are not so gallant after all. If they like a person's shoes, they demand 'em off his feet. All excise due has had to be paid to them, instanter. They're pilfering and threatening and beating up for volunteers. We think they'll march to Loughborough for London. Their advance guard has already secured the pass at Swarkstone Bridge. In short, my fighting ladies—is there not a female prizefighter called Bruising Peg?—you had best cease thumping each other, for the thumping promised us all is now a catastrophic one. Your ladyship had best go downstairs again —what were you doing up here?—and leave this foolish young woman to tear my character to shreds as she pleases." Then his voice rose to a roar, as if he had had more than he could stand. "Get downstairs, ma'am. I have had enough of this. Oh, I'll deal with this young woman—I have been waiting the opportunity for some time, but I do not need an audience, and this tittering and giggling drives me nearly out of my mind."

The old lady did not appear to resent this rudeness. She looked at Mary, who was sitting there motionless, head bowed, cheeks suffused—and a wide anticipatory grin appeared on her face. She said, "What will you do to her, Ventnor? What will you do to her?"

He said roughly, "That is my affair. Get downstairs."

"Oh," she said in a whine, "I'm only a poor old woman, ain't I? What with my rheumatics and all, I can't move as quick as you young ones. I need time to get my breath, pox take you—you ought to be ashamed of yourself, bullying me at my age—a nice, dutiful son you are to be sure, your father'd turn in his grave if he heard you——"

"Your rheumatics got you up the stairs," said Ventnor in a snap, "they can damn well get you down." His hands descended on her shoulders. "Out! Out, I say——"

"I'm going," she said, nodding her head from side to side to that with her black eyes and red cheeks she resembled some mechanical doll. "Oh, I'm going. There's no need to bellow at me, is there? Sounds like a bull, don't he, Mary?—a mad, mad bull——"

"Will you go?" said Ventnor. There was a whiteness round his mouth.

She looked again from him to Mary, then back. "I'll be missing all the fun," she said; then, in mock pathos, her snapping eyes contradicting every word: "Can't the poor old woman sit down for a minute to get her breath back? Can't she, Ventnor? Oh, what a hardhearted, savage boy it is, to be sure——"

He said in a whisper, "Get out, for God's sake!"— and at that she began to shuffle towards the door, groaning and puffing as she went, one hand on her hip as if it hurt her. "Oh, oh!" she moaned. "Oh! It hurts cruel, cruel! Oh——"

He waited until she had shut the door behind her. Still he waited. They heard her limping steps go heavily down the stairs. Then he turned to Mary, who still sat there, one hand twisting the clasp of her reticule.

He said quietly, "You will never listen—— Give me your diary, please."

She did not answer. She did not even shake her head. Her humiliation weighed her down like a ton weight. If she had looked up at him, she might have seen that his face, far from being filled with savage mockery, was haggard and drawn. But she did not look up. Only her hand, plucking at the clasp of her reticule, had now automatically unfastened it, and had crept into the bag, as if in hiding it, she was hiding herself.

He said again, "Give it me, please."

"No," she whispered. "No."

She heard his indrawn breath. Then he said, "I do not give a damn what you have written about me. I know well enough what you think of me. To you I am a murderer and everything that is vile. That point you have at least made plain, and I will not dispute it. But you *must* give that diary to me. Can you not understand? No, of course not. It is of no matter. Give it to me. Do you believe I will not take it? Do you really intend that we should tussle like a couple of children? You know perfectly well that I can take it in a minute. I think you might spare us both that indignity. Give it me!" He added bitterly, "Considering I am every kind of brute and bully, you should surely find it wiser to obey me. What did you say of me? 'He is a man who would sink to any depths of vengeance'——"

She had hardly heard what he was saying, except for the reiterated "give it me." But she heard the last. It was to her the final straw of degradation, that he should hold her private diary in his hands, and read it out to her. He would certainly not spare her. Those foolish things she had written down to amuse Nan would be spoken aloud in his deep voice. It would be like being stripped in public. Then vaguely in her confused mind floated the thought that she should not have written them; it was childish and impertinent. But she could no longer think coherently at all. The only thing clear to her was that he should not see the diary; when he had gone, it would be destroyed; no one should ever see it again.

She heard him swear below his breath. She had not once looked up at him, but she could imagine how angry he would be. "For the last time," he said, "will you please give it me? Do you not know how dangerous it is? Has your hatred utterly bemused your wits?" Then his hand shot down towards her wrist.

Perhaps her hatred had bemused her. She scarcely knew what she was doing. But suddenly with her free hand, she jerked the little pistol out of the reticule, and in one swift movement was on her feet, moving a pace backwards. *You put your finger here and press so——* He had said that. Or was it Horace? She had never used a weapon in her life. Shooting was not, after all, part of the training of a vicar's daughter. But she held the little gun up, and looked now to see his face so utterly astonished and incredulous that she almost wanted to laugh.

He stared at her, the hand that had been intending to pin her down swinging at his side. She had never thought to see him so disconcerted. But it was only for a second. He leapt forward, crying out, "Put that down, you little fool!"—and at that instant her finger slipped. There was an explosion that to her horrified ears sounded so loud that she thought the room around her must go up in flames. She had never meant to fire. It was cocked, of course—she remembered vaguely that he had said so. She dropped the pistol to the floor, and burst into tears, crying out, "Oh, God, I've killed him——" Then, nearly fainting, turned her eyes to where his corpse must be undoubtedly lying.

It was a minute before she could focus clearly. Then she saw that the corpse was still upright, staring at her with a most uncorpse-like expression, one hand holding the other, down which the blood was running.

His voice came to her from a great distance away, booming oddly in her ears. "For a murderess," it said, "you seem to me well intentioned but inadequate. Do you imagine that I shall now support you? Faint if you must, but I'm damned if I'll do anything about it."

The mist cleared before Mary's eyes. She came at last to her senses. She forgot the diary and her humiliation. She could only see the blood pouring down his left hand. She said in a severely practical voice, "That must be bandaged immediately. Wait——"

She ran to her cupboard and pulled out a dozen handkerchiefs. She was long past seeing any absurdity in the situation. She could not bring herself to raise her eyes to his, but she was aware that he had sat down rather hurriedly, the injured hand extended on the table. Her own hands were shaking uncontrollably. The bullet, she saw, had not penetrated—only grazed the side—but the flow of blood frightened her. She made a temporary tourniquet round the wrist, then began to bandage it. It was a business she was well enough accustomed to, for her duties had often involved first aid, but she had never thought to treat a wound that she had made, herself, and the tears running down her face did not help.

His silence did not help her, either, though she could

see that this was scarcely the moment for polite conversation. She supposed she would now be given into the charge of the nearest constable. But at least his death would not be on her conscience. His hand lay motionless between her fingers. When she had tied the last knot, she did at last give him a despairing glance. His face, she saw, was blank and rather pale, the eyes very wide.

She stood in front of him. She said, "I really did not mean to——" Then, aware of the inadequacy of this remark, fell as silent as he.

He said at last, fingering the bandage, "I do not believe that such an excuse would hold water in a court of law." He put his undamaged hand to his forehead for a moment. Then he said sternly, "And now, please, I want that diary, without any more of this nonsense. And your pistol."

She looked at him once in complete despair, then handed him the diary which he placed upon his knee, thumbing the pages. He said, almost as if nothing had occurred, "You believe I am going to read this, don't you? You believe I want to know your estimate of my character? You think that would give me pleasure. Do you really imagine—even you—that I propose to spend the rest of the night reading page after page concerned with my own misdoings? However, I suppose nothing would convince you to the contrary. You have a picture in your mind that no words of mine could destroy." He paused, wincing a little as if his hand hurt him. He said, "You deserve nothing from me but instant dismissal— but if I hand this diary back to you, Mary, have I your word that you will destroy it tonight?"

"Yes," she said wretchedly. She could think of nothing else to say. The circumstances were past all imagination. She had always believed she could deal with any situation, but this was beyond her.

He held out the diary. "I do not know why I should trust you," he said, "but I beg of you, for your own sake, to keep your word." He added, "Let us hope that the depths of vengeance to which I sink are not as fathomless as you seem to imagine." For a second his mouth twitched.

Then he said, "You have forgotten the pistol, have you not? I want that too, please."

She picked it up. The very touch of it made her face whiten again. She could not believe that she had ever fired it. She saw that he was watching her, and found the tears coming back to her eyes. She was dreadfully ashamed. She could not imagine what her father would think of such behavior.

He took the pistol in his unbandaged hand, examined it, then slipped it back into his pocket. "I do not propose," he said, "to have an armed companion about the house, especially one whose finger lies so softly on the trigger. Did you intend to kill me?"

Mary said almost inaudibly, "You take it very calmly! No. But why should you believe me? There is, after all, nothing that I can say."

He said with some asperity, "I should hope not. But there is a great deal I could say, if I had a mind to." Then to her amazement, and a little to her anger, too, he laughed. "We spoke," he said, "of the hazards of a companion's life—— I did not consider that an employer's life might have its dangers, too."

She said in choked voice, "I am sorry. You'll not believe me, but it was the purest accident. I—I was a little out of my mind. I did not know what I was doing. I have never even handled a pistol before."

"You did very well," he said, "for a first attempt."

"I never meant it to go off. I'll never forgive myself. Only," added Mary, feeling that somehow she must assert herself, despite the tears she could not stem, "you provoked me so dreadfully. I should never have written such things, I know, but it was mine, it was private——"

"Are you so sure?" he said.

She did not understand this, only repeated, "It was private. Of course I should not have lost my temper with your stepmother. But she snatched it from me, and she read it out—— You were going to do the same. I could not endure it, I could not—— To be so mortified——"

He did not comment on this, only surveyed his bandaged hand. Then he rose to his feet. He was still very white. He said curtly, "I've had enough of this: Spirit is all very well, but you are employed here to keep my mother company, not to indulge in tantrums. There will be no more diaries, Miss Mary. Your opinion of me you can keep to yourself until you return to Derby which, if you continue like this, will be soon enough. You can then regale your family and neighbors with tales of the monster of Wardwick Hall. The monster has, I think, shown creditable self-control. In future you will do as you are told, and when the desire comes upon you to walk about our corridors in the middle of the night, you will think twice about it, and confine your perambulatings to your own room. There'll be no more scenes with my step-mother, neither, or—or I'll shoot *you*. You ought," he said, with a faint break in his voice that she was too confused to notice, "to be ashamed of yourself. Is this the kind of thing that goes on in your father's vicarage? Do you shoot parishioners at matins, and draw and quarter them before evensong? I can only suppose that in the evenings you and your little sister indulge in target practice. You'd best not indulge in any more here. It is not safe. And one more display of temper from you, and you go——— Unless, of course, you wish to give in your notice?"

There was nothing she would have liked to do more, but her purpose fettered her to Wardwick Hall. She said nothing. She felt shamefully like a scolded child. However, this rating was part of the price she must pay for her father's salvation; as such it must be accepted. In all honesty she had to admit that his lordship had taken her appalling behavior in surprisingly good part. But he was a violent man, himself—perhaps he accepted violence as part of the normal run of things.

"Well?" he said. "Are you not giving in your notice?"

Mary said in an unhappy voice, "I should prefer to—to stay, if you will permit it."

For some reason this seemed to provoke the temper he had so far kept leashed. He caught at her shoulder with his right hand. He said savagely, "So that you can spy on us further, no doubt——— But you'll not. You'll not! What do you hope to find? Tell me!"

"Spy on you?" she repeated. She could feel the color dwindling from her face, and knew that he must notice it, but her voice was almost normal again. "You are quite mistaken. There is nothing I hope to find. What could I find? Why should I want to find anything?"

"You'll find yourself a grave shortly," he said, releasing her. He began to walk towards the door, adding, "I do not know which of us is the worser fool." At the doorway he halted. "I had forgot—I came up to give you this letter. I did not realize I should be shot in the process. You may as well treasure it. It will be the last you will receive for a very long time. The weather and the Pretender's son have severed your last link with home. I think you might do well to brood on that."

And with that he placed the letter down on the table, and left the room.

She did not at once pick it up. She only sat down at the table and rested her head upon her arms. She looked at the diary, and the full memory returned to her, of the old lady's reading it aloud, of Ventnor's listening. She saw herself standing there with the pistol in her hand, like the heroine of some play, defending her honor. Sick humiliation overcame her, and remorse, too. She seized hold of the diary, and began savagely to rip out its pages. No historian should benefit by this. She could never bear to see a line of it again; her memory, however, was truer than her eyes, and her tears flowed faster and faster as she remembered what she had written.

It lay at last in her fireplace, a mountain of torn paper, a memory of humiliation insupportable to endure. It was only then that she saw the other piece of paper lying on the table.

She picked it up mechanically, opened it.

"Oh, dearest Mary," wrote Nan so ecstatically that the words all ran into each other, "so wonderful a Workbox! I have never, *never* owned anything so exquisite, so beautiful, so *magnificent,* and with all the Wood, too, you always think of everything for us———"

Mary repeated aloud, in a dull voice, "All the wood?"

"It has been shocking cold for all of us, this winter, and Papa with his usual Cough, but this is much better, thanks to you, though once it quite alarmed me. Hannah is pleased, too, and says we have suficiant to keep us in Fuel for all the cold Months. . . . How is your handsome Lord? You do not tell us much of him, but I expect that is your Caution, and we shall hear all your News at Christmas Time when you come Home. I shall be quite cross if you are not at the very *least* promissed in Mariage to him——"

Mary let the paper drop into her lap. "Wood costs money," she had said. That was all. It seemed sometimes as if his lordship's left hand did not know what his right hand was doing—— And, that brought back the memories again. His lordship had virtually no left hand for the moment, and that was her doing, because she had shot him—— She saw again his white face, devoid of expression, and the blood running down.

She lay full length on her bed, her face buried in the pillow. It was not until the small hours of the morning, when the cold clawed at her like an icy hand, that she thought to undress and creep beneath the coverlets.

IV The Younger Son

She could not sleep. Early in the morning she rose from the bed, dressed herself and came quietly out into the corridor. She heard the library clock chiming six. She did not think now of going up to the attic. She could only flinch beneath the weight of mortification at her breast; it was even heavier than it was last night. The thought of facing the family at the breakfast table made her sick, yet the solitude of her room was even less bearable. The diary lay in ashes in the grate. The pistol, no doubt, was in Ventnor's room. But the memory of what had happened was in her, and burnt within her like a flame.

She stole down the stairs. Ventnor, if he heard her, would think she was spying again, but in her unhappiness nothing was further from her mind. She could only think of home and Derby, wish to God she could go there; never had her courage been at such low ebb.

It was a little ironic, then, that as, in the snow-filled twilight of the early winter morning, she crept into the library, she should meet the last person she wished to see, who was standing by the window, staring out.

She gave an involuntary gasp of protest, and at that he turned slowly round. She felt the color scald her cheeks, but she met his gaze as well as she could. The whiteness outside—the snow seemed to have fallen again during the night—shed a luminous light upon him, draining the color from his face, so that he seemed like some penciled drawing, gaunt and washed of blood, bony outline flung into gray and white, with the black, untidy hair overtopping it.

She would have retreated, but he said, "Good morning," and she could hardly reply and then run away. She came up to him and said in a shaking voice, "Your hand—— Is—is it any better?"

He laughed, and not as if he were amused. He too looked as if he had not slept. The haggard look was not entirely due to the gray light. "Oh, gentle murderer!" he said. Then: "It pains me like the devil. What do you expect? You have taken half the skin off. Are you pretending to be sorry?"

"I am sorry," she said. Then, desperately: "Will you not let me undo the bandage and bathe it for you?"

He shrugged his shoulders. "You are very tender to your victims. Which are you salving—my hand or your conscience? If you can drown your remorse so easily in a basin of warm water, you are welcome to do so." But as she turned thankfully towards the door, he seemed to change his mind, and said roughly, "I'll not have this preposterous nonsense. I don't need a nursemaid. All this womanly solicitude is, I suppose, to convince me what a sweet creature you really are. I'd as soon have Jael or Judith as handmaiden. Leave it be, for God's sake. It's only a scratch. Next time you shoot, my dear, aim at the belly. An inch to the right or left there scarce matters, and you can be happily sure that your victim will die in the greatest agony."

Mary, finding herself near tears again, gave him a weary, bitter smile. "Don't you see," she said, "that I am so ashamed of myself that I do not know what to do? I admit there is no reason why you should be merciful, but it would be the greatest kindness if you would permit me at least to make sure that the wound is not festering, and put on a fresh bandage. I suppose," she added, speaking now with the candor of utter exhaustion, "that you imagine I wish to gloat over it. I assure you I would not do that to my dearest enemy. I do not like causing pain to anything, and I have been brought up to believe that all violence is unpardonable. I do not know what my father will say to me—— I think I must have been mad. Please permit me to re-bandage your hand." Then she began to cry again, for she was so very tired. She sobbed, "It should not s-spoil our enmity, and after all, it will be easier for you to c-cut my throat later on, if you have b-both hands at your service."

He said, after a pause, "Have it your own way. You are exaggerating, of course, like all your sex. But never mind. And for God's sake, stop crying. I should be crying, not you—— You will find linen in the cupboard in the hall. We keep it there for emergencies. I suppose this can be termed an emergency."

Mary unwrapped the bandage, seeing to her relief that the wound was clean, but realizing that it must be excessively painful, for there was a great flap of skin hanging down. She fastened the bandage as neatly and gently as she could; Ventnor chose to accompany this process with a barrage of comment. "You will," he said, "use this for future applications for posts. You will say, 'I can turn the pages of a novel with one hand, and shoot my employer with the other. If the damage is not mortal, I am an excellent nurse and can tie a workmanlike bandage; if mortal, I can weep as efficiently over his grave as any professional mourner'——" Then the injured hand unexpectedly tightened over hers. She did not struggle, for fear of hurting him, only looked up at him, disregarding the tears that trickled down her cheeks. "Oh, I think you take this too hard," he said. "You must not grudge me some small retaliation. Why do you go on crying? I do not believe this is on my account." Then, with an abrupt change of tone, "No. It is nothing to do with me." He released her hand and moved over to the window, saying with that strange inconsequence that was sometimes his, "When I was a child, and the world was wrong, I used to go to that cottage on the moors that you once thought was our home. You were righter than you knew. It was my home, the one place where I was safe and alone. I could blubber there and, by God, I needed to. There are not, if you consider it, so many places to weep; such privacy is a luxury. So there I went, to howl, if it pleased me—to batter my fists and heels against injustice. And then one day my stepmother discovered my rat hole. When I arrived, she was waiting for me. It is a long time ago—and I am still alive. And so are you, Mary.

And so is your father. Humiliation fades like love, like happiness, like everything else."

She said in a choked voice, "You dare to speak of my father——"

"Yes," he said, "for he has endured a humiliation far worse than ours. We at least did not have a hundred onlookers to stare at us."

"How do you know all this?"

He turned his deep-shadowed eyes on hers. "I was in Derby," he said. "I wish you will tell me exactly what happened."

"I will not," said Mary.

He took a step towards her. "You had best do so. For your own sake."

She said in a whisper, "So you are threatening me again. Ah, but I am not your young brother, my lord. I am not so easily moved by rough words and menacing gestures."

"There are times," he said slowly, "when you would do well to be afraid. You seem to me a very foolish young woman. You should remember that here you are out of your own world, with a killer loose upon the moors, a rebel Prince not so many miles away, and the snow to fetter you."

She was as coldly angry as she was coldly afraid; she forgot now her shame and remorse. "Fear," she said, "is undoubtedly a potent weapon, but it can lose its edge through misuse. One day, sir, you will overreach yourself, and I can only pray that you will receive more mercy than you show to yours about you."

"You damned hypocrite!" he said, and laughed. "I suspect your prayers are quite otherwise. But of course you have been speaking to my stepbrother. I had forgot."

"I have eyes to see," said Mary, "and ears to hear, too."

There was a silence. Then he said in a suppressed voice, "Have I three kingdoms, and must you fly in my eye?"

"And what does that mean, pray?"

"Did the abecedarians not teach you history? That is the remark of his Majesty, King James I, great-great grandfather of the young upstart in Derby, when a rebellious insect invaded the royal eyelid. I am in my kingdom here. I should be inviolate. Do you—a little girl from the town, a chit scarce out of swaddling bands, and my mother's paid companion—dare attack me with words as well as bullets?"

"I beg your pardon if I have forgot my place," she said in a tone which did not match her words.

He looked down at her. She suspected that he was grinning at her, but the light was too dim for her to be sure. "Well, my little fly," he said. "So you have summed me up in your prim judgment, and found me wanting. But even you cannot take my kingdom from me—— Look! Come here, I say, and look!"

She came towards him, unwillingly. He caught at her arm and swung her round so that she faced the window. "Look!" he said again, and compelled her to stare across the bleak, barren whiteness which stretched further than her eyes could see. Then he cried out, "You must tell me about your father—— Why are you here? What are you planning in your nutshell of a mind?"

She wrenched herself from his grasp. She said, "You have the audacity to ask me that—you, of all people. Do you not know? Can you look at me and swear you do not know? But we will not discuss it further. It is an insult to my father's name that we should do so."

"You damned fool!" he said, with so black a look that she grew terrified. He raised his hand; she thought for an appalled second it was to strike her; but he only brought it down on the latch and pushed the window open so that the bitter dawn wind from the moors blew in upon them, lifting Mary's petticoats, tugging at her hair, laying its icy palm across her cheek. She shuddered. She stared out, resentful, afraid; shivering at the desolation that swept past the window. She said nothing.

Ventnor said savagely, "You'll regret this. You do not know how you'll regret this. God save us from women and fools. Look, you stupid slut—look! If your town-cramped eyes can see—— The moor gives the long sight, and that is better than the second sight of the Highlanders. Look! Can you see nothing?"

She stared, narrowing her eyes against the harsh

brightness; it seemed to her that for an instant something moved against the skyline.

"It is our killer," he said. "Sam lost three more sheep this morning, and a chicken, too. They say the bitch has whelped, and now has pups to feed."

"I hear," said Mary, trembling, "that there are other killers abroad."

She regretted the words as soon as they had been uttered, but indeed she was in such a state as to have no control over her thoughts or speech. She saw to her astonishment that this time he was undeniably smiling; the smile broadened into a brief laugh. "That is true," he said, "but I do not know if you can blame a killer if the sheep extends its throat so recklessly. But we will discuss this further, some other time. It can wait. This cannot——"

She cried out, "Your hand——"

"Oh, damn my hand!" he said, and with that he left her. She heard him crashing into the hall. A moment later she saw him running across the moors, a gun in his hand. His long legs covered the ground at an incredible speed, in the direction of the moving dot against the snow.

She pushed her wind-blown hair back with a shaking hand. She knew she should not have spoken so. The weight of her mortification was increased now by the colder weight of fear. She had not intended to reveal so much of her knowledge to him. Even if he did not realize fully what she planned, he would at least appreciate her insolence. His momentary mood of tenderness had been shattered, and she knew well enough now that he could make an ugly enemy; he was not a pirate for nothing.

Of that she was not left long in doubt.

At first it seemed that the old lady was too preoccupied with the arrival of the Pretender's son in Derby to remember last night's happenings; it seemed that Ventnor had told her nothing of the shooting. Mary, feeling very young and horribly insecure, slipped into her place at the breakfast table. She would have preferred to have hidden herself beneath it. She sat there, her eyes fixed on her plate. Then something impelled her to raise her head. She met the gaze, not of the old lady who was excitedly scrabbling among her newspapers, but of Ventnor who was staring at her with open mockery. To her fury she flushed deeply. She looked away, permitting herself one brief, sideways glance at Nicholas who seemed as embarrassed and unhappy as herself.

The old lady said in glee, "What price His Highness of Cumberland now, Ventnor? What price dear William Augustus now? There's our bonny lad, God bless him, tucked safely in his little bed in Exeter House, and all the gentry falling head over heels to accommodate his friends. I see Lord George Murray is staying with Mr. Heathcote in Full Street, and Lord Pitsligo with the Meynells. Oh, that I was there to see! How gallant he must have looked, riding down Friar Gate into Queen Street. We'll have the drinking glasses out at dinner, Ventnor—the ones with the roses on—to drink the darling's health, and, long may he reign." Then, to Mary's astonishment she burst into song. She had a voice as screeching as her laughter; it was not a voice to sit kindly on the digestion at eight in the morning:

> *"Let howlet Whigs do what they can,*
> *The auld Stuart's back again!"*

And as she caroled, she swiveled her fat body round, to meet in turn her stepson's blank, unresponsive stare, her son's look of dejection, and Mary's expression of anguished embarrassment.

She broke into a howl of rage. "Damned hypocrites, the lot of you! Loyal, ain't you? Loyal to your fat German king! Staunch Hanoverians, ain't you?—all looking to see which side your bread is buttered on. Oh, you'll miss the butter, all right, and how I'll laugh! You'll have a better king than your wee German lairdie, and you'll be all groveling on your knees, ay, and undoing the button so's you can kneel bare-knee'd, as loyal subjects should. And then, you pox-ridden fools, you'll be kicked back where you belong, or hoisted on to the nearest tree, with tallow in your eyes to light the world to traitordom!".

She paused for breath. No one replied. Then slowly her black eyes turned to Mary who sat rigid, praying she would be ignored.

"Ah," said the old lady in a caressing voice—she likes a mouse to play with, Ventnor had said. "Ah. But o' course the girl's father was set in the pillory for Jacobitism, so the slut must play the loyalist, and look down her pious little nose at us. What else you been putting in that precious diary of yours, miss? Eh? I'll have to get another look at it, that I can see. Bring it down here. D'you hear me? Ventnor! Make her bring it down here——"

Mary said, shaking, "There is nothing left for your ladyship to look at, unless you wish to scour the ashes in my grate."

Ventnor broke into a sudden laugh, and at that her color flared up so that it nearly choked her. But she would not look at him.

The old lady shrilled viciously, "So we're not good enough to read it, miss! Such insolence I never heard, God damn it—— And after saying such fine things of my dear stepson and all. Oh, you didn't see the half of it, Ventnor. You should've done. She summed you up proper, the little dear. Finds you handsome but a devil, just like what Nick gets me from the circulating libraries. Probably head over heels in love with you. Are you, miss? Are you? Do you dream of him at nights? Do you kiss your pillow for him? Do you——"

Mary rose to her feet. Her temper had almost submerged her shame. She cried out, on a sob, "I'll not be so spoken to. You had no right to look at the diary. Nor you, neither, my lord. It was mine. It was my one piece of privacy. I had the right to say there whatever I chose. I could say, if I wished, how I hated you all. Perhaps I did. You'll never know. But you need not worry about the love, ma'am, for there was none. There's many as marry for position and money, such as—if you'll forgive the liberty, ma'am—yourself, but rather than saddle myself with a man who has the manners of a pirate and the look of a killer, I'd as soon go into a nunnery and never see a man again. I love my father, ma'am. And it seems to me plain blasphemy to mention even the word in connection with a man who——"

Ventnor at this point leaned across and gripped her arm with a violence that made her gasp, and checked her in full spate. At this the old lady burst into her great hysterical laugh. "You deal with her, Ventnor," she cried. "You deal with her. The damned impudence of it! In my young days, if a girl dared so to speak to her employer——"

"We are scarcely interested in your young days," he interrupted. "We are, God knows, immersed in present disaster, and bygone flummery has little attraction. But I'll certainly deal with this young woman. Go into the library."

"You dare speak to me like this——" she began in a whisper.

He stared at her in silence, his hand still gripping her arm. She saw no alternative but to obey. It seemed that, if she did not, she would be dragged from the room. But she cast one look of appeal at Nicholas. Ventnor, intercepting this, said roughly, "There's no help there. He's not the guts to defy me openly. Will you go?—or must I carry you?"

Mary, jerking her arm away, walked to the door without another word, across the hallway, and up the stairs to the library. She heard his footsteps following her. In the library she turned to face him. He seemed to her enormously tall. The expression on his face flickered oddly in the winter sunlight. For one strange moment it seemed to be more of fear than of anger. But the next instant he had caught at her shoulders and was shaking her violently. He said in a harsh whisper, "Have you no sense? No sense at all? Even after last night? If I had let you finish——"

She replied, her teeth chattering, "If you had let me f-finish, I might have said more than you would want your family to hear, p-perhaps——"

He turned away so that she could no longer see his face. She stared at his shoulders. She would once again have given the world to be able to say, I must leave, I

will go now. But she would not—she could not, not with
her purpose unfulfilled, her memory of what had happened, her apprehension of what might still come. It was
surely ironic that she, who was proud, must now wait in
terror lest his next words dismiss her.

It was as if he read her thoughts. He said, always
without looking at her, "I should send you packing. Will
you never learn to hold your tongue?"

"Even if you sent me away," said Mary, "you would
not curb it."

And now he did turn to look at her. His face was quite
expressionless. "Tongues can be curbed," he said.

"Would you murder me then?" she asked, then went
scarlet at having asked such a question. She said irrele-
vantly, her voice shaking, "Did you—did you get your
killer?"

"No. She was too cunning for me. The falling snow
blotted out her tracks. But killers do not escape for long."

"No," she said. "No. Not for long."

He came up to her. She folded her hands before her,
a half-smile on her lips. She could see that her reply had
disturbed him. She was glad. This, after all, was the
man responsible for her father's suffering. And then, with
an inconsistency that shocked her, she thought, he does
not look like a murderer. His mouth is generous. His eyes
are kind. He has been extraordinarily forbearing about
last night—— She cried out, "Well? What will you do to
me now? Will you use violence on me? There is after all
a law in this land——"

"Not here," he said. "Not here. Here the moors are
your dungeon, your gaoler—and your shroud, too, if
need be. Mary——"

She was angered by the use of her name. Had he not
said there was to be formality between them? She answered stiffly, "My lord?"

He said, "Will you not forget about your father? It is
over and done with. Vengeance is a barren thing. No
one knows that better than I."

"I will never forget," she said. "Never. My lord, I saw
him as they brought him home. And I saw him in the
market square. He was in the pillory for two days, sir.

And not a soul dared to cast a stone at him. They shed tears. So did I. But not he—— He accepted his martyrdom as he had accepted happiness; for him it was the will of God. It was only later, and when he was sleeping, that he rebelled. Night after night he would cry out. But in the mornings he was always calm again. I am not so calm. I will never forget. One day I will find out who was responsible. And then——"

"And then?" repeated Ventnor.

She did not reply, only held out her hands.

He said, with some difficulty, "I apologize for having shaken you. I—I did not mean to hurt you——"

"Why, sir, it is nothing," said Mary, her gaze bright and hard. "You are the master here. You owe it to yourself to keep order among your dependants."

He looked at her in a way that made her instinctively draw back. But he only said, as if to himself, "The manners of a pirate and the look of a killer—— You have a pretty turn of phrase, Miss Mary." He saw her flinch, and laughed. Then, his fingers on the door handle, he glanced at her once more and roared out in his great voice, "By God, I could—I could strangle you—— How much more stupidity must I endure? And to be forced so into the role of shepherd—— It is not my trade, it is not my trade!"

And with that he banged the door behind him.

She could not face a return to the breakfast room. She crept upstairs, as softly as she could, put on her cloak and, wrapping it tightly about her, walked through the bare garden and out on to the moor.

It had stopped snowing, but the sky was still leaden with promise of further falls to come. The way was treacherous, but less so than the path she would now be compelled to steer in the house. She almost felt that death in a snowdrift would be preferable to further humiliation. But this was cowardly thinking, and she was certainly not going to die, if she could help it. Her purpose was burning within her. Her one great fear now was that Ventnor might dismiss her; she refused to think that anything worse could happen to her.

She stumbled on, so intent on her thoughts that she did

not look where she was going. She stepped on to an icy
patch, and would have measured her length, had not
Sam, enveloped in sacking so that he appeared like some
kind of tent, emerged from behind a snow-high bank,
and caught her.

He said, quite roughly, "This is no weather for you to
be out in, girl. And there's more snow to come. These
moors are treacherous to strangers. You'd best go home."

Mary cried out involuntarily, "Oh, I wish I could, I
wish I could——" then, to her utter shame, burst into
tears.

He at once put his arm round her, in so friendly and
fatherly a way that she could not possibly take offense.
Indeed, it was the most comforting thing that had happened to her, so far, and she leant against his chest, trying with her numbed fingers to find a handkerchief.

He said, "There, there——" as if she were a child;
she would scarcely have been surprised if he had offered
to blow her nose for her.

Presently, when she could speak again, she said, "Sam.
Will you tell me something?"

He grumbled, "This is not weather for talk. You'd best
go home, girl, and get a tot of brandy inside of you.
What the devil do they think they're doing to let you out
with ten-foot drifts to drown you in?"

"Please, Sam."

"I got my work to do. Three more sheep with their
throats open in the snow—— And the lambs dying the
minute after they're born—— Such weather. It seems
the popish boy has brought a murrain with him. Well?
What is it? You'll not take my advice. You should go.
This is no place for you."

"Just tell me this," she said. She was beginning to
tremble. "There was a murder here, wasn't there?"

He stared at her. The sacking hung ludicrously over
his eyes. He said at last, "I told you to beware of *him*.
He is not what he seems. You talk of murder, lass. It's
an ill word. There's been throats plucked out here, and
not of sheep, neither. There was a young woman before
you. Some sort of cousin she was. A plain girl—couldn't
get herself a man, so took a job, instead. And as she

hadn't a husband to keep her in order, she went nosing round—and a fine long nose she had and all, enough to keep any husband at bay—but not death, girl, not death. They found her on the moors with her neck broke. We know who did it. We have always known. But what is our word against the gentry's? She found out something she weren't meant to know, and then she got more than she asked for. She lies in the churchyard down there. There's a pretty writing on her headstone. It don't do her no good where she's gone. Go home, Miss Mary. It's cold here, but it's colder down there. He's been blooded now, and more than once, maybe. Once a killer gets the taste, he's done for. Go home."

"Was she young, Sam?"

"Oh, ay. A slip of a thing. Like yourself. She couldn't help being plain, poor lass."

"Do you think he would kill me, then?" asked Mary, staring; she had grown very white.

Sam cried with sudden violence, "Girl, I do not know. How should I? I'm his lordship's chief shepherd, ain't I? —not a fortune-teller. But there's always been a madness in him. He takes what he wants. And if anyone stands in his way——"

"He might murder his own brother, then?"

"It's not for the lack of trying he ain't done so," returned the shepherd, then, as she exclaimed in horror, "Go home! You're a good lass, but you're not in your own world. Go back to Derby."

She turned away without a word. She glanced once across her shoulder, to see him staring after her. Then he pulled the sack more firmly over his head, and, turning his back on her, stalked across the moor.

She met Nicholas at the door. He was looking more distraught and wild than she had yet seen him. He said in a whisper, looking around him as he spoke, "My brother—— Did he hurt you? What did he say? Tell me. I must know."

"No, Nicholas, of course he did not hurt me."

He said, in the same suppressed voice, "I must speak to you. This afternoon. He will be out then. And my mother rests after dinner. There's an attic room at the top of the house, above your bedroom. We'll not be disturbed. Promise you'll come. It is for your own sake."

She waited with bitter impatience for the afternoon. It seemed that at long last she would see the attic. She had never been able to endure waiting. ("Oh, Mary," Nan used to cry, "you fidget so—— Why can't you sit still and be patient?") But when at last she faced Nicholas in the attic room, she thought for one second of something utterly irrelevant. At dinner he had offered her a glass of wine. And, as she glanced at his hands, she saw to her astonishment—her affront, even—that they were entirely at variance with his gentle, melancholy face. They were his mother's hands—coarse, broad, splay-fingered, brutal hands, ruthless hands. And Ventnor—— She remembered that his were, despite his nature, the hands of a gentleman—sensitive, long-fingered and strong.

Nicholas's hand was held out to her now. For some reason she preferred not to look at it. Instead she glanced round the room. It was plainly the lumber room of the house, with a truckle bed at one end, littered with oddments and rubbish; boxes on the floor, and at the far end a big, old-fashioned Jacobean cupboard.

"We kept our toys there," said Nicholas, following her gaze. "Sit down on one of those boxes, Mary. I fear there is no chair to offer you."

She seated herself. She did not look again at his hands, only thanked God that in this unnatural household there was at least one person she could talk to and trust. She said, "I was indiscreet, this morning—I know it. But I was so angry and distressed. You heard about last night?"

"My mother is not inclined to keep things to herself," said Nicholas dryly. "And we lead a quiet life."

She saw that he, too, had heard nothing of the shooting. She did not wish to tell him. Instead she said abruptly, stirring the floor dust with the toe of her shoe, "Is it true that he has tried to kill you?"

He gave her a strange look, then walked over to the window. It was bolted, with iron bars in front of it, as if to prevent a small boy from falling out—or perhaps to keep a prisoner caged in. He said without turning, "I know you despise me for my weakness. God knows, I despise myself. But you cannot know—— If he has tried to kill me, it is only the logical end of what he has been trying to do, all my life. My father died when I was a child, and Ventnor seventeen. If you knew what I endured at his hands—— I was brought up to blows and abuse and worse, everything that could break the spirit. Even now—— But I do not know why I tell you of these things. I have never spoken of them to a soul. And a year ago, there was an unhappy accident. A cousin of ours——"

"She was found dead, wasn't she?"

"Who told you that?" There was a shrillness in his voice. He jerked round to face her.

"Sam."

"Ah? Yes, it's true. She was found dead. It is dangerous to explore too closely into this Jacobite household of mine. The Prince is at Derby, but the fortunes of war are precarious, and if there is eventual defeat, there are— things here my stepbrother might not care to see the light of day. You ask, has he tried to kill me? How should I know? Guns go off by accident. Rocks topple down the hillside. In the rains there are dangerous bogs—— I do not know. But I know that he hates me. We live close, and hatred walks between us. Can you not smell it, Mary? Can you not sense the hate that is our heritage? They call us the mad Ventnors. You know that. Why have you come to us?"

"I have to earn my living."

"Oh!" He burst out laughing. "Is Wardwick Hall your only hope of employment? How is it your father permits you to come here? Does he not know our reputation? Or have his sufferings unhinged his mind?"

"He would survive anything," she said proudly. "He is a good and brave man. Sir—— You told me your brother was in Derby, last March——"

Nicholas's eyes flickered away from hers. "Yes," he said. "Why do you ask?"

She hesitated. At last she said, "You know what happened? Your know my father was pilloried. It was in

the *Derby Mercury*. But not all of it—— They came to
search his house. And in his study they found a letter
which was enough to hang him. Oh," cried Mary—and
the tears began to pour down her face—"that they could
accuse him of treason!—— But the letter: Would you
not like to know what was in it? For indeed I know it by
heart. I can recite it to you." For a second she put her
knuckles to her eyes. Then she continued, "This is what
it said:

> *'After the success which Providence has granted to
> me, I think I cannot do better than enter England
> where I have always been assured that I should meet
> with many friends equally disposed to exert their loy-
> alty to their native King, and to shake off a foreign
> yoke under which the nation has so long groaned.
> The particular character I have heard of you makes
> me hope to see you among the first. I am persuaded
> you will not baulk my expectations, and you need not
> doubt but I shall always remember to your advantage
> the example you shall thus have put to your neigh-
> bors, and consequently to all England. . . .'*

There was a great deal more. It was signed: Charles P.
R.—Charles, Prince Regent. You will see," added Mary
more quietly, "that the purport of the letter could not be
misunderstood. It was addressed to 'V.' Simply the initial.
One day I will find that person."

"And then?" said Nicholas, as his stepbrother had
done.

"He shall find me a hard enemy," said Mary. Then,
her voice soaring up: "Before God, I'll see him strung up
on the gallows. He may be six foot, for all I know, and
put the entire county in fear—but I can be as bold as
he."

Nicholas said, almost in a passion, "You do not know
what you are up against. Go home, I tell you. Go back
to Derby, attend church on Sundays, watch the Derwent
flowing by, dance at the Assemblies. There are rogues in
every county. Why must you concern yourself with
them? Do you, too, want a broken neck? The Prince will

do you less harm than that which may happen to you, here."

She was to remember this. But she brushed the warning away. She said, "Next time it may not be the pillory. It may be the gallows." Then she looked down, and sighed. "I am not at heart a vengeful person. But I cannot endure injustice. I cannot bear it that a kindly, generous, charitable old man should be so used, and all for the whim of—of some devil who has pushed his own guilt upon him, and who is perhaps even now laughing at his own cleverness. I would like to break this person. He shall feel all my father has felt."

He said, "Are you being wise?" There was the faintest slurring to his words.

"Oh, wise! If one were always wise, one would be better dead."

"Sometimes if one is not wise, one *is* dead."

She thought of Ventnor with the gun in his hand. She did not like the thought. She said suddenly, "What would he do if he hears us speaking together in this manner?"

"My stepbrother? He would half-kill me," said Nicholas. "And you—why, you would be lucky if he threw you out into the snow. Mary. Listen to me. What is the good of planning vengeance if the only result is your own death? Come with me now. I think we could make the nearest village, despite the snow. And later you could return home."

"And Ventnor?" demanded Mary, looking at him steadily. It was the first time the actual name had been mentioned between them. She saw Nicholas's face shutter down, and realized with something of a shock how much he hated his half brother. She went on, "Do you imagine that if he is as you say he is, and as I think he is, he would let us escape him? No. Come what may, I will stay here. And you will help me."

"What do you wish me to do?" The old nervous look was back on his face. He picked up a mat lying on the table, and began to twist and wrench it in his powerful fingers.

"Does he not have some place for his private papers?"

"I do not know."

"But you must! He must, after all, have his farm accounts, the rents of his cottages, and so on. Where are they?"

"I do not know."

"Oh, Nicholas!" she said, in complete despair.

He dropped the mat and came so close to her that he almost touched her. She felt his breath on her cheek. "I do not know," he said, "if you are brave or foolish, but you cannot, you must not do this. You do not know what he is capable of. You think you can ruin him. But you'll not do so. You will only kill yourself. And that I could not bear—— I know that I am no one, nothing, but I do have feelings, you know, and I am going to say what I should not say. I love you. No. Don't say anything. For, you see, there is nothing to say. I am not the man for you, or indeed for any woman. But at least I have met you, talked with you, and that is enough to know that you shall not throw away a life that is far more precious to me than my own. You do not know my brother. How should you? But I know him. And I know he is growing suspicious and, therefore, afraid. I have seen him looking at you. Mary, for God's sake, go——"

"Poor Nicholas," she said gently, and at that he gave a kind of groan, and his hands swung out, almost as if against his will, and gripped her arms above her elbows. She did not move away. Only she found herself thinking a little wearily as she had thought before that men thought a deal too much of kissing, and that really this was scarcely the moment. Yet, staring up at the face descending on hers, she was faintly bewildered at the change that passion had made in it; it was no longer boyish and afraid; but smooth, smiling, a little blown, the eyes unwinking and hard.

She waited almost with resignation. His mouth came hard on hers. She had, of course, been kissed by young men before. Not very often, for she was sparing of her kisses, but she had occasionally permitted it, and been rather ashamed of herself afterwards. However, it had happened, and it had been pleasant enough, bringing the color to her cheeks, making her heart beat, and giving her a delightful feeling of superiority. But now, to her surprise, she felt cool and composed, with no feeling in her but pity, tenderness and—how cruel! but she could not deny it—the faintest twinge of contempt, a kindly contempt, but none the less unmistakable. He was holding her very close. She could feel the violent pumping of his heart. His hands were moving now in a proprietary manner that did not please her; she tried gently to free herself. "Nicholas," she said, rather as if rebuking a child, "Nicholas——" But his hands gripped her tighter; she was amazed at his strength, and, for the first time, a little alarmed. Her fastidiousness, too, was affronted by the greediness of his hold, by the insistent mouth that searched for hers, by the rasping of his breath. She said sharply, in her best schoolmarm voice, a little shrill through unease, "Nicholas! For God's sake! Suppose your brother comes up—— What would he think of us?"

He released her suddenly. She could almost have laughed at the instant effect of her words, then thought, with a flash of shame: What a slut I am; what has happened to me? If Ventnor came in now, God help them both, but it was not so much apprehension as the realization of her own shocking behavior that made her speak more angrily than she had intended. She said quite shrewishly, "I am not your fancy girl. Have you no sense of propriety at all?" Then she saw his scolded look and was at once both irritated and penitent; indeed, her own behavior had been equally as free as his. She put out her hand which he at once seized in both of his, turning it over, and kissing the palm frantically. She protested, half-laughing, "Don't eat me! Nicholas. I think this is my fault, but it is not at all seemly. We should go downstairs. Not only would your brother be extremely angry——"

"Angry!" said Nicholas, in a muffled voice. His eyes slewed towards the door. "Angry! My God——"

"But," she continued, "it would also put a stop to all my plans." She wished again that he were not such a coward. He was, after all, surprisingly strong for his build, and even if it came to a standup fight, could surely hold his own. But she went on, "For he would certainly dismiss me, for which one could scarce blame him—and then I would be back in Derby with no chance in the world of finding out what I want to know."

He said almost sulkily, "I think that would be a very good thing."

"Not for me!"

He turned towards her. She thought he was going to take her in his arms again, and she moved hastily backwards. A curious revulsion seized her. She did not want his arms round her. But he only said, very sadly, "No, Mary. I am not going to touch you. I frightened you, didn't I?"

"No, no."

"I know I did. Can you forgive me? Oh, Mary, you must forgive me, or I shall go mad."

What a fuss over nothing, said the detached, practical side of her mind. But she saw that there were tears in his eyes. She said uneasily, "Of course, I forgive you, Nicholas. Don't be absurd. It's as much my fault as yours. We are both a little overwrought."

He whispered, "I love you so much."

She was growing more and more conscious of the absurdity of the situation, and also—to her secret fury—of a terror that Ventnor should suddenly appear in the doorway. The thought of what he would say or do in such circumstances made her stomach turn over. To see his brother embracing the young woman who had tried last night to shoot him—— Then, disconcertingly, she realized that she would be not only terrified but ashamed. He might half-kill her, or kill her entirely, for all she knew—but it was not only that; she did not wish him to see her in so unbecoming a situation. She looked at Nicholas with something approaching dislike. Men were all the same. They could never discuss anything serious with a woman, but must be perpetually kissing and cuddling —— His mouth was a little open, his eyes glistening with tears. It was not—it was not *manly*. However, she was a kind-hearted girl, and she did not wish to hurt him; besides, she was afraid that if she spoke to him sharply he might break down entirely—and that she could not endure.

She said soothingly, "I know, but it's only because you

are upset. I like you very much too, and it is wonderful to feel that I have a friend here, but——"

"Oh, Mary," he said.

"I must go now, Nicholas. It would really be most unfortunate if——"

"I know, I know. But listen, my darling girl, listen—— Oh, God, how lovely you are——"

"I am not in the least lovely," said Mary crossly. "I am rather plain."

"You are beautiful."

"Nonsense! Nicholas, please——"

"Just one moment," he said. "There is something I must say. Hear me out, Mary. I'll not be long. You can't remain in this house, you know. It is too dangerous for both of us."

"But——"

"And the—the evidence you want is not here."

"Is that true?" She was staring at him.

"Do you think I would lie to you?"

This was not a question to which, tactically, one could reply in the affirmative. Yet Mary, her senses sharpened by emotion and fatigue, was not sure; she did not reply.

Nicholas said in a wretched voice, "You despise me, don't you, for being afraid of *him*. I despise myself. No one could reproach myself more bitterly than I do."

Mary, though filled with compassion could only wish that Nicholas would not choose this minute to indulge in self-recrimination. Any moment now she expected to hear a heavy footfall on the stair. She moved nearer the door. Her mouth had grown unmistakably dry. She could not but admit to herself that his lordship, though he was far from being a desirable character, had the power of inspiring a hearty respect in his household.

And there was Nicholas going on and on and on, as if they had all the time in the world. She could have boxed his ears. "I am ashamed of myself," he was saying, "but I shudder from violence. I always have done. And he—— I must not frighten you, my dearest little girl."

"Pray don't distress yourself on my account," said Mary with a rather acid smile and, resigned now to what fate could offer her, sat down on the edge of the ramshackle bedstead, her hands folded in her lap. If Ventnor came, he came, and that was all there was to it; let him assume the worst, and no doubt he would do so.

He sensed the irony in her voice. He shot her a hard look that she did not see. Then he said, more calmly, "I am boring you. I'm sorry. I'll come to the point. When I said I knew nothing, that was not true. Only I—I wanted to protect you. However—— When you journeyed here, Mary, you must have passed the shippon. Do you not remember?"

"Why, yes." She looked at him in some surprise. "It is haunted by an echo, or so your brother said. You don't mean, surely——"

"Yes. Why not? Nobody goes there. It has an ill reputation. You know how it is in country places—people are very superstitious."

She had risen in her excitement. For the moment she entirely forgot her fear of Ventnor. She began, her voice shrill in her excitement, "Do you mean——"

"Hush, sweetheart. Yes. There is enough there to hang us all."

She said, "Then I am going there. Now."

"In this weather, alone?" He raised his hands. "There are drifts ten feet deep. You would never reach it. But I will take you, Mary."

"You!"

"Yes. Coward as I am, I will take you."

She was very moved, and ashamed too that she had so misjudged him. She said, her voice a little out of control, "Oh, Nicholas! But what will happen to you if he finds out?"

He gave her a rather wry smile. "I think we shall have to take very good care that he does not find out until it is too late. Listen, Mary. We will go tonight, when the household is asleep."

"But he will hear——"

"No. I'll ensure that he sleeps soundly."

"What can you mean?" Fear rounded her eyes. "Surely you——"

"Oh, I'll not poison him! Do you think so harshly of me? I'll just put a sleeping draught in his wine. He'll be none the worse for it, next morning. Will you be ready at midnight? I'll come for you, and we will go together. With any luck we'll be back before anyone is stirring. There are fortunately no servants on the premises, except for old Betty, and she's as deaf as a post."

"Your mother——"

"Oh, she sleeps like the dead. Anyway, her room faces the back of the house. You need not be afraid," said Nicholas. "And then you will have all the evidence you want, and you can tell Ventnor simply that you wish to go back to Derby. He'll suspect nothing. Why should he?"

Mary did not answer. Ventnor seemed to her to be of a singularly mistrustful nature, and she was not well-trained in deceit. Her mouth went down at the corners. Something in her rebelled. It was all perhaps a little too glib. Her eyes wandered again to the cupboard against the wall. Surely if one wished to hide incriminating evidence, one would choose to do so where one could keep an eye on it, not in some outlandish spot where any chance tramp, who would care nothing for local superstition, might spend the night, and examine the premises in the hope of finding something of value. But then if Nicholas were right, how shocking it would be if she missed this opportunity——

She said at last, without much enthusiasm, but with considerable firmness, "Very well, then. I will be ready at midnight."

"So we are fellow conspirators," said Nicholas; then, before she had the faintest idea of what he would say, cried out in a sudden loud voice, "Mary! Mary—will you marry me?"

Men, really——"Oh, Nicholas," she said, like any shrew, "please do not be so absurd."

"Is it absurd? I love you so very dearly. We could get married tonight, Mary. There is the Peak Forest Church not very far from here. I believe we could reach it. The minister there is his own surrogate, and grants marriage licenses to runaway couples. There is even a special book for them—— It would be a real marriage. You don't imagine, surely, I am suggesting a Fleet marriage for us? It is a recognized thing. Anyone here will tell you. Oh,

Mary, I know you do not love me as much as I love you, but I swear I could make you do so, I have enough love for the two of us, and——"

"Nicholas!" Then she put her hands over her face, saying in muffled tones, "Dear Nicholas, this is quite preposterous. You do not have to marry me to help me—— No! You must let me speak. We scarcely know each other. Why—why, what could we live on?" Her voice broke into laughter. "Do you think perhaps your brother would make us an allowance?"

He plainly did not find this amusing. He said sullenly, "I could work——"

"And what do you imagine Ventnor would say?" She spoke the name deliberately, then was penitent at the instant change in his expression. She said gently, "Shall we talk about this some other time? Be sensible, Nicholas. Marriage is not something that can be decided in an hour's conversation. Besides, if you talk like this, I shall begin to think twice about letting you escort me to a deserted cow-byre in the middle of the night——"

"You are quite right," he said, catching at her hand. "You are always right. Tonight we will search for those papers. But we can talk of this again, can't we? Can't we?"

"Yes, of course," said Mary absentmindedly; thinking: Perhaps tonight I shall know at last, perhaps the world can be told the truth——

"You do love me a little, don't you?"

"Of course I do——" To be able to say: Papa, it is all over, everybody knows how shamefully ill used you have been——

"Then may I kiss you once more? I only want to kiss you. You are so sweet——"

Mary turned on him an exasperated face, in which sweetness was singularly lacking. She said coldly, "If you insist. It is really not seemly, but as the whole business is shocking, I suppose it does not matter."

He kissed her very gently, so gently that she was sorry, and wished she could love him more. But then she said, "We must go down now. And I will go first. If I am challenged, I will think of an answer. If we are together, I fear it would be impossible to explain."

He said, with a half-laugh, "You are the better conspirator of the two of us. Very well, my darling. Be ready at midnight, and make sure you're warmly dressed. I think it would be advisable if we are not seen talking together for the rest of the day. But I shall be there. And you need not worry about my dear brother. He will be having the best night's sleep he has had for a long time."

She did not like this. She wished she were more single-purposed. However, she spent the rest of the afternoon reading aloud to the old lady, who was in one of her romantic moods; this did not stop her swearing at Mary for the undeniable number of mistakes she made in her reading, which even included turning over two pages at once, and going on as if nothing had happened.

That was bearable. But supper was not. Her gaze wandered continually to Ventnor's glass of wine. When he picked it up, she could not bear to look. When she glanced at him again, his glass was empty; the look he bestowed on her, however, was not; she could not read its meaning, but it brought the guilty blood to her cheeks. She was thankful when the meal was over, and she could go up to her room again.

But the solitude and waiting were unbearable, too. Never had she regretted any decision more heartily. Never had the hours to midnight crawled by so slowly. She struggled to read, but could not take in a word. She had derided Nicholas's lack of courage, but it was nothing now compared to her own. When she heard Ventnor's unmistakable footsteps coming up the stairs, a little after eleven—the family kept early hours, for they were usually up at daybreak—she had to bite her hand, to keep some vestige of self-control. She was almost certain that the steps paused outside her room, but she could not be sure, and almost immediately she heard them moving away, and then the shutting of his bedroom door.

She slipped on the cloak Aunt Briarcliffe had given her. Aunt Briarcliffe would have hysterics if she knew that her niece was planning to go out at this hour with a young man—— Mary was not far from having hysterics, herself. She sat down again by the fire, her fingers intertwined. At the back of her mind was a small, nagging ache of fear that she had not yet permitted herself fully to consider. It was nothing to do with Ventnor. That fear was all-engulfing—how flattered he would be, she thought. No. It was not that. It was more the thought of the journey—alone with Nicholas, to a deserted cottage. He was so very uncontrolled, so very much—apparently —in love, and so very strong. Mary could not but realize how angry she would be if Nan, her young sister, at a later date, did anything so foolish. It had to be done at night. She could see that. But it was not wise. She did not believe Nicholas meant her any harm, but he was very young, and there would be nobody within call——

"I wonder," she said aloud, voicing at long last the suspicion that had never quite left her, "if those papers really are there?"

There was the faintest knock at the door. She jumped to her feet. She was committed now—and she had never lacked decision. She pulled the hood over her head, and opened the door.

Nicholas crept inside, moving stealthily in a way that irritated her; it was like a stage melodrama. The suspense, the fear, the warring doubts, had the inevitable effect; she began to giggle.

"Ssh!" he said. "For God's sake! Are you quite ready?"

She recovered her gravity. Heaven knew it was serious enough. She said she was ready; then: "Your brother——?"

"Dead to the world," said Nicholas, with a flash of the vindictiveness that she found so distasteful. He looked at her. "How pretty you are! Let me kiss you once before we start."

Her face tightened with fury. "No," she said sharply, remembering, however, to keep her voice down. "Certainly not. Have you no sense at all? If you talk again of kissing, we shall stay here. I am not going out into this bitter night to kiss, but to save my father's repu—— Nicholas!"

She was so utterly helpless. She could not, of course, make a sound except gasps of spitting vituperation. But she did not even dare to struggle as she would have liked to have done, and there were his arms wrapped round her, her body pinioned against his, and she could only twist her face aside, tightening her lips, screwing up her eyes too, wishing she could kill him, mad with fury and humiliation.

She heard nothing. But suddenly Nicholas jerked his head back; then, with a choking sound, half-oath, half-whimper, almost let her drop to the ground, the color blazing into his face.

Ventnor stood in the doorway. He stood there, legs astride. He was still dressed, in shirt and breeches. He said nothing. There was no need for him to speak. Fury, amazement, and something else that Mary could not define, flared blackly about him. Meeting his blazing, enraged eyes, she began to blush as scarlet as Nicholas. In the diary of her mind she thought frantically: A fine guilty pair we look, dressed for running away, embraced in each other's arms, both as red as apples—— A less suspicious man than his lordship might have been entitled to assume the very worst; what Ventnor must now be thinking simply passed all imagination. Oh, God, she thought, oh, God—— This could not be happening to her. The girls who had come to her with their stories of shame and disgrace—— She had said, gently enough, but reasonably: It is your fault too, you know. There is no reason to find yourself in such a situation—— A little common sense, she had said, might have prevented it. You have been very foolish, she had said, one must after all have pride and decency——

Pride and decency—— There was, of course, nothing to say. Nothing at all. She was thankful when at last he spoke. He did not immediately look at her, but turned to his young stepbrother, who had now backed against the wall, in the most abject fear, and was standing there, all color gone from his face. Ventnor said softly, "So you are up to your tricks again. But I warned you—— Get out! I'll speak to you, later."

Nicholas stammered, "You—you do not understand. We—we love each other. We are g-going to get married——"

"Married!" The word came out in a roar that must surely, thought Mary, crack the very windows. But she was equally appalled by Nicholas's remark—the boy must be mad. She cried out, "No! That is not true!"

Ventnor said, with a savage smile, "You do not seem to be in complete agreement. Perhaps the marriage ceremony was not to be insisted on?"

Nicholas, plainly panic-stricken, ignoring Mary, stuttered again, "You don't understand——"

"Do I not? Do I not!" Ventnor stepped forward at this, and shooting out his right arm, caught his brother by the collar and threw him towards the door, so that he fell on to his knee. He said, his breath coming in gasps, "Was not once enough? Did I not warn you of what would happen if this occurred again? Get out——!"

Mary, forgetting her own fear, sprang forward. "Oh, don't," she began, half crying. "Don't. You'll hurt him——"

"You are perfectly right," said Ventnor, in the same fierce, bitter voice, then to Nicholas, "Will you get out, or do I have to put you out? You will have plenty of time to explain yourself. I doubt if any explanation will be a plausible one, but I only hope for all our sakes that it is."

Nicholas seemed beside himself. Mary staring at him fearfully, grew aware that the expression in his face was not entirely terror. There was an enraged, frustrated look to him like—the image flew into her mind—some wild animal at bay. Afraid, yes—but it was a fear that could turn to attack, a fear that concealed a knife half-drawn from its sheath; he was looking from side to side, his mouth parted, the sweat out on his forehead. He did not at once move. He cowered there, head sunken, eyes roaming from Ventnor to Mary, then back again.

She could not bear it. There was something debased in him that appalled her. She said, "Oh, please go—— Please!"

Ventnor at this gave a harsh laugh. "You see. The lady begs you to go. She is about to create a tragic and dramatic scene. To weep, protest her innocence—— Get out, for God's sake, before I do you a mischief. She and I are both swelled with drama." Then his voice soared up to the pitch which could quell even his stepmother's appalling laugh. "Get out!"

Nicholas met such a look that his courage failed him altogether. He backed into the passage, slamming the door behind him.

It was not a gallant exit. Mary, now well in the firing line, for a second closed her eyes. Her father had once said, "If you are about to be unjustly accused, never speak first. It gives you time to collect yourself, to know what to reply." But her father was a patient man, with a powerful will—and she was young, impatient, and dreadfully situated. Ventnor's look of bitter scorn took her breath from her, and nearly her wits, too; she could control her speech, but not the color in her cheeks, nor the mortified tears that blurred her eyes.

He said with the quietness that presaged a storm, "This has all been exceeding clever. You must have planned it most carefully. First a powder in the poor devil's wine, to knock him into sleep——" The storm burst in a thunderclap. *"What* sort of fool do you take me for? What sort of fool? To be trapped by such a child's trick—— Oh, I know my brother. As I am beginning to know you—— When he offers me wine with so polite an air, so steady a hand, why, that wine is not for me—— And you watching to see me drink, so delighted when you saw my glass was empty—— How you must have congratulated yourself. And so you were going to get married——?"

"No," said Mary faintly, then wished she had not spoken, for the truth would be to Ventnor far worse than this false assumption; she was left with the bitter knowledge that it would be better to admit to gross impropriety than a spying that might cost her her life.

"Then what were you proposing to do?"

It seemed that silence was her only weapon. And so she was silent, and stood there, feeling as if she were guilty of every crime in the calendar, and wondering what she would do if he struck her, for she had never even considered such a thing, and he looked as if he were considering it at this very moment.

He said, "Have you no lie ready for me? You *were* going to get married. Where were you going? To the Peak Forest Church, perhaps?" He saw her lashes flicker. "Ah.

So you were. All this time, while you have been playing
the meek little girl, the dutiful companion, you have been
planning this move. A fitting end to your excursion away
from home—— To come back with a handsome husband,
and the chance of a title, provided you could get me out
of the way. I suppose that was the next step? How were
you going to manage that? You would have come back
together, I suppose, and said nothing to me. And then
—— What then? You have no pistol any longer, but I
assume that could be arranged. Or would it be another
powder that would make me sleep a great deal longer? I
am sure that you and Nicholas between you could contrive something vastly effective. And then a brief period
of mourning, and the new Lady Ventnor would rise, a
brilliant star in the London sky—the vicar's little daughter
would trespass on the fringe of the *haut-ton*, and all
would be golden, all would be like the end of a novelette."
He paused for a moment. "It would have been a fitting
punishment if I had left you alone, shut my ears to all
this shuffling and whispering, hush, hush, don't let
Ventnor hear us——" He stared at her, his face gray in
the dim light. "You would have crept down the stairs,
hand in hand. To kiss perhaps on the doorstep. To laugh
a little at the damned, deluded dupe upstairs, snoring in
his drugged sleep. You'd not have laughed for long——
But you would have stolen out into the snow, dreaming
of the gold ring round your fingers, the gold coronet on
your hair, the golden days and nights of London, with
balls and masquerades and all that your heart could wish.
And he—— Shall I tell you what he would have been
dreaming of? Shall I, Mary? You will forgive the lack
of formality, I am sure. After all, as a potential sister-in-
law you should be addressed by your Christian name."

She wished to say a great many things. But she could
only see herself as Ventnor saw her, and the words choked
in her throat, and the tears burst from her eyes. The
strange, reasonable side of her that still functioned, even
in this moment of catastrophe, whispered to her: How
can you blame him? Her mortification was like a physical
blow; she had never imagined herself, the self-possessed,
cool, composed Miss Mary Vernon, in such a discredit-

able situation; she struggled for self-control, but she could not stop the bitter, ashamed tears from rolling down her cheeks.

He said, "Am I making you cry again? I'll make you cry a great deal harder before I have finished with you. Cry by all means. Howl if you will. I have a most invulnerable heart to cheats and sluts and hypocrites. Well? Shall I not tell you my half brother's private dream?"

"You must," sobbed Mary in a compound of fury and despair, "tell me what you please."

"So I must! But perhaps that is a dream that should only be told in the full light of day. There is a wayside cross on Kinder Scout. Of course you have not yet seen it. It is a speciality of the county. There is always room for more." The derisive tones cracked in a fresh storm of anger. Outside the snow was flung in whiteness across the moors, but Mary, in her wretchedness, was not aware of it, could only stare at him. "You slut!" he cried out. "You designing, contriving cheat! To think that all this has been weaving in your fine sharper's mind—— Saying, yes my lord, no my lord, reading so sweetly to my stepmother, chopping logic with me, looking with wide, grave eyes—so that, upon my soul, I believed in you, and even thought the pistol shot was truly an accident—— That misfired, did it not? But you bandaged me so charmingly and feigned such penitence that—let this afford you what satisfaction it may—I believed every word of it, every word, I, the worst fool of all. And all the time, whoring after him—— Are harlots so cheap in Derby? It seems they must grow two a penny. Cozening me and cozening him. How do you do it? Does one take a course at a seminary, on how to lie, how to deceive? What are your methods? Answer me! This sniveling is of no use now; surely you have the wit to see that. Be brazen, Mary. Tell me the truth at last, so that there can be something between us that is not lying, before we part."

At his last words, her eyes widened, but she could only mutter, "Whatever I say now, you will not believe." And then, before she could prevent herself, "I don't blame you. No one in his senses would believe anything but the worst of me."

He stared at her. "Always the play acting—— So utter frankness is now your weapon. I fear the edge of it is blunted. But you still do not answer. What are your methods? I hope you will not encourage me to use mine. My stepbrother is not too old to be corrected, but neither are you, if I had my way." Then before she could even attempt to answer, he crashed his damaged hand down on the nearest chairback, so violently that he must have reopened the wound, crying, "God, God, God! I cannot believe it—I cannot——"

Then oblivious of the pain that must have scorched through him, he advanced on her. Her aghast, down-slanting eyes saw the redness creeping through the bandage. She forgot the menace of his attitude, and exclaimed, "Your hand! Look what you have done. Have you no sense at all?"

He held the hand up. The blood had now stained the bandage across, and was beginning to trickle into his palm. He whispered, "Such solicitude. Such true, feminine solicitude—— The lady shoots me with one hand, and binds me up with the other. I have no doubt, my dear, that when you have poisoned me, you will run to my bedside to lay cool cloths upon my brow." He broke off. He met her miserable, resentful gaze. His own color flared up. He said, "But I have been the fool. I should have known. It seems one always keeps a vestige of one's youthful *naïveté*. But it is gone now. There is no one to trust. No one." Then he said in a hard, abrupt voice, "Enough of all this. I had intended—— I do not know what I had intended. But you act better than you know. You have so young and ingenuous a face, Mary, and the tears are poignant, and you are very little, after all, and it seems I cannot deal with you as you deserve. But you will go. You will leave immediately."

She had of course expected this. It was inevitable. But this did not make it any the less appalling. She began to stammer, "But it's the m-middle of the night——"

He mimicked her. "Yes, my dear. It is the m-middle of the night. Your wedding night, as I understand. But is one brother worser than the other? You were proposing, were you not, to set out for Peak Forest Church? In the m-middle of the night. And now instead you shall set out for Derby with Robert. Or Robin, if you wish to be more familiar. Why not? Hugged in his arms—oh, hugged most tightly, I assure you—all the way back to Derby, and in the m-middle of the night, too. Will that be sufficiently romantic for you? I cannot promise you kisses, but I swear to hold you as you have never been held before. We'll not stop. We'll carry all before us. By this time tomorrow you should be on papa's doorstep again."

She cried out, forgetting everything except that she could not leave, she must not leave. "No! No, no, no!"

"Oh, yes," he said. He was staring at her, half-smiling, the breath coming violently between his teeth. "Yes, indeed. Are you worrying about your salary? It shall be paid to you. But I'll not have you another hour in this house. Start packing your things."

She looked at him wildly, clenching and unclenching her fists. His smile widened. "This is not quite what you expected, is it?" he said. "Upon my soul, I believe you thought to cozen me, even now. Have you no pretty words with which to melt my heart? Could you not go on your knees to me?" Then he shouted at her, "You confounded little bitch! Pack your things, or else you go without."

Mary fought a desperate, agonizing battle with her pride. To be so spoken to, to be sworn at, to be turned out of the house like a misbehaving servant—— Papa, she said to herself, papa. I must think of him, not of this —— She forced to her mind the picture of how he had looked when they brought him back to the house. Papa —— Then she raised her face to Ventnor, and began to sob, deliberately, noisily, vulgarly, clutching at him with her hands. She wailed, "Don't send me away! Oh, don't please, please don't! I'm sorry, I'm sorry, I've behaved disgustingly, I know, but I never will again, I swear it. Forgive me this once, let me stay! Oh, you can't do this, you can't be so cruel—— What will my father say to me? Oh, oh, oh——!"

"I trust he'll beat you soundly," said Ventnor, jerking away from her. But he was disconcerted. She could see that. His eyes widened as if he were genuinely astonished.

"He will!" sobbed Mary—papa, who had never struck either of his children in his life! "He'll kill me. Oh, please, my lord, don't send me away. Give me one more chance. It'll never occur again——"

He infuriated her beyond measure by breaking into laughter. "That it'll not," he said, "you damned play-acting little slut! Trying to bam me—*me!* There'll be no more kissing, my girl, and no more eloping, neither. Start your packing, or I swear I'll give you something to cry for."

Mary at that moment could willingly have killed him. She forgot her role of blubbering penitent. She glared at him, white with rage.

He met the glare. He returned it with a brief, hard smile. He said softly, "And all for nothing—— That hurts, doesn't it? All for nothing!" Then he added grimly, "Will you go and pack, please? I shall not ask you again."

She swallowed hard. It was unbelievable that one moment of impulse should utterly wreck her plans. She said, the words as painful as a mouthful of nails, "Could you not overlook this? It was not as you think. Your brother——"

He said in a whisper, "You'll be out within the hour. I overlook nothing. As for my brother—— But that is no concern of yours. For the last time—pack. You had best obey me."

She walked over to her portmanteau. She had no choice. He watched her for a minute, then walked out of the room. Now that she was alone, she wept genuinely and bitterly—wept for the inglorious end to her schemings, for her father, for her own disgrace, and for something else that hurt more than all the rest combined. And as she wept, the tears flooding her face, she hurled her clothes savagely into her box. But standing there, a handful of garments under her arm, she thought suddenly of the cupboard in the attic. The room was disused. Perhaps even now at the eleventh hour—— She opened her door—to be immediately thrust back by an iron arm, to hear a voice saying coolly, "Well, Mary? Is there anything further I can do for you?"

She stared into his eyes. She did not trouble to feign surprise or distress. The time for pretense was gone. She said, "It is your victory, my lord. But, believe me, it is not the end."

"Is it not?" he said. "Why, Mary, if it is really not the end, then it is none of your doing. The end is upon us sometimes before we realize it."

She said, turning her face aside, "I suppose you know what you mean. But, 'faith, I do not."

"I do not suppose you do," he said, "for you are an excessively stupid girl who leaps to conclusions with the most unerring inaccuracy—— But I believe I told you to pack. Why are you not doing so? Are you going back to your room, or must I carry you there? I should," he added, with a smile that angered her beyond bearing, "rather enjoy that."

She went into her room again in silence, her color high. She stuffed her belongings into her box. When at last she emerged, she found him still at the top of the stairs, rather as if he were a watchdog. He took the portmanteau from her—an unexpected courtesy which surprised her—shoved it on to his shoulder and carried it downstairs. She half suspected he would have liked to do the same with her. In the hallway he said, "Wait here while I saddle my horse." He added with a threatening gesture, "And you'd best do as you are told, this time."

She stood there, fighting still her despairing tears. She wondered if Nicholas would contrive to say goodbye to her. She did not really want to see him, but it would have made a difference to hear a few kindly words of farewell. But it seemed that she must swallow her disgrace undiluted. There was no sign of him. The house was as cold and still as the grave. The only sound was that of the library clock chiming two.

She watched drearily as Ventnor crossed the hallway. He opened the door. The bitter air blew in on her so that she shuddered; it seemed to penetrate through all her clothes. She waited for him to speak, to summon her. But he said not a word, only stood there, motionless, his vast shoulders blocking the doorway.

At last, impatient, she stepped to his side.

The snow was blown before them in a wild blizzard. It blotted out the world. It lay high and heaped by the door, reaching to the top so that she could not have seen over it, had Ventnor not kicked some of it away. The outline of the moor was scarcely to be seen against the white, flurried sky. Only Kinder Scout was visible, rearing itself up like a vast shoulder, Atlas supporting the world.

He turned his head slowly. She saw the bleak rage and despair in his face. Joyful triumph flooded her own. She said, her voice soft and quivering, "Why, my lord, it looks as if I must trespass on your hospitality for at least one more night."

He still said nothing. And then she began to laugh. Her laughter pealed across the blanched silence, hurtling itself against the soft whiteness that streamed before her eyes.

He caught at her shoulders. His fingers dug into her. She believed he would hit her; she rejoiced and was unafraid, so far had she come from Miss Vernon of Derby, the vicar's daughter who had gone to war, and who now, at the moment of defeat, saw victory. But he only looked down at her from his great height. He said, "God save us, what a fool you are."

That was all. He released her. He walked away. Her laughter ceased. And now she was afraid again—afraid of the north wind that clawed at her, the emptiness, the barrenness, the unbearable whiteness of the snow. And as she stared across it, she saw a small gray dot move over its surface. She broke into a great cry that arrested his progress halfway up the stairs.

"Ventnor!" she called, her breath sobbing, "Oh, Ventnor! Fetch your gun, my lord. Your killer is abroad again!" And turned to bury her face in her crooked arms, against the doorpost.

V The Killer

What passed between the stepbrothers Mary did not
know. It was not, perhaps, as violent as she dreaded.
Ventnor, as she was beginning to realize, was less drastic
in his methods than in his speech. But she could not know,
and she was very much afraid. She walked upstairs to
the little room she had never thought to see again. As
she halted for a second on the stairway, she saw Ventnor
fling open the library door, heard Nicholas's voice. Then
the door shut. She clasped her mittened hands on the
banisters, leant over a little. She waited for sounds of
violence, raised voices. There was a sickness in her
stomach. But she heard nothing. Yet she could not rid
herself of fear. In this wild household anything could
happen; the Ventnors were a law unto themselves, and
the moors their kingdom.

He had said to her, Have I three kingdoms and must
you fly in my eye?

I'll fly in your eye, she thought, going back to her
room and sitting down on the bed—oh, I'll fly in your
eye. But how short was her time. The moment the snow
ceased she would be rushed back to Derby. Ventnor was
not the man to go back on his word, and it was plain that
he was in a mighty hurry to be rid of her.

Somehow that put heart in her, and she was so low in
her self-esteem that she badly needed the restorative.
She pulled off her cloak and bonnet, threw them on the
bed, and came softly out of her room, looking up the
rickety stairs that led to the attic. It was God knew what
hour in the morning, but she was wide awake to the
point of feeling she would never sleep again; Ventnor
was closeted with his brother, and probably would feel
that after the set down he had given her she would be

crying in her room, her spirit temporarily crushed.

As she stood there, hesitating, she heard the library door open. She started guiltily, then, glancing down, saw that it was Nicholas.

He turned his eyes in her direction. In thought he was plainly still in the library. There was so white and frustrated a rage on his face that she could scarcely credit it. For the second time tonight it struck her that Nicholas, too, could be dangerous. The next instant the expression vanished, to be replaced instantly by the dreadful hangdog look she had grown to associate with him.

Pity stirred in her heart, and again that unwelcome flicker of contempt. How could he be so afraid? She would never be so afraid of anyone—no, not even of Ventnor, though tonight he had given her enough cause.

"Nicholas!" she whispered; then, "I am so very sorry."

He gave her a look that seemed to her startled eyes to be one of dislike. Then he raised his hands in a dramatic gesture of despair. She saw again his great, wide, violent hands; they made her wince. They were wrong. They were not in character. If they had been Ventnor's——

"Well?" said a deep voice behind her.

She did not turn. But she was horribly taken aback, for she had assumed he was still in the library. She had forgotten how silently he could move. She saw Nicholas disappear across the hallway like a flash. She said, calmly enough, "Well?" But she was trembling, beyond all control.

He was saying, "So you are up to your mischief again —and again, and again. I thought I had taught you a lesson. I thought that after tonight you would not be so eager to meddle. But it seems I have underrated you. You certainly do not waste your time. Look at me, please. Where are your manners?"

She turned at this, leaning back, her hands still clasping the banisters. She was so angry that she forgot to be afraid. She said, "So you must continue to discipline me? Your household is growing sadly out of hand, my lord. Your young brother forgets to behave like the twelve-year-old you take him to be, and I—why, I am become the town slut you have always rated me; I plan an elopement, I do not wilt before you, I presume to speak to you saucily. I see you are still keeping an eye on me. I trust it is not the eye I have flown into."

He said grimly, ignoring this, "I am keeping an eye on you, my girl, until the moment you leave this house. And that, I hope, will be soon."

"How afraid you are. How afraid that I shall find out something you would not wish me to know."

"Yes," he said, "I am afraid."

This admission disconcerted her. She stared at him.

He went on, "I give you fair warning, Mary. I'll not have you spying on us any more. Is that understood? God knows it ought to be—I have surely made it plain enough."

"Yes, my lord," said Mary, with a bright, hard smile.

"*Don't* call me—— Look, my girl. I am warning you. Do you believe me? I am not the man to threaten and do nothing. If you have any wisdom in your featherhead, you'll listen and obey."

"Yes, my lord."

His breath was coming swiftly. He gave her a sideways glance, and suddenly she was afraid again and in good earnest. She shot a frantic look round and down, to see if there were anyone in the hall.

He said, quite mildly, "You see. You are a stupid girl. There is no one within hearing. No one to help you. There are no servants, and my stepmother, if she thought I meant to treat you as you deserve, would risk her rheumatics and everything else to act as spectator. And Nicholas—I should not depend too much on him if I were you. Suppose I chose at this moment to put my hand on your waist—so, and bring my other down on your shoulder. Like this. I am considerably stronger than you, Mary. And larger. It would not take a breathing space for me to tip you over the banister. There are stone flags beneath. There would be a paragraph, perhaps, in the *Derby Mercury*. A regrettable accident, etc. I should, of course, pay for your funeral and attend it in person."

She knew at this point, despite the terror that swallowed her breath and brought the sweat out on her body, that he was shamelessly laughing at her. She could not understand it. She grew wildly angry. His face was grave enough, and threatening, too; the hands touching her had tautened as if for action. But there was something in the eyes so near hers that suggested not murder but a deep and unregenerate amusement. She stared back, refusing to flinch, refusing to utter one word of entreaty. He released her. He said abruptly, "At least you have courage. It is often the fool's only virtue." A new note came into his voice. "Mary, if I said to you that I had nothing to do with your father's betrayal, if I swore that——"

She cried out, "I'd not believe you if you swore an hundred oaths."

His voice changed, and his face too. "Very well," he said, "we will leave it at that. Since you are so determined to make me out a villain, why, I'll endeavor to play the role to your satisfaction. I hope tomorrow to return you to your father. I shall do it in person, to make sure you do not escape me. But meanwhile, if I catch you again poking your nose into things that do not concern you, I'll break your back for you, and possibly your neck too, and I mean it. What is more"—his voice was quivering with temper so that she instinctively drew back—"if I find you and my young step-devil hobnobbing together, kissing and so forth, I'll so deal with the pair of you. You'd not enjoy seeing him humiliated, would you? Or enjoy his seeing your humiliation? And I am not likely to restrain myself. Then I suggest that for his own sake you leave him alone. He does not need you. And you——"

She interrupted in a clear voice. "I could forgive you for speaking so to me. But Nicholas is your half brother. How can you treat him so? You are far kinder to your horses and your sheep. Have you no kindness for him? Are you not afraid that one day he may turn on you? For if ever a man invited murder, my lord, it seems to me that you are he."

"Murder," he repeated, looking fixedly at her. Then he gave a sigh, almost as if in despair, and turned away. He said over his shoulder as he went slowly and wearily down the stairs, "I mean what I say. If you are wise you will keep to your room or stay in my stepmother's company. I would not like, for your own sake, to find you investigating the contents of our bureaux and cupboards. And I should find out. I am not so easily hoodwinked as you seem to imagine, and when I am angry I am not particularly nice in my methods, neither. I might give you the shock of your sheltered life."

She could believe that. But she was already prepared to disregard his warning. She was afraid of him, but her time was nearly eclipsed, and her desperation overrode her fear. But it seemed that he would give her no opportunity for doing what she wanted. For the rest of the day she was never left alone. Once, when her eyes turned towards the attic stair again, she started to find him silently at her elbow. He said not a word, only took her arm and led her away, not leaving her until she was safely in the sitting room.

The old lady appeared to know nothing of what had occurred. And, fortunately for Mary, who was beginning to feel as supervised as a prisoner on his way to the gallows, she was mainly preoccupied with the news of the young Prince at Derby. She greeted Mary with a shriek of delighted laughter, apparently not noticing her pale, strained looks.

She cried out, "Did I not say that a Highlander without shoes or stockings would fight better than all your Hanoverians with their gaiters and pigtails? Did I not, miss? And now James III has been proclaimed king of England, Scotland, France and Ireland. O that I had been there! And Lord John Drummond has landed at Montrose with a thousand Irish and Scottish troops. There is even good news from France, not that I'd trust those Frenchies myself, dirty lot of foreigners that they are. There's a council of war in Exeter House today. Oh, he'll be in London within the week, God bless him, and we'll go there to salute him. What the devil's the matter with you?"

Mary, who had been letting the words flow over her head, started and flushed.

The old lady surveyed her with a shrewd, unkindly eye. "You're looking precious sorry for yourself, ain't you?

Been having a set-to with my dear stepson? He's sometimes a little rough in his ways, and you mewling town
misses don't perhaps like it. What's he been doing to you?
What's he been saying?"

"Nothing," said Mary stiffly. "You are mistaken,
ma'am. There has been no disagreement between us."

"Then what ails you? You ain't paid to sit there as
pale and peaked as a cream cheese. You're paid to
amuse me. If you don't do your job better, my girl, I'll
get Ventnor to speak to you. He'll sort you, I'll be bound.
Might as well sit with a headstone for all the company
you give me. I'm a poor old woman, ain't I? I'm a widow,
ain't I? I need taking out of myself, and all I get is a
puking chit who sits there mum and glum and don't say a
confounded word to me." Her voice rose into its familiar
screech. "Well? What you got to say for yourself, miss?
Eh? Eh?"

"I'm sorry if I displease you," said Mary, and to her
shame the exhausted tears sprang into her eyes.

"Oh, I'm sorry if I displease you," mimicked the old
lady in a dreadful refined accent, then burst into a great
oath which, Mary felt, would sooner have distinguished
one of Cumberland's dragoons than this relict of the
aristocracy. "You'll be sorrier in a minute——" Her
voice slurred into a whine. "But then I'm only a poor old
creature. Nobody loves me. Nick would push me over a
hill as soon as look at me, and Ventnor—why, he'd ride
over my grave, never mind whether I was dead or not."
She looked up at Mary from beneath heavy brows. The
face sunken in folds of fat was brutal, ugly. "You'd best
do as I tell you, miss. You want to go home to papa,
don't you? You'd like to see Derby again, wouldn't you?"

"What can you mean, ma'am?"

"Never mind what I mean. I knows what I mean.
You'd best not be too saucy, miss. We don't like saucy
sluts here. Nor them as what goes sticking their noses into
what don't concern 'em. You've never seen *him* in one
of his rages, have you?"

Mary made no reply; she refused to show fear, but her
heart was beginning to quicken.

The old lady continued with some faint flicker of

emotion, "There was the other one. She had a long nose too. For ever peering and prying she was. She don't peer nor pry no longer. I want to play bezique. Damn the girl, she ain't no good as a companion. I want to play bezique, I tell you."

They played bezique. The day dragged interminably by. Mary's only solace was that the snow was still falling and showing no signs that it might stop. She half longed to be away and back in Derby, for the atmosphere was such as to frighten a braver person. Nicholas came in to meals, but addressed no word to anyone, and scarcely ate, sitting there slouched in his chair with his chin sunk on his chest. Ventnor, plainly in a vicious temper, baited him mercilessly, only pausing to address an occasional remark in a similar vein to Mary, who colored but made no reply.

The old lady seemed at first delighted with all this byplay, then it was suddenly as if she had grown apprehensive. Mary saw her glance several times at Nicholas, then finally fall into a glum silence.

If this goes on much longer, thought Mary, I shall go mad.

And the snow still fell, and the killer was still at large, and murder, opening its slitted eyes, began to creep and stir about her.

The next afternoon she saw Nicholas and Ventnor, side by side, prepared to scour the drifts for the killer bitch. Mary had scarcely slept; such sleep as had come to her had been ridden by fearful dreams. She looked at the brothers in a kind of nightmare despair. Civility had been taken from them; there was nothing to say. She had wanted to stay; she must stay, but the atmosphere was insupportable, and her humiliation of the morning before ever present in her mind. She stared miserably at Ventnor's six foot towering over Nicholas, who, himself reasonably tall, only reached his companion's shoulder; as he was slight of build, he wore a childish and sheepish air beside him. The only point of resemblance was their clothes; they both wore fur-collared leather jerkins, riding breeches and thick, high boots up to their knees, to protect them from the snow.

They both returned her gaze, Ventnor in bitter anger, and Nicholas with a kind of sullen dislike that she felt was undeserved. But then doubtless he had considerably suffered on her account. She smiled at him, but he would not smile back, only turned his head away.

It was Ventnor who intercepted the smile. He said in a low, savage voice, "The moment this damned snow clears, out you go. Do you imagine I have forgot our conversation? If I had my way I'd not have you one second longer in this house. If any horse could reach Derby in this blizzard I'd have you across the saddle this very instant." He swerved round on Nicholas, and the anger of his look increased until his whole face seemed to darken. "You're waiting your time, are you not?" he said. "Oh, I know those looks of yours. A timid boy, indeed. Though not too timid to—— A fine pair you make! I should have left you on the moors with the snow for your bridal bed, and the north wind to cover you. But there'll be no more mischief between you. You, brother, are coming with me now. It is an errand that should suit both of us—an errand of death. You"—and here he turned back to Mary—"you no doubt think this is your opportunity. But you are mistaken. Go down to the sitting room."

"Her ladyship is sleeping," began Mary.

"Then for once her ladyship can stay awake." He caught her by the arm and propelled her into the sitting room, where the old lady, engaged on some ploy of her own which concerned a sheaf of *Derby Mercurys* and a pile of letters, started rather guiltily at the sight of them, and then turned lobster-red with temper.

"Write to your little sister," said Ventnor. "Tell her again what a brute I am. And keep my stepmother company. It's what you're paid for, is it not? Here. Here's notepaper for you. Ink. A quill. Sand. And myself for inspiration. Write! And let me find you still here when I come back, or it'll be the worse for you."

The old lady said nothing, but the apoplectic flush suffused her face to its very eyeballs. She sat there breathing heavily through her nose, her lips so tightly compressed that they seemed sucked in out of sight.

She watched Mary for a while, who had obediently started to write, scribbling down phrases in a letter which she knew would never be posted. When the old lady suddenly screeched at her she turned round to stare. The words were the last she had ever hoped to hear.

"Get out!" shrieked the old lady, almost dancing in her rage. "So Ventnor's put you here to spy on me, has he? The dirty bastard! Get out! I'll not look at your damned mealy face an instant longer."

Oh, thank God, thank God, thought Mary, and, laying down her quill, fled from the room. She heard the key turn in the lock after her. She paused briefly to open the front door and peer out. There was nothing to be seen in the haze of snow. Then she ran upstairs as fast as she could.

When she was a little girl, back in the good days when papa had his church and life flowed by as sweetly and sanely as the river Derwent, she had played sometimes with Horace and the neighboring children the game of hide and seek. She remembered now that intense moment of excitement when pleasure and fear were indistinguishable, when, concealed in her corner, she had heard them coming after her. The agony of apprehension had been such that she had never been able to play the game to its end; she had always screamed, "I'm here, I'm here— oh, please find me!"

Up at last in the attic room she remembered this. The same feeling was on her now. "Mary is so *silly*," Horace had said. And now she might be hiding for her life. She knew Ventnor was out on the moors. She knew the old lady was safe in her room three floors below. She knew that old Betty would never be interested enough to come up to investigate. The house was still, as only a country house in the winter can be still. In Derby there would be the sound of carriages, the cries of the link-boys, the calling out of "Chair, chair!" The flow of noise that swelled a city. But here there was silence, the silence of the moors, the silence of the cold, the silence of the snow.

The silence, perhaps, of the grave.

The attic room, unheated, unused, smelt of dust and

mould. Mary, standing on its threshold, was shivering
uncontrollably. The little window was tight-shut and
barred, its bolts rusted. The truckle bed, on its iron feet,
was littered with rubbish that had been cast down on it—
old clothes, a curtain, a walking cane, a dog lead. The
floor, uncarpeted, was covered with boxes; she pushed
back their flaps, inch-thick with dust, but they contained
nothing to her purpose, only more clothes, unframed
pictures, and some books. She picked up one of these in
instinctive interest; coming from a household where the
library was the focal point for them all, she could never
pass books without at least one glance.

It was an edition of Shakespeare, much thumbed. On
the flyleaf was written in a bold, sprawling hand, "Robin
Ventnor, His Book, God help anyone who touches it,
June 16th, 1727." And at this, despite her fear and the
feeling of urgency, she had to laugh. Seventeen twenty-
seven—eighteen years ago. He would be twelve and she
one month old. He had drawn a little pattern round this
defiant inscription. She flicked open the pages; they fell
apart at the beginning of *Hamlet;* a deep line was scored
by the sentence:

> "How weary, stale, flat and unprofitable
> Seem to me all the uses of this world."

A strange sentiment to appeal to a boy of twelve! An
uncalled-for picture flashed into her mind of a dark,
fierce little boy with fists raised against the world. And
who, now in 1745, was ready to murder her.

Mary dropped the Shakespeare and turned her attention to the cupboard. It was locked, but in such bad
condition that she thought she could probably force it if
she had the time. A terrible excitement came upon her;
for the moment her fear was gone. She knew now that
what she was looking for was here. Nicholas had been
wrong. Or perhaps he had tried to lead her away from a
danger which he recognized only too well. She tried the
drawers beneath the cupboard. They were empty except
for a few oddments. In the last drawer was a skewer, of
the kind used for turning meat over the fire. She held

this in her palm for a moment, considering its possibilities, then crept back to the door to listen.

There was no sound. The brothers would be away on the moors, fighting their way through the snow, not speaking to each other perhaps, with a mountain of hate and mistrust between them. But in this crisis their farming instincts would come first; they would be searching for the killer dog which would be slinking away in silence too.

The silence weighed on her ears. Her breath began to come swiftly between her lips. She was afraid—I'm here; oh, please find me!—how afraid she was. There was a cold, implacable enmity about her. But this was not the time for hysterics. The weather might change, tomorrow she might be on her way to Derby. This was her one chance, her only chance. For her father's sake she could not fail now.

She inserted the skewer in the lock. It was a stout piece of steel intended to support a massive joint; the wood splintered as she wrenched it round, desperation giving her an unaccustomed strength. For a few minutes she thought she would not succeed, then, to her dismay, it was not the lock that turned, but a panel of the cupboard that fell in.

She looked at this and grew cold to her very blood. This could not be repaired. The person concerned would see this the moment he opened the door. Panic flooded over her like icy water; she closed her eyes, striving to calm herself. Then, setting her lips tight to still her chattering teeth, she put her hand through the cavity and pulled out a small sheaf of papers.

It was all there. She could scarcely believe her eyes. After all, she had never been certain. It had been pure guesswork and that much-despised feminine intuition. The letter "V" could stand for a hundred names. The Ventnors had been suspected of Jacobitism; they had been in Derby at the time of her father's impeachment; they had been seen near her house. But there had never been the slightest legal proof, nor indeed proof of any kind.

And now the proof lay in her hand, a hundredfold, damning, inconfutable. "Ventnor" the letters were headed

—not "V" but "Ventnor." They were signed, as her father's letter had been signed— "Charles P.R." She could not examine them closely; there was no time, but even a cursory glance told her that here there was enough treason to hang a man. Not only were there various letters telling the recipient whom to contact, but there was also a black list of Derbyshire Jacobites here that would shatter the Court of St. James—the Cavendishes, the Stanhopes, the Curzons, the Fitzherberts. There were even the parole words for various days—"James and London" for December 4th; "John and Bristol" for December 5th; and so on.

As she was looking down at these, her face twisted, her fingers moving queasily over the crackling paper, she heard the first footsteps downstairs.

She gave a great sobbing gasp. Her heart began to beat a fierce rhythm in her ears.

The footsteps were coming weightily and slowly up the stairs. Mary, almost whimpering in the extremity of her terror, turned her head wildly from side to side. The window could not be opened, and in any case the bars were firmly fixed. The cupboard gaped accusingly at her. She tried with frantic, slippery fingers to fit the panel back, but it would not go in. Then it slid from her trembling grasp and fell to the floor with a crack that to her appalled ears sounded like a pistol shot.

The person coming up the stairs presumably heard this, too. The footsteps paused. That pause, that cessation of sound, that sudden complete silence, was the most terrifying thing that Mary had ever experienced in her life.

The person at last continued his way up, moving, it seemed, with a deliberate, remorseless precision.

Mary heard the measured tread of those feet, now apparently on the first landing. There was no hope of her reaching her own room; the person would see her as she came down. He would be ready to meet her. This time the pirate would know well enough where the lady had been and what she had been doing.

"I would not like to find you," he had said, "investigating the contents of our bureaux and cupboards."

Mary, blind with panic, knowing that it was murder that walked towards her, her mouth dry, her legs giving beneath her, stuffed the letters into the bosom of her dress and looked helplessly around for somewhere to hide. Fear had stripped her of pretense. She heard those remorseless footsteps ascending; she wanted, as she had done in her childhood to burst out of the room, to cry, "Here I am; kill me, kill me."

The footsteps had arrived at her bedroom landing, the floor below. The instinct of self-preservation restored to her a last vestige of sanity. The truckle bed stood raised on its iron claws from the floor. She dropped down and wriggled underneath, pulling down the curtain over the side of the bed, just as the person began, unhurriedly, to climb the attic stairs.

She was dreadfully cramped. Her heart was beating so violently that she thought it must be heard; she wondered that the bed was not heaving up and down with its pounding.

The footsteps paused outside the room. Mary, the sweat streaming down her face, watched with dilated eyes as the door began to open. Her head was wrenched sideways on to her shoulder, weighed down by the bed frame which cut into her neck. The door and the pathway before it was the only thing within her line of vision.

She saw the slow pencil of light widen as the door opened. Thump, thump, thump went her heart—O God, he must hear it, he must—it was beating a sick tattoo in her ears. She fought to control her breathing, which was nearly choking her.

Then, as the person came in, she saw the toes of his boots. It was all she could see; the bed cut across the rest. She saw the toes of his boots, great heavy-soled boots, with a little frozen snow still in the hand-sewn caps.

The boots came into the room and stopped dead in the middle of the floor. The boots were close together, as if the person were standing at attention, looking round him.

There was a long pause. Then they moved again, came over to the bed. Lying there, her eyes screwed up, her lower lip caught so fiercely between her teeth that the blood dribbled down, she heard a soft, swishing, fumbling sound as if the person were tossing over the various articles that lay on the bed. The curtain, which she had draped over the side, fell off. One boot kicked it under the bed, missing Mary by such a fraction of an inch that she thought it must have touched her, that her hiding place was discovered.

The person then decided to sit down on the bed, which creaked and groaned beneath his weight. One heel swung back; she could have touched it simply by extending her fingers.

Suddenly the heels shot together and the person rose with some violence. Mary, nearly fainting, thought with such of her swooning senses as remained to her, that he must have seen the cupboard.

The person walked across the room. She could no longer see anything, but she could hear a variety of little movements as if he had opened the cupboard, were fumbling about inside.

Then again there was silence. She heard nothing now but her wrenching heartbeats, that seemed as if they would tear her body asunder; but she knew the person was there, standing stock-still, perhaps with his head a little on one side, listening.

She knew she could not endure much more. She had not known there was such an extremity of fear in the world.

The person gave a deep prolonged sigh.

Then she saw the boots making their way towards the door. She saw the door open. She saw the door close. There was another pause as if the person were standing outside, waiting, listening. Then the footsteps went briskly downstairs. To her horror she heard them stop outside her bedroom door. She was sure he tried the handle. If she had been there—— But then, at long last, she heard the person continue his way downstairs; a door opened and shut.

She thought afterwards that she must have fainted, but, if so, it was brief. She lost consciousness for perhaps one or two minutes at the most. But for a little while, cramped and anguished as she was, she could not move; her body was too weak and exhausted to obey her. She could only lie there in the dust and dark and cold, letting her breath out in sobbing gasps, listening to the drumbeat of her heart, bathed in the icy sweat that crawled over her.

At last she crept out on her hands and knees, and with a monstrous effort managed to stumble to her feet, ripping her dress on the iron of the bedstead as she did so. She rubbed her forehead frantically. "I must not faint again," she said aloud. "Oh, I must not faint again." The room shivered round her. There was blackness swirling before her eyes, a rushing in her ears. Her head drooping, her hands dangling at her sides, she managed somehow to walk out of the room, down the attic stairs and along to her bedroom.

As she opened the door she thought suddenly that the person might be waiting for her. She raised her head in a dull apprehension. Her fear had been too extreme for her to feel any more violent emotion. Death had laid his finger on her shoulder; for a few brief moments she had smelt the savor of his charnel house. She was utterly exhausted. If the killer had stepped before her she would not have had the strength to scream.

But there was no one there. She staggered over to the washstand, sluiced her face, then poured herself out a glass of water. She drank greedily of this, gulping it down so that it slopped over her, and an icy trickle ran down the neck of her frock. This reminded her of the letters; in her terror she had forgotten about them. She pushed them further down her dress. They scratched her abominably, but they represented her father's salvation, and she would wear this salvation if it were a bunch of thorns.

She felt a little revived. She put on her cloak and wrapped a thick scarf around her neck. The tightness of it made her think of other things and her head began to swim again, but she pushed this weakness from her as if it were some tangible thing, for she needed all her strength for what she had to do.

She stepped across to the window and pulled aside the curtain. The snow had stopped, except for a few soft, white flakes that fluttered across her vision. In the fading light of the December afternoon the moor looked as cold and grim and bleak as death itself—but then, never before had death stood so near, and she knew that somehow she must get away and immediately, for the killer would not miss a second time.

She took nothing with her. She prepared to make for one of the shepherds' cottages that dotted the moor. If she arrived, they would surely help her. If she lost her way in the snow—why, then she would die, and there was an end to it. At least it would be a kinder death than having one's breath squeezed out between a murderer's fingers.

She shook her shoes off and, holding them in her hand, stole downstairs. In the hallway she could hear the sound of voices from the old lady's sitting room. The pirate would never dream that she would try to escape. In such weather even the shepherds did not stir far from their homes, and he would know better than most how little chance there was of her finding her way.

She knew this, too. She shivered. But she crept to the door, and there, standing on the thick mat which mercifully swallowed all sound, put her shoes on again.

As she stooped down to fasten the laces, she heard the old lady cry, "But surely you don't have to *kill* her."

Mary shuddered convulsively, the color brushed from her cheeks. She could hear the murmur of a low, masculine voice, and then the old lady again, "It's not safe, I tell you. It's not safe. You always was a damned fool. Do you think *he* won't do anything about it? He ain't such a fool as you take him for, and he's sweet on the slut, and you know that as well as I do."

Oh, poor Nicholas! thought Mary, her hand stealing to the latch on the door. Poor Nicholas! He may be sweet on the slut, but he is bound hard and fast in some hideous chain of his own contriving and he will do nothing.

She did not wait to hear any more. She opened the door and stepped into the snow. She dared not shut the door behind her for fear the click of the latch might betray her, but she wedged a stone beneath it lest the wind should blow it to.

She crept down the path and out on to the moor. Once she looked behind her. There was no one there. It seemed that there was no one in this whole white world.

For the moment she was safe from pursuit, for the mountain-high drifts which might easily prove her death were also ironically a guarantee of her security.

The snow had stopped altogether. Mary, staggering on, up to her waist in snow one second, stumbling over some hidden obstacle the next, was dazed by the bright whiteness which seemed all the more dazzling for the advancing twilight. She knew well enough how small her chance of survival was. She did not know the moors. She had only the vaguest idea of her direction. The drifts were deceptive. One never knew if the surface would support one's steps or treacherously sink one past all hope of recovery. But the fear behind her was greater than the terror that lay in wait. From time to time she put a hand to her breast to make sure the letters were still there. Perhaps, even if she died in the snow, the letters might be found on her body.

She thought of Ventnor. And, strangely enough, she thought not of his harshness, nor of his ruthless urge to kill, but of a little boy who had written a defiant inscription in his book and then scrabbled so bitterly against the lines which expressed his misery and despair. She thought, too, of what had occurred two nights before, and wished with all her heart that, murderer as he was, her murderer as he planned to be, he had not caught her in a situation which, even to kinder eyes, must seem shameful, insupportably vulgar. And finally she thought of his face when he had threatened to push her over, a face so startlingly near laughter. But then on top of this came the memory of those few minutes in the attic, and for the first time since she had left Wardwick Hall she was filled with pure blind panic. For he would come after her, of that she was sure. He would never dare to let her go. She gave a little childish wail of fear and stared around her. There was nothing in view. Nothing, nothing, nothing. It was growing dark, but the sky was hard and bright above her, with a full moon that made eerie, blue shadows on the snow. Mary, in her exhaustion, began to sob weakly. And as she sobbed she looked round again and saw something moving towards her.

She stopped dead, as if by so doing she might obliterate

herself from view. An icy gust of wind blew her hood back and the hair streamed from her head. And as she stood there motionless the moving thing came into full view.

She looked down at a small, lean, dirty gray dog, which stared back at her in as much fear as herself. It was painfully thin, with every rib showing. Its ears were back, the whites of its eyes showing, as it cowered there. There was an open sore on its flank where one of the shepherds must have winged it, and its muzzle was scarred and naked of hair as if at some time it had run into barbed wire.

She knew at once what it must be. She stared at it in compassion. She thought: Human killers go free, but this wretched thing has all the world against it. She said aloud, "You poor thing!" and at the sound of her voice it gave a curious whine as if the kind, human tone brought back memories of the days when it had lived at peace with mankind. Then, before she was aware of what was happening, it shot past her, taking her so by surprise that she lost her balance and slithered down the snowy hill until her clawing hands brought her to a standstill.

Then she saw the cottage.

It was the derelict building she had passed on the evening of her arrival. How long ago it seemed, though in actual fact it was barely a month. ("Good God!" he had said. "Do you think we live in a rabbit hutch?") She could see now what a ruin it was, with its shuttered, boarded windows; attached to the side was what was presumably the shippon. It was not a prepossessing sight in the bleak, bright night, but if it had been a superb mansion with her father himself there to welcome her, it could not have been more pleasing to her view. It was neither warm nor comforting, but it was shelter, and she was at the end of her resources. In the bygone days in Derby she had been Miss Vernon, the vicar's daughter, a calm, composed young woman with a sharp tongue who could manage her own affairs, and everyone else's if need be. "It is not," Aunt Briarcliffe had said, "as if Mary is going to find a husband easily." Husbands did not care for strong-minded females; they preferred them weak and clinging. Mary could scarce visualize a husband at that moment;

the only arms waiting for her, it seemed, were the skeleton ones of Death; but alas for feminine pride! She did, cold, exhausted and terrified as she was, long most passionately for a shoulder to lean on; never in her life had she felt less capable of dealing with the situation.

She stumbled towards the cottage, the tears—O God, she seemed to do little but cry these days!—pouring down her cheeks.

The other killer, the person with the boots, had in the meantime discovered that Mary had gone. He was very angry with himself. He should have searched the house more thoroughly. He had even discovered where she had hidden herself, for he had returned to the attic and found the torn fragment of her dress by the bedstead. It had never entered his head—for he was a big man—that anyone could have crawled there. To think that she had been lying there all the time, within an inch or less of the heel of his boot. If he had only known he could have pulled her out. He would have enjoyed that. And then he could have finished her spying and prying for always. She was only a little thing; the slightest of pressure would have sufficed, and then he could have rolled her body under the bed again until he had decided where to bury her. In his mind, his strange, angry, frantic mind, fact and fantasy were constantly shifting, so that he could feel her throat beneath his hands, see the terror in her face, imagine the desperate hands plucking so uselessly at his. The black eyes would be staring now, unseeing—the black eyes. But hers were not black. He was confusing her with the other, who had presumed to deliver him a lecture, who had dared to interfere, to tell him what to do—him, *him*. Oh, he had had more than enough. These people who tried to thwart him—— Well, the old lady who had plagued him so many times would plague him no more, or indeed anyone. The person, though now in the state where he would endure no opposition, was still not hardened enough to care much for the look of her as she lay there in her chair, with her bezique cards scattered on the floor where her flailing arms had hurled them. He would if he had had time, have covered her face, for the protruding eyes were hideous in rage and terror, and her bloated face, with the folds of flesh pushed up by his extinguishing fingers, appalling to behold. But there was nothing to cover her with, and he had not time to look for it, neither. The girl must have had a good start, but her progress in the snow would be difficult, and she had probably not the faintest idea where to go. But he could no longer delay; he must be gone before his brother returned.

He set off swiftly down the path. The snow and dark held no fears for him. The moor was his kingdom and Kinder Scout his archangel. And his purpose was a flame within him; he was power and brain and righteousness; he was a killer who could kill with impunity; he was God. Mary's footprints lay plain to see, an erratic zigzagging trail of small-soled shoes. He followed them with down-bent head and a little smile on his lips. The wretched fool, to think she could thwart God. She should be snuffed out, and rightly so, as all his enemies had been —all, all. There was only the other to deal with now. The other. As he thought of this the person lost his smile and looked briefly the killer he was. The other should not wait long. This time he should get what he deserved. And then —ah, then!—the person would be king, as in his mind he had been for a long time now; he would join the other king at Derby, and they would reign side by side, and God would look down approvingly upon them.

And, thinking excitedly of this, the person came at last within sight of his goal.

Mary, gasping for breath, was now at the cottage door. She wondered for a second if she would be safer in the shippon. But the hay which stuffed the baulks was rotten with damp and smelt abominably; the sods of peat which had comprised the beasts' beds were overgrown with fungus, gray-green with mould. Two disused hurricane lamps lay on the floor, the rest of which was covered with wood.

She turned away and flung with both hands at the cottage door. The wind was rising again, and flurries of snow blew against her face. She was convinced that Ventnor was near her. He must by now have discovered her flight. He would not dare to let her escape. Terror rose in her in a great surge, melting her bowels, churning her blood, pounding her heart, until she thought her swimming head would burst.

If the door had been bolted she knew she would have gone mad, shamefully screamed her panic to the moon. But it drove in before her, and she flew in with it, nearly landing flat on her face, bruising her hands and knees, the breath buffeted out of her.

She stumbled to her feet and stood there staring round her.

There was no lamp, no candle. But the stars, diamond-bright in the chill vault of the sky, gleamed down, and the moon filtered through the shuttered window, making strange shadows everywhere. She could not bear the shadows. They moved. They were constantly where they had not been the minute before. A ghost, he had said, a poor thing, a little boy, afraid and angry, a wretched puling brat not even worth the shooting down. She thought for a second that she saw him—a thin, fierce little boy with enormous eyes and tangled black hair hanging over his face. Robin Ventnor, his book. God help any-one who touches it.

"Robin," she said aloud, "Robin——" But that was Robin at twelve years old. And now, eighteen years later, Robin was coming to murder her. In a fresh outburst of fear she tugged at the shutters. The locks, long rusted, gave easily to her frenzy and flew apart, so that the moon-light streamed through. She swung round to make sure the door was shut. She could not endure that the killer should creep silently in without warning.

Her footsteps clattered on the stone flags. Now she was soaked in fear. Fear swept round her from the snow-covered moors, the merciless sky, the white, bright, pri-meval world which hid her enemy. And, as she moved, a fearful noise burst on her ears, as of an army charging into the cottage, with a smashing of boots, a tumult of people. She gave a scream, so faint that it whistled off in the wind. Forcing herself to move, she opened the door. "Who is there?" she cried; then louder, "Who is there?"

There was no answer but the cold northern wind that howled across the moors, rippling down the snow. There was nothing to see but moon and snow and stars, a milky world of unutterable desolation.

A sudden thought struck her. She shut the door again. Then she stamped her foot, clapped her hands and waited. A few seconds later there was a violent thudding and clapping, as of some devil audience. It was some diabolical trick of acoustics that caught the sound and shot it back a moment later. But even now that she knew what it was, she was afraid. At first, in defiance, she behaved as children did; she shouted out, "Hallo, there! Hallo, there!" Back, so unexpectedly as to make her jump, came the echo, derisive, hoarse, "Hallo, the-e-ere!"

"Damn you!" she cried on a sob.

"Damn you!" cried the echo, and sobbed too in dreadful mockery.

At last she dared neither move nor speak. She huddled by the fireless grate, trying to pray, trying to compose herself, trying to push away the fear that came over her in great shuddering waves, trying to still her convulsive shivering.

Then she heard the footsteps.

They were real footsteps this time, no echo. She heard the measured crunching on the snow. She turned her white, agonized face towards the sound. This, then, was the end. This was her murderer. She had sometimes wondered how she would behave at execution. The Duke of Monmouth, so they said, had been dragged shrieking to the scaffold. Others, worse than he, had died more gallantly, with a jest, a noble oration, or a tavern tale upon their lips. There was, perhaps, some last resource in the human spirit, some final strength of will, to force composure on the shuddering soul. And this for her seemed to be true. As she waited for the person to emerge, with death in his glance, murder in his outstretched fingers, she grew still, almost calm. She did not scream nor leap to her feet. She stood motionless, cold, her eyes wide.

The door opened. Then for a second she closed her eyes. What would he do? Would he shoot her? She hoped so. It would be quick. Or would he strangle her? She felt already the hands at her throat, the relentless pressure, the breath of the murderer on her cheek as his fingers pressed the consciousness from her.

A voice that she knew well enough said in explosive anger, "Damn this confounded snow! Is it never-ending? And what a place to hide, my clever general, what a place to hide! With your tracks in the snow indicating the way like an arrow, and a cottage open to the four winds so that your enemy can come at you from all quarters of the globe, and not a soul for miles to help you. You are a fine, intelligent girl, Mary. Why, there are even ten-foot drifts to bury you in, so that you can lie undisturbed till the spring. God save us, I'm cold. Is there no wood here to make a fire?"

Ventnor stood in the doorway, frowning at her, his dark face darker yet with the cold, his black hair in wild disorder, and melting snow running off his boots. Despite her terror, she could not honestly say that he had the look of a murderer, for all he carried a pistol in his hand. He had, indeed, more the air of an exasperated man who was tired and cold. He tramped across the floor, then checked as the echo hurled his footsteps back at him, and his final words, "Make a fire, a fire, fi-i-ire."

He began to laugh. "All right, old mole. I'll make a fire. We'll have to open the door a little. That is the secret. The echo only functions when it is shut. Where's that bloody wood?"

"In the sh-shippon," stammered Mary, then in a weak cry, "Must you warm yourself before you kill me?"

"Before I——?" He stared at her, holding an armful of wood that he had gathered from the adjoining cowbyre. He looked more irritated than murderous. "What did you say?"

She began to cry. It was as if the tears would never stop. She could not say anything, only sobbed and sobbed, rocking herself as she did so.

He crouched down beside her, spilling the wood over the floor. "What the devil is all this? I'll not say you don't deserve murdering, but I have no intention of being your executioner. Did you think *this*"—and here he shook his pistol at her—"was for you? But that is your prerogative, my dear. It is you who are handy with a weapon. So you imagine that I have made this damnable journey, up to my neck in snow half the time and down on my backside the other half, for the pleasure of shooting you? Ah, but I had forgot. You believe everything that is bad of me. I am vindictive and brutal, am I not? Ready to sink to any depths of vengeance. Come. Pull yourself together. This is nonsense. Your tears will freeze on you. Come! That's enough." And here, to her amazement, he stretched forth his hand and patted her cheek as if she were a child. He went on briskly, "Well, before I murder you I must thaw my fingers, for indeed I could scarce press the trigger. Help me put the wood on, there's a good girl, and we'll have a blaze going in no time."

She obeyed. She was too bewildered to realize fully what she was doing. The wood flared up quickly. She looked across the leaping flames at Ventnor, who crouched before them, his pistol on his knee. She met his eyes and slowly began to blush. As he saw this he smiled, still saying nothing, but watching her with great, dark eyes which held both amusement and derision, yet also, as she could not help but see, some amount of tenderness. They were not the eyes of a killer. Her blush deepened. She bowed her head, looking away from him.

His next remark was not a murderer's remark, neither. He said, "Do you want an apple? It was all I could lay my hands on. I was rather in a hurry once I saw your ladylike tracks in the snow." He held the fruit out. "Well? Are you going to accept it from me? You could imagine yourself as Aphrodite. And it is not poisoned."

She took it. Her mind was in such confusion that she could not even thank him.

"At least," he said, taking a vast bite of his apple and speaking with his mouth full, "we can now talk without skirmishing, snarling and threatening. The things I nearly did to you——" Suddenly he laughed, nearly making her drop her apple. "A fine act you put on for me! Such sniveling and howling—I was almost taken in. Not that it would have made any difference. If the weather had not blackguarded me I'd have you back in Derby now, my girl. And I swear at this moment you'd not be sorry, neither. There are worse places than home, and I daresay papa is not quite so harsh as you have led me to believe. Indeed, he seems to me to have made a sorry job of your upbringing. I would have done a great deal better." Then he cried out in exasperation, "Have you lost your tongue? Here I am doing my damndest to provoke you and you say not a word, only sit there, peaked and mum, nibbling at your apple as if you were a mouse. It is true you have no pistol, but surely you can shoot words at me, call me a brute, bully and worse, or, if your invention has really failed you, at least address me by my title. You know perfectly well that drives me to the point of madness. Mary, I am longing to be given the opportunity of shaking you as you deserve, and you say nothing, nothing at all. Come. Be brave. You have lacked sense, manners and decorum in your time, but I have never yet known you fail in courage."

Mary at this point did something she had never intended to do. She did not think that the letters were at her breast, and her enemy barely a foot away. Without a word she held out her hand to him.

He did not take it. He looked at it. He said, "What is that for? A token of apology or resignation, or—or what?"

She said, "I am so cold and so miserable. Will you please not take my hand? We have not been friendly, but I am so tired of quarreling with you. I cannot do it any more. I once thought I knew everything. Now I don't know what you are or even what I am. Only, if you don't hold my hand I think I shall die, because I have had more than I can stand."

"Well," he said consideringly, "I suppose I have no alternative." He laid the pistol on his knees, then took her hand in both of his. The firm clasp was comforting. "It is true," he said, "that you and I have not spoken much in the way of civility to each other. But you cannot really blame me. I was never a good-tempered man, and it is in any case a little souring to the disposition to be condemned at first sight as a murderer or worse. Every time I tried to speak to you, you glared condemnation at me, so that kindness withered within me, and I was left with little but a strong desire to beat you. Which would scarce have helped. But now we must wait together."

"Wait?"

"Certainly. I should prefer to meet our next caller here. I'd not like to feel he was at my back in the snow. He'll not be long. You've left as fine a set of tracks as any hunter could desire. It was a pleasure to follow you. I see that you fell down. Did you hurt yourself?"

"No."

"You deserved to. You really are a plaguy silly girl, and God knows why I should imagine myself in love with you. But of course——"

She began, "Have you taken leave of your senses?" and thought she must have done so herself. The color swept again across her cheeks.

He nodded coolly, as if she had not spoken, "——you have courage. You are not pretty as the world rates it, but that never mattered anything to me, and there is a great deal in your face that pleases me. Besides, you stand up to me like a cornered mouse. And now I suppose you are full of vainglory at having accomplished your purpose. I am not, of course, referring to my loving you. That was not, I believe, in your scheming. Or was it? But never mind. You have your letters. A fine mess you've made of our cupboard, too. Did you take a hammer to it? Give them to me."

"No!" she said in a whisper, and her hand went up instinctively to her dress.

He saw this and laughed. "Oh, clever girl! The woman's inevitable hiding place! Don't be a fool. Give them to me at once."

"No!"

He let her hand fall and gripped her shoulder. "Do you not realize he'll be here at any moment? Give them to me, I say. You surely do not imagine modesty will restrain me from taking them?"

She saw he meant what he said, and knew she had no chance in the world against him. She pulled out the bundle of letters and handed them to him in silence.

He flicked them over, glancing at her as he did so. "A

fine quire of treason," he said. "A fine daisy chain to hang a man."

She said, with great difficulty, "I think I—I have maligned you. But these are your letters, are they not? Perhaps you did not mean to ruin my father. Perhaps it all happened by chance, and you had no alternative but to let the justices assume the letter was his. But you must have known what you had done to him. How could you——" Her voice faltered and died away.

Ventnor, after a pause, said in a suspiciously mild voice, "Because, ma'am, I am a devil and a brute and a traitor and other things besides, which I leave to your fertile imaginings to tell me." Then he roared out, "So I ruined your father, did I? So I had him set in the pillory?" He unfolded himself from the floor as he spoke. "So I cheated and lied and betrayed and tortured? So I——"

"Stop!" cried Mary, for he was now standing over her, talking at such a rate and volume that she was all but defeated. "Oh, stop!"

But he went on remorselessly, "So I am every kind of filth and vileness. So I would smash the world to get myself ha'pence. So I would put on the throne a popish boy with the corrupt Stuart blood in his veins, and in my effort to do it betray my country and sacrifice anyone and everyone. So I would murder a silly girl—and, by God, if anyone asks for murder you do, with your slanders on my honor, my decency, my humanity. Why are you not cowering away from me? Do you not see this?" He waved his pistol in her face, then suddenly lowered it so that it pointed at her breast. "Do you not feel that? It is loaded. I need only press my finger, so, and then—why, you'll be straight among the angels, my dear, to look down upon us from your heavenly throne, and pity us for the fools we are. Well? Are you not going to whine and snivel? To cry for mercy? Or do you realize that with someone of my temperament it would be useless? Well? I am waiting. I have always desired to have a woman on her knees to me. It would satisfy my brutal vanity."

Mary did not move an inch from the pistol clapped against her. She said faintly, "I'm sorry."

"You're sorry! And do you imagine that is enough?

Surely your feminine sense of drama can produce better than that?"

She began to laugh, if a little hysterically. She pushed the pistol aside with one hand, came up to him, put her hands on his wrists, and said, "Please, I'm sorry. But how was I to know?"

"How are you to know now?" he said, staring at her uncompromisingly. "I am the same as I always was, though indeed I swear I'm nearer murdering you than I have ever been."

"Your hands," she said. "Your hands——"

"What the devil do you mean?"

"His were the killer's hands. When he suggested we came here for the papers——"

"So that's what you were doing, were you?"

She met his eyes, then closed her own. She whispered, "Would he have killed me—like that?"

"Of course. He was afraid of you. He read your precious diary—oh, yes. That diary of yours! God!" said Ventnor, clutching at his forehead, "you may well blush. The imbecility of it! And, of course, as if that were not enough, you had to confide in him. You did, didn't you? You poured out the whole story to him——"

She was seized with a fit of shuddering. She remembered those boots coming over to the bedside. She huddled again by the fire, putting a hand to her cheek.

He resumed his former position, turning a little sideways so that he could keep his gaze fixed on her. The firelight tilted the shadows in his face, indented the lines by his mouth, deepened the dark eyes. Mary could not avoid looking at him with pleasure; it was a handsome face, and she was dreadfully ashamed that she should so have misread it.

He said reflectively, "You have never known Nicholas. You saw him as a gentle boy, did you not?—brutalized by his wicked stepbrother. I have no doubt that he painted for you some black picture of a youth of cruelty and victimization, of blows and insults, and everything else his imagination could contrive. Is that not so?" His voice grew harsh, as it had been at their first acquaintance. "Is that not so? Answer me."

"Yes, he did. But I still do not see how I was expected to know——"

He said, a hint of anger in his tone, "I am not in the habit of brutalizing children. Though you would credit me with every vice, no doubt. But it is true you could not know. There is a kind of madness that delights in cruelty. It is not my kind, though half the world holds me to be mad in my own way. There were so many things, and of a sort, perhaps, that would not please your ears. There was his dog—he tried to shoot it once because it had disobeyed him. He only wounded it. He called it to him by its pet name and shot it dead. And so on—not only dogs. There was your predecessor, as meddling as yourself, and less fortunate. I should have handed him over to the authorities a long time ago. But he is my half brother and we were brought up together, and in an odd sort of way that you would not understand there is a kind of affection between us. Though he has tried to kill me too. But he did it very clumsily. His heart was not entirely in it. Now I think it will be. He does not like to be thwarted. And the day I found you together—even now I do not believe you realize how fortunate that was. From that moment I fancy my death was as planned as yours. Mary, I—I could have done anything and everything to you. In a not particularly even-tempered life I have never been quite so angry. And I could not even get you out of the house."

She said unsteadily, for the memory still hurt her bitterly, "You could have explained a little more. You ordered me out as if I were some servant girl caught rolling in the hay."

He laughed. "Was there all that difference?"

She said, near tears again, "You must believe me. I really thought we were going for the papers. I did not expect him to kiss me. I was furious. And then you came in." The tears began to flow down. "I could not bear you to think of me as so cheap a slut."

He stopped laughing. He said in some surprise, "Does that matter so much to you?"

"It matters more than all the world," said Mary. "I know I was a fool to believe him. But I was so desperate. I never for one moment suspected he intended to kill me."

Ventnor said grimly, "Naturally not. Your attention was entirely focused on me. Of all the stupidity——"

She said with more spirit, "I still say that if you had explained a little more——"

"Explained! You have the impudence to say that to me! Did I not try? Did you not say that you'd not believe me even if I swore a thousand oaths?"

"It is difficult," said Mary, "to accept an explanation from a man who has just offered to throw you over the banisters. It does not give you the type of assurance needed."

"I see," said he, looking at her sideways, "that you and I will get on prodigious well. How fortunate it is that we are alone in this derelict cottage—though I believe we will not long be so—and I can indulge my piratical manners to their utmost without fear of interruption. I am now going to kiss you." With that he reached out a long arm and pulled her towards him. He said, "I have put up with a great deal too much from you. It is high time it stopped."

She did not resist him. It was true that men thought too much of kissing, but she had been thinking a great deal of it herself for the past few minutes, and she could not discover in herself any feeling of resentment; indeed, she found to her surprise that she was quite anxious for him not to stop. He did not stop for some time. Mary made not the slightest attempt to move away. He said at last reflectively, "How forward town girls are. They kiss one brother after another. In the country we are more coy; we say, 'Get along with you, do,' and only give way after the correct prevarication. But no doubt one learns the habit on the banks of the Derwent. They say it is a charming river."

She was furious at his first remarks and had already struggled to move away; at this last she gave a cry of protest. But he held her tightly; she could feel his shoulder begin to shake. She said in a rage, "I suppose I might have known! Only you could have behaved so."

"Keep still," said Ventnor. "Is this another tantrum?" The laughter was surging up in him. "Keep still. Did he get to dry land again?"

"You would not care! He might have drowned!"

"Oh, I knew you'd rescue him if need be. You seemed to me a very strong-minded young woman. Keep still! If I'd known what I know now, I should probably have thrown you in after him."

"You are like all men," said Mary, "impossible, dictatorial. Robin Ventnor, his book!"

"Oh, we have our uses. *What* did you say?" And here he held her away from him so that he could look into her face.

She laughed at him. "I would like to take that book with me when I go back to Derby. To remember you by."

"So," he said, "this is the grand scene of renunciation." His arms came tightly round her. "Do you think I kiss for amusement's sake? Is that what you are doing?"

"No!" She was suddenly terrified by the force of feeling that had risen in her. It seemed that her whole independence was threatened. She said, "But I—I needed comforting so badly. I have been so afraid."

"Comforting!" he repeated. "I have no doubt you were afraid. So was I. If you but knew—— And this damned snow, and I couldn't get you out. And you staring at me as if I were the devil incarnate, and only waiting for my back to be turned to go running your head into the nearest noose available. I could have killed myself for ever having brought you here."

"That book," she said. "You must have been so unhappy."

"Well," he said, moving his shoulders, "it was not very gay. But there were consolations. There were always the moors."

She glanced out of the window and shivered.

"Oh, you—you are a town girl," he said impatiently, "a silly slut who likes the dirty streets, the stinking kennels, the narrow houses fencing you in so that you can scarce breathe. But I was born here. I spent my childhood on these moors. To me they are a new miracle every morning. But of course one sometimes needs another kind of consolation when one is young, and even when one is not so young. There are other miracles. Such as this———".

With this he kissed her again, so violently and so lengthily that she had nothing to say, only stared at him, thinking suddenly of that appalling moment when he had found her with Nicholas, terrified lest he should still think her light and treacherous, yet unable to protest.

He released her, rising to his feet. He sat down in the chimney seat, long legs stretched before him, the pistol on his knee. He saw that she was looking at the weapon, and smiled, an odd, youthful smile that swept the harshness from his face. He said, "You look at this emblem? It is nothing, but it is a comfort to hold it there. It will not necessarily prevent our dying, but it should at least ensure us a companion when we ferry across the river. I hold it there because I like the grip of it between my fingers. And now, this dramatic renunciation of yours. I gather you do not choose to marry me."

"You have not asked me, my lord. Besides———"

"If you call me that once again———" began Ventnor; then, "But if you wish for a formal proposal you shall have it. Will you marry me? But I remember. You think of marriage these days as a business proposition. You said so on your arrival. I have not forgot."

"And so it is," cried Mary. "One sees it in all the newspapers. A marriage between So-and-so and an agreeable young lady with a fortune of a thousand pounds."

He said coolly, "Do you have such a fortune?"

"No, of course not!"

"Then I see not the faintest ground of comparison."

Mary, not knowing how to take this, said weakly, "You propose with the pistol cocked." Then she said, her voice strained, "You once said there had been enough mismarriages in your family."

"There have been indeed. It is time the matter was rectified."

"I do not know," she said. "I have never felt like this before. To decide now—in such circumstances———"

He said in his most aggressive voice, "Well, either you'll marry me or you'll not. I've only proposed the once before. But she played the fine lady with me, said yes when she meant no, and then, to plague me, the other way round. I shouted out my feelings and she did not like it. I spoke my mind and she liked it even less. We quarreled. To her it was nothing. It was part of the game. But, you see, I never came back. She may have been grieved. I do not know. She told me to go and I went. That was all. You, I gather, are now telling me to go, too."

"I am not," cried Mary, before she could stop herself. "Oh, I could not. But let me go back to Derby. After a month or so, when we have both had time to reflect——"

"Very well," he said indifferently. He added, as if he were making polite conversation, "Did you know that the Pretender's son is reported to be in retreat from Derby?"

She stared at him. "Then my father——"

"He is safe enough. I could have told you that if you had asked me. I do," he said, "fulfill my obligations."

"What do you mean?"

"Oh, it does not matter. Yes. Sam tells me they set off early this morning. His forces are apparently moving towards Loughborough, in the direction of Ashbourne. And Charles now rides behind. Strange. If they had marched over Swarkeston Bridge, I swear that James III would have been proclaimed king in London within the week." He looked at her downcast face, unmistakably the face of one who at that moment was not interested in history—then suddenly grinned. "You will always fly in my eye, will you not? Charles turned back, God knows why, but I shall not follow his example. I am set on my path. Whether or not you choose to accompany me is your decision, not mine. There's someone coming." As he said this he rose to his feet, narrowly avoiding cracking his head on the low beams. The firelight shot his shadow before him, engulfing Mary in its blackness. He said, "I think you should talk with him. I am not so generous a man that I wish you always to have a suspicion that I might be a murderer. I have not killed—yet. You shall see and understand. Are you afraid, Mary?"

"Yes. Oh yes!"

"You had more reason before, and you were not. I shall be here. I'll not let you be killed. But I want you to *know*. Meet him, my girl. Talk to him. You kissed him once. It might have been the coldest of embraces. Here he is. I recognize his footsteps. This is the end. He has done that which no man can do and escape scot-free. He will dissimulate no longer."

"What has he done?" she whispered.

Ventnor slipped into the shadows at the far end of the room. His voice came very low. "I had no reason to love her. But she loved him in her own strange way, and perhaps understood him better than any of us. It is an unhappy death to be killed by the one thing you love."

His voice died away.

A hand pushed at the door.

Mary came forward to meet him.

Nicholas stood in the doorway and looked at her. She wondered how she could ever have been so foolish as to think him innocent. For his face, concentrated now on what he had to do, was slurred a little sideways, the face of a human being who has strayed beyond humanity. It was the face she had known, youthful, rounded, a little weak, but the eyes were wild and mad and overbright; his mouth was parted and the lower lip was wet.

He came slowly in, almost smiling, but it was not a smile, only a greedy anticipation. He held out his hands to her—strangler's hands, with the thick, strong fingers curved. He came up to her as she stared at him, very pale. The flames enlarged the grasping hands as if their shadow would descend on her, flatten her like a fly to the wall.

He said in a petulant voice, "I have been looking for you everywhere. You really are a most tiresome girl."

She said nothing. Her mouth had grown very dry.

"Such weather to come out in," continued Nicholas. "What made you run away from me? We have always been friends. You used to write in your diary that you were sorry for me. Why, Ventnor might have found you, and you know what would have happened then."

She still said nothing.

He looked at her from beneath his brows, head a little lowered. There was that in his eyes which brought the sweat out on her body. He said in a little soft voice, "Give me those letters."

"I do not have them," whispered Mary.

"Give me those letters."

"No."

"If you give them to me," he said in a bright, reasonable tone, "I promise not to harm you." He added, "You cannot believe that I want to hurt you. Only, you see, I must have those letters. You do see that, don't you?"

"Yes—yes."

His mad eyes were fixed on hers. A prickle of moisture gleamed on his upper lip. "Come," he said, "there's a sweet, dear girl. Give them to me."

He was almost on her now. She said quietly, "Why did you make my father suffer?"

He checked, flinging up his head as he did so. He was barely a foot away from her. She could see that he was shivering from head to foot.

He said after a pause, in a slurred, sulky voice, "Why not? Is your father of any importance? He is only a little man, a common little man. Little people like that do not suffer. They do not have the sensibility. Besides, he should have been grateful to me. He suffered for his king, did he not? And me—me!" A sly smile came to his lips. "I was really extremely clever. I crept in. It was while you were all at church. Your maid left me in the study. And I put the letter among his papers. Don't look at me like that! How dare you look so at me? You are privileged to have spared me suffering. For they were after me. They had to be sidetracked. They are always after me. They are there now."

"Who? Who are they?"

"*They*—they are always there." And Nicholas jerked his head round to stare across the moon-covered snow. "They think they can outwit me. But they cannot. For when they try I kill them. She was one of them. She thought herself so clever. She did not think so any longer when I caught her. It served her right for getting in my way. Even the other one——" Here he fell momentarily silent, his mouth open, his eyes wandering, unfocused, perturbed. "She didn't want to die, neither. But she should not have interfered. She would not be quiet. She is quiet now." He began to laugh. His laughter tittered up, rising until it was a giggling falsetto. "Oh, I am too clever for them. And now my king and I will reign together, and the whole world shall bow before us. How clever I am, so clever, so clever. No one can fool me. But I fool them. I fooled you, didn't I?" His eyes narrowed. "Give me those letters."

"No, Nicholas," she said. She was faint with horror, but her voice came out surprisingly firm.

"Then," he said, "you give me no choice." He stepped towards her, his hands swinging free. His face had grown expressionless as a mask. But, as he came within touching distance, the voice from the corner spoke.

"Well, Nick?" said Ventnor.

Nicholas gave a little shriek, an odd feminine sound. He spun round, then flung out both his hands, his fingers spread wide. His face turned greenish-white. "You!" he said. "Always you! Don't touch me. Do you hear? If you lay a finger on me, my king will avenge me——"

"Your king!" said Ventnor. "Your king is halfway back to Manchester, boy, and the shadow of defeat trails after him. He is lost. As you are lost. As you have always been lost."

Nicholas sprang back against the door, banging it shut, and shrieked again. The echo caught at the shriek, tossed it and tormented it, so that it ended in a terrible wail like a child's crying. Then he flung the door wide and ran out into the snow.

Mary, sick and shuddering, covered her face with her hands. She heard two shots. Involuntarily she let her hands fall and came outside, with faltering footsteps. She saw the two black things lying in the snow. As she stared down she heard other footsteps behind, and swerved to see Sam and Ventnor standing side by side, looking at each other in silence.

Presently Sam said, "Poor bitch. Looks half starved, don't she? And him—you couldn't let him go, man. Not now. Once a killer gets the taste—— It'll not lie heavy on my conscience, but it'd have lain mighty heavy on yours. You was always too soft, lad, that's your trouble." He produced unexpectedly a massive pipe from his pocket and set it between his lips. He said quite placidly, "The weather is going to change. It seems the lad brought the snow with him. Take the girl away, Ventnor. Don't you see she's near to fainting? I reckon the snow will be half melted by tomorrow night. For God's sake don't stand there gawping. What's the good o' looking? He's better dead, ain't he? Take the lass away. This is no place for fine town misses."

Mary, in the blackness that engulfed her, saw as her last sight Ventnor's face coming towards her as he caught her in his arms.

VI Epilogue

Derby: December, 1745

The last two days at Wardwick Hall were so dim in
Mary's mind that afterwards she could scarcely remember
them. The old lady was dead, and Nicholas—
Nicholas was dead, too, translated by the hand of death
into a very young boy who lay there, sprawling in the
snow, innocent, surprised face upturned to the stars.
One could say of him that his wits had been diseased,
that he was no more responsible for his actions than a
child—but Mary could only remember how he had
looked when he came towards her in the cottage, and
she shuddered at the memory.

During those two days she hardly saw Ventnor at all.
He was not a man—or so she had believed—particularly
hampered by the conventions, but of course his behavior, from the point of view of propriety, was ad-
mirable. He did not speak to her of love or of marriage;
he did not indeed speak to her at all, being out all day
and half the night, too; the thaw that Sam had prophesied had set in, and the work involved was enormous.
She could not help thinking that he seemed precious
anxious to avoid her. She had hoped with a quickening
of the heart, that they might talk together in the evenings; the kisses that she had once so despised were now
never absent from her thoughts. But there were no
kisses, and no talks, either; it was almost as if he wanted
to be rid of her. Probably he regretted his rash proposal;
now that he was the last of his line, he would plan for
himself a more important marriage. Mary had given a
great deal of good advice to the lovelorn in her time; this

did not prevent her from weeping angrily to herself at nights, and moping about the house in the daytime.

Left in the Hall to her own devices, she wandered around at her will. There was no one now to stop her looking at whatever she pleased. Once, trembling, she returned to the attic. It was nothing now but a lumber room, with no ghostly traces of the young girl who had cowered beneath the bed; only she looked at the broken cupboard, and her eyes widened a little. She only stayed there for a moment, but before she left she picked up the volume of Shakespeare that had belonged to Robin Ventnor, aged 12, took it down with her, and guiltily packed it at the bottom of her box.

Once or twice she met him on his way out. He glanced casually at her. "You'll be able to go any moment now," he said. On the second day he said, "Your father will be waiting for you at the George Inn. I have taken a seat for you on the 'Derby Dilly'. You will be ready early to-morrow morning, and we will ride down to the *Jacob's Ladder.*"

"What are you going to do?" she said. "Will you stay on here?"

"Always," he said. He took a deep breath as he said it. "Always. This is my home. I could never endure to be away from it."

Mary was a town girl. She had lived all her life in Derby. She raised her head now and stared across the moors which had once so frightened her. The tears filled her eyes; she averted her head lest Ventnor should see them. She could not bear the thought that she might never see this again. Wardwick Hall, despite her ill memories of it, was the most beautiful house she had ever seen, and now, with the wind blowing cleanly through it, scoured by the brightness of the sun and the cold, it was free at last of its taint, it was to her, incredibly, home.

But she said nothing, and when at last she was riding towards the *Jacob's Ladder,* in the thawing snow, she wondered again, and looked about her in a kind of despair. The stretch of moors, the shadow of Kinder Scout, and Ventnor's arms about her, blurred into one. She could not speak, and he apparently did not wish to do so; he held her firmly enough, but with efficiency rather than tenderness; his face was impassive and singularly unloverlike.

He set her down at the inn. He said, "There is a little while to wait. Would you rather go into the parlor? There are sometimes people here who plague young female passengers. You see," he said without a smile, "I have become schooled in courtesy."

Mary silently raised her face to him. She did not answer, but stayed there in the courtyard. Presently he began to pace up and down as if he were anxious to be away, cracking his riding crop against his boot, looking everywhere but at her. He said at last, "By this time next week the moor will be green again."

It was no good. She swallowed her pride. It went down remarkably easily. She said, "When are you coming to Derby?"

He turned his great dark eyes upon her. He said negligently, "Derby? Oh, I cannot say. There is a great deal to do. Business to settle, and so on. I shall be very occupied."

She could have sworn he was laughing at her, for all his face remained grave. She grew angry again, all the more so because of her despairing consciousness that she could not endure to be away from him for any time at all. She said weakly, standing there in the slushy yard. "Perhaps after all——"

"After all," he said, "I must have time to reflect. And I did propose to you, and you said 'No' to me."

"I did not——" Then she realized how very ungenteel this was, flushed, and grew silent.

"You said I was proposing with the pistol cocked. You were most maidenly. And, as you rightly reminded me, there have been enough mismarriages in our family, ever since great-great-grandfather Robert ran off with the gypsy from the common, and injected violent blood into the rest of us."

"You are being very cruel," said Mary, nearly in tears. She had expected nothing like this. "Would you have had me fall into your arms and protest my love for you?"

"You could have done worse. Though I know your sex despises such a wanton show of feeling. But then I am of rude country stock. When we love, we say so. We do not hesitate. We are not coy. We do not make a leg and throw in pretty speeches. But that is obviously too direct for you. Indeed, I think I would not suit you at all. You want some pretty gallant to escort you to the ball, write you little verses, languish beneath your window, die if you frown at him and leap to the stars if you smile. I do not care for dancing," said Ventnor abruptly. "I cannot write verse. I'd be through your window rather than beneath it. And if you frowned at me, I should so scowl back that you'd be frighted head over heels into the Derwent, like your stout little gentleman who was so forward. From which I should not rescue you—I have no time for these fripperies. Find yourself a genteel townsman, and lead a genteel life."

She summoned up her spirit. Never in the whole of her life had she been so spoken to. "Very well," she said, "I will." Her chin was trembling, but she stared at him in defiance. "Indeed, I could not endure life with such a boor. I would prefer a husband who would be civil to me, one who'd shout at me all day and bully me and perhaps beat me. You will be happier without me, my lord."

"Undoubtedly, ma'am," he said.

"Then why," she cried, forgetting the people about her who were also waiting for the coach, and who were staring at her in the frankest interest, "did you ever propose to me?"

"Perhaps," he suggested, "I like to be unhappy."

"Then you will not be unhappy at my expense," said Mary in a wild fury. "I will say goodbye to you now."

"Goodbye," he said cheerfully, and now there was no denying that his cheek muscle was twitching in a most offensive manner.

"There is no need for you ever to come to Derby."

"Naturally not."

"So you had best advertise for another companion."

"Such an advertisement would look prodigious well in the *Derby Mercury!*"

"——Who likes sheep and moors——"

"And bullies and boors. Poetry, you notice. Perhaps I could write verse, after all."

"Oh, you are quite impossible!" cried Mary. This was not in the least how she had planned it, and now it seemed it was goodbye, indeed, and she would never see him again. The tears began to flood down her cheeks. She swung away, praying he would not see. The elderly lady at her left, however, remarked this quite plainly, and her eyes shone with excitement at the drama that was being played out beside her.

The "Derby Dilly" was coming round the corner. This was the end. In a moment she would be away from him for ever. But if that was how he wished it—— She could not say goodbye. She could not speak at all. The tears were running into her mouth. She took a blundering step towards the coach. The next instant she found herself picked up in arms that almost squeezed the breath from her, and such final breath as remained to her was then soundly kissed away. She was released as suddenly as she had been seized and, before she could summon up the strength to voice her fury at this outrage, saw Ventnor swing himself up in his stirrup, and ride away as if possessed.

The elderly lady was quite enchanted and told her grandchildren all about it the moment she arrived home.

Mary on the way home thought of little else. For a girl who had always known her own mind, who had thought falling in love foolish, who had organized her way through life, she was in such a state of longing and indecision that she did not know what to do.

She wanted to go home and she did not want to leave. She stared miserably out of the windows at the vanishing moors now smoothing into the softer contours of the dales, and thought, not of her father, not of a Nan wild with excitement, but of deep-set eyes that had once looked tenderly upon her, of hands that had held her, of a voice that had derided her—everything indeed that was foolish, sentimental, ridiculous, and which still brought the tears flooding down her cheeks. Yet at the back of her mind was always the wild hope that

Ventnor might be waiting for her. It would mean riding like the devil, but he was surely capable of doing so, and it would be a flamboyant gesture after his piratical heart.

The passengers were all talking of the Pretender's son. He had now left Derby well behind him, would perhaps be over the Border again, going back and back into the Scottish Highlands which had risen so gallantly to his support, and which would—if the stories of Cumberland were true, the bloody butcher they called him—bitterly regret it. "A little essential bloodletting," he had grimly promised them; God knows they must already have had that. People said that Charles had ridden sullenly behind his men as they retreated, his head sunk on his chest like a chidden boy; he had cried out, "I would rather be ten foot underground than turn back." It seemed strange that this popish boy, no worse and no better than a hundred others, should so have influenced her life, thought Mary. But for him she would never have come to Wardwick Hall; but for him Nicholas and the old lady might be there today; but for him she might never have met the Hall's piratical lord.

Mary wanted to weep again, and then for the first time her grief vanished from her. They were in Derby now, driving down the North Parade, past St. Alkmund's Church, across St. Michael's Lane, down Irongate to the market place where the young prince had had his glory for so brief a time. They were coming up to the George Inn, and there—she was now leaning out of the window to the peril of her neck—were three familiar figures staring in her direction, one of them beginning to wave its hand frantically. Not the tall figure she had been hoping against hope to see—ah, he would be riding his moors, no doubt, doing whatever people did on moors in this season, preoccupied with his own affairs, pitting his wits against the thaw which must be rushing down the side of Kinder Scout; no time to waste on a silly girl who so belatedly had fancied herself in love with him—but no matter, no matter, she was not going to break her heart for that, after all. There was Nan, darling Nan, surely a good deal taller than when she saw her last, and —Good God! of all people—Horace, definitely stouter, yet so homely and comfortable that she at once forgave him for everything he had ever done to annoy her.

She jumped down from the coach, to have Nan's octopus-like arms flung about her neck; she grabbed at her father, crying, laughing, immersed in a tangle of welcoming arms and kisses, so that her hat fell sideways, and her portmanteau thudded on to the roadway.

Mr. Vernon said calmly, "This is a great to-do, Mary. You must go away more often. It seems to make you appreciate us. Well, daughter? How do you do, after this shocking absence of one whole month?"

"One month?" She drew back a little to stare at him. "Is it only one month? It seems so very much more. Oh papa, how glad I am to see you again——"

"And me, and me!" Nan was crying. "Do you not remark how I have grown? And do you not like my new hair style? I am not a little girl, any longer. Say you like it—— Oh, Mary, you look well, you look wonderful, were they kind to you, and are you not going to marry him? Is he very handsome, and is he as mad as they say? Hannah has baked your favorite cakes—— The workbox was lovely, lovely—— I've put flowers in your room. They say he rides the moors like the storm, it sounds prodigious exciting—— How tall is he? Did they feed you well? Did they work you to death? And——"

"Oh, darling, for pity's sake!" Mary, laughing, nearly in tears again, put out a hand to ward off the questions. "I'll tell you everything, later. And your hair is up—you look such a young lady. But it's a little severe, Nan— could you not bring it more across the cheek?" For Nan had indeed shot up since her brief absence, and her hair was now screwed into an imposing knot on top of her head. She had grown thinner, too, with the coltish thinness of her age, with elbows that shot out, and long legs that moved awkwardly. But the spate of questions was still Nan, as was the wide smile, the bright eyes, and Mary hugged her, thinking that perhaps the month had been hard for Nan, too, with her father to care for, and all the household tasks on her shoulders.

"The Chevalier was here," Nan was crying. "Oh, Mary, he was here. I went down to Exeter House to see him. Do you know, his Highlanders threw our mayor down the steps?—he was in such a state that instead of asking to see the Prince, he asked for the Pretender, and the guard gave him such a kick that he fell down, and he said, 'If you want to see a Pretender, go to the court of St. James!' And I saw *him*. Oh, he was so handsome, far handsomer than your silly old Ventnor, I'll be bound, and he smiled at me—I swooned, Mary, I did indeed!"

"You are a complete goose," said her sister, "and I will not believe you did anything so missish. And," she could not help adding, "he is not more handsome than Vent—than his lordship, though I daresay he seemed more civilized."

"Oh?" said Nan. "Oh, indeed——?" And seemed about to say more when Horace broke in, in a sulky voice, "And what about me?"

"Oh, you are more handsome than the two put together," cried Mary, at which he said crossly, "I did not mean that. You are funning me. Aren't you glad to see me at all? For, 'pon honor, you have scarce looked at me."

"Of course I'm glad to see you. You know I am. It was wonderful of you to come to meet me." And she kissed him, adding, "You have put on weight, you know. Is this what London life has done for you? It's all that wine, I expect, and all the pretty girls who are encouraging you."

"Horace takes after his king," said Nan, but her cousin chose to ignore this, and only said to Mary, surveying her with a gaze that was both shy and appraising, "You're fatter, yourself."

"I? Oh no!"

"Well, you look different, anyway. You seem to be oh, I don't know. Does she not look different, Uncle Edward? Softer, not so vinegar and lemon——"

"Horace! A fine greeting for me!" She turned, laughing, to meet her father's eyes.

"Yes," he said. "You have changed, my dear. It must be the good country air." He watched with interest the flame sweeping up her cheeks. "You used not to have such a color. Nor that light to the eyes. There's an air of—— How shall I put it? I think perhaps that when my parishioners have strayed, as indeed they so often do, they would not mind telling you about it."

Mary said, with some asperity, "I do not know what you can mean by that, papa. I have never set up to be a moral mentor. You of all people should know that I am excessively broadminded."

"Yes," he said, "perhaps so. But I sometimes suspected that you were overconscious of it. But we are blocking the way here, and now the emotion is over. Give Horace your portmanteau, and we will walk back to the vicarage."

They walked down the street, Nan hanging on Mary's arm, whispering, "Something did happen. You must tell me. Oh, I can hardly wait——" And suddenly in Mary's ears was ringing another voice which said: She has come all the way from Derby to teach us gentility, and again the sick longing swept over her to hear that voice again, to see him striding out of the house in his rough riding clothes; she thought shamefully, Oh, God, I wish I were back, I wish I were back——

"Nan," her father was remarking, "takes her duties very seriously these days. She has been a good girl, Mary. She has looked after her father, troubled herself about the parishioners, spared herself in no way, and run the household as to the manner born. She plays the hostess so well now that it is quite alarming."

"She is far too interested in politics," said Horace. "It is not seemly in so young a girl. Such matters should be left to the gentlemen."

"Ah!" said Nan, grimacing at him behind Mary's back. "There he goes again, the little Tory overlord, loving the Elector of Hanover, stuffing himself on German cakes, and winning the war in the gaming rooms."

Mary ignored this. Horace and Nan had always bickered. She only said in a small voice, "You keep on talking about parishioners, papa."

"I had hoped you would at last notice. But you seemed so preoccupied—— Yes. I have been reinstated a few days ago. It appears that I shall even receive an official apology from the Bishop."

"Papa!"

"The world has decided that it was all a little mistake." He gave her an ironic smile. "Everyone is so sorry. All the ladies who turned their genteel shoulders on me, now run to bring me samples of their cooking or horticulture. We are, indeed, all making the most diligent effort to behave as if nothing whatsoever had happened. You must not keep stopping in the middle of the street, my dear. Hannah has the most superb dinner waiting for you, and will be very angry if you are late."

Mary said—the lump in her throat seemed as if it would choke her, "How did—did this happen?"

"I do not know." He looked steadily at her. "Someone appears to have worked very hard on my behalf. Whoever it is seems to have that power of getting things done, for it was all incredibly swift. By the time the Pretender's son was here, I was back in my church. It was perhaps as well. There were some unpleasant incidents. I owe a great debt of gratitude to this stranger; I only hope that one day I can thank him in person."

Horace, presumably following his own train of thought, said suddenly, "What was the fellow like? Is he as mad as they all say? You never wrote to me, you know. He must be half crazed to live in the middle of the moors like that. Did he treat you decent?"

"Yes. Oh, yes."

"No familiarities?"

"Certainly not!"

"You never know with people like that. They think they are still living in the old days, with feudal rights and all that sort of damned nonsense. Especially a Jacobite——"

"He is not a Jacobite!"

"Well, there's no need to get miffed, is there? I was only asking."

"You are always asking," interrupted Nan. "Really, Horace, you are the most tiresome boy. You want a world composed of people like yourself, and Lord, how dull that would be——"

Horace cried out, "In a minute I shall slap you. And pull down that hair you're so proud of—— You're only a spoilt little girl after all——"

Mary, under cover of the squabbling, said in a low voice, "Papa, it's true what you said. I feel I have changed very much. I do not seem to know any longer what I think about anything. It is all dreadfully confusing. One does n•t know where one is at all. I do not feel efficient, any more. I do not believe I ever want to be. What is the matter with me? Do you think I will ever get over it?"

They were outside the vicarage now, and Nan and Horace had run ahead to open the door; they shouted each other down as they did so.

Mr. Vernon said, "I do not suppose you will ever recover. The illness is, I believe, incurable. You did not tell me much in your letters, Mary, but I gathered that something of the kind was happening to you. Even Nan began to suspect. But I dare not tell you her prophecies. They would make you angry because they would coincide so strictly with your own."

"I could not write much. I wanted to, but it was—difficult."

"Oh," he said, "some day you shall tell me all about it. But shall we not go in? It is a pity that you cannot infect Horace with a little of your disease. He always knows so indisputably that he is right that it grows quite alarming. But of course he is my sister's son. I should warn you that he is offering for you again. Twice a year he feels it is his duty to be married, and this time you are to be the sacrifice. He will doubtless propose this evening. Perhaps by the banks of the Derwent."

"Then I shall turn him down."

"There's my daughter. Yet one cannot blame him. You have grown quite pretty, Mary. But perhaps it is just my partial eye. However, you need not distress yourself on Horace's account. He is not one of those who will die of a broken heart. Come, Mary. The weather is mild enough now, but I still think you should come indoors. Come—— I am beginning to believe you are some fifty miles away."

She looked at him, half uncomprehending. He is not one of those who will die of a broken heart. He had kissed her at parting, but that was doubtless his way of saying farewell. If he really loved her, he would come to Derby instanter; if his love were so poor that it must be overridden by his duties, why then he was no lover at all. She would not die of a broken heart, neither. And around her for a brief instant was a vast desolation of moorland, with Kinder Scout uprearing to the sky, and again that deep voice, saying, I had not thought I was bringing a vixen into the chicken house——

Then hastily she followed her father in.

She was after all human. She had lived here all her life. It was not possible not to respond to the welcome that had been planned. The unhappiness momentarily fled from her. This was home, with a wonderful smell of cooking in the air, and Hannah wiping her hands on her apron, scolding her, "Now hurry up and wash your hands, Miss Mary, the dinner is all spoiling——" And Nan still quarreling with Horace, who was shouting, "The Chevalier, indeed! I warrant you'd not find him such a hero if he lacked a few inches of height and had a receding chin!"

"Like you, Horace," replied Nan; perhaps she had not grown up so much after all, then she added in a falsetto so that they both spoke together, "There's no need to get so miffed!"

At dinner everyone talked at once. Horace talked about London, and Nan about Derby and the Chevalier; her father spoke of his parish, and Hannah stood there, crying shamelessly, scolding Mary from one course to another, and pushing as much food in front of her as would have fed the rebel army. Only Mary herself said little, and at last when they had eaten, her father looked at her and said, "You must be tired. Why don't you go to your room and lie down for an hour? We have all the time in the world ahead of us. Sleep for a while and, when you are rested, come down to my study. The children can solve the history of the world, and I will start my sermon."

Mary went slowly up the stairs. She heard Nan crying

out, "You and your Elector of Hanover! Now take James I——"

Mr. Vernon remarked, "We are lucky that she does not start with Robert the Bruce. But she has been such a very good child. You can have no idea how she looked after me. Even you could scarce have done better. Though you did not let the distance impede you, daughter. The wood you sent us saved our lungs, if not our lives."

"It was not I who sent the wood, papa."

"No?"

"It was his lordship." How angry Ventnor would have been! She found the phrase sweet to utter, and resisted the temptation to repeat it. But she only said, "He is a good man, papa. He was very good to me."

Then she went into her room.

She lay down on her bed. It was true that she was very tired. She had not slept well for some time, and the journey had been long, and disturbing to her heart. But she could not sleep. She closed her eyes and beneath the veil of her lids her thoughts arose and thumped and thudded on her attention, calling up always Ventnor—Ventnor angry, derisive, striding out of the house, watching her in the cottage. She remembered the touch of his lips on hers, the feeling of his arms about her, the waiting together, perhaps for death, when it seemed sweeter to wait so than to be alone and live.

She grew angry with herself. Somehow she must dispel these insidious dreams, and to lie, stretched out on her bed, half-asleep, was inviting those dreams to become stronger than reality. She rose to her feet, slipped on her cloak again, and came downstairs.

She could hear the sound of voices from the parlor. They sounded amicable enough. Presumably Nan and Horace had thrashed out the question of England's kingship, and were now playing cards. Horace in his heart had always been fond of Nan; his intellect at the age of nineteen was about on a level with hers at twelve, so conversation was easy between them. From her father's study there was a complete silence. She would not dare to speak to him just now. He was too shrewd; he knew

her too well. She could not quite endure that he should
know her secret. Later—oh, later, when she had forgotten, and Ventnor had grown to be a shadow among
the other shadows that comprise a life—but not now,
when that shadow loomed dark upon her, obscuring
everything else.

She moved secretively, therefore, unlatched the door,
and stepped out on to the road that led by the banks of
the Derwent. The weather was soft and mild, as often
happens in a country that boasts of its snowbound De-
cembers and its sunlit springs; this might indeed have
been a spring day, except for a sharpness to the air
which hinted at cold, once the sun had set. It was growing dim now at four in the afternoon, but was still warm
enough to walk slowly in, and Mary strolled along,
wrapped in her thoughts, until at last she came to the
river.

She sat there on the bank for a long time. There was
no one about. Horace might come to seek her later, or
Nan, but now they would believe her asleep in her room;
they would not think to look for her. She stared into the
water. The river was dark, reflecting the naked boughs
that overhung it. There was no sound. The birds had
gone, long ago; the wild things that lived on the bank
were submerged in their winter sleep.

She threw a stone into the water. The sluggish ripples
ringed it round and, as they did so, stirred the surface
of her thoughts so that all resignation sank with the
stone, and strange, piratical ideas swelled to the rim of
her mind. To stay here, and end her days here, in this
little country town, with the church bells ringing, and
the small talk, the small thoughts, the small life flowing
easily about her—— I cannot, she thought. I cannot. If
he will not come to me, then I must go back to him——

She heard the steps. She knew of course who it was,
but she could not believe it; she dared not turn round,
only sat there, her head drooping more and more, her
hands tightly clenched on her knee. The steps stopped
close beside her. Still she would not turn. Only at last the
silence became unendurable, and angrily, fearfully,

joyfully, she looked up prepared to do battle, and prepared equally strongly to be defeated.

He was standing over her. He looked quite disreputable, so much so that for a second the Derwent vanished, and the trim woods with it; the wind of the moorland took her breath away. His boots were thick with mud, and his breeches spattered with it. He wore, as might have been expected, no peruke. He said, in a voice of the utmost exasperation, "I was wondering when you were going to notice my existence. I had a change of heart, Mary. You should acknowledge this rarity. I decided for once in my life to accommodate myself to female vapors, and settle this matter once and for all. I planned to reach Derby before you did. I should have been at the inn. But this damned weather! Of course, I was too clever. I took what I thought was a shorter route. I should have known better. I had forgot the thaw. The land is streaming with it. It was like riding through a river. I was up to my knees in it, half the time—— Look at me!"

She looked. She said nothing.

"I had even meant to change," he said. "I have after all relatives here who would have housed me. They do not approve of me, but I do not think they would have turned me from their door. I had a fancy to put on the peruke you value so highly, and sail out to do my courting in proper style. And here I am, like any groom. But that is how you know me. You may as well see me as I am, after all. If a little mud displeases you—why then, my courting is done with before it is begun."

And saying this, he sat down beside her, his long legs stretched before him, his hands on the ground. There was a distance of perhaps a foot between them. He made no attempt to bridge it.

Presently he said without looking at her, not, it appeared, finding her silence singular, "Now. If you marry me, you have as your dowry Wardwick Hall, for I will never live anywhere else. You have—I have forgot the exact number—a great many acres of moorland as your private property. You have some several hundred sheep, an equal number of cattle, and the other livestock on my farms. I can enumerate them, if you wish, but it would prove tedious. The cottages around belong to me; I collect the rents. The exact amount I have written down—— Wait." He began to fumble in his breast pocket, and at this Mary cried out in a strangled voice, "I do not propose to marry for a man's possessions—— What is this? Have you gone out of your wits?"

"No," he said, "I believe I am quite sane. Only you regard marriage as a business proposition, and I felt I should set the matter fairly to you. In due course we will come to what you can offer me, and that may prove a little more complicated—— You also must take me. Why do you look so offended? I am a farmer. We do things this way, at the market. Must I take marriage more lightly than a financial transaction? I admit that I am the stumbling block, but I'm not quite so bad tempered as you think, and only roar every other hour or so. Besides you have not seen me fairly. I am not usually so provoked as I have been this past month, what with knowing that every second my back was turned you would be running yourself into murder, not daring to sleep at nights for fear of hearing your latch lift, and frighted half out of my wits every time you opened your foolish mouth. Oh," he said, "I could have broke your neck a dozen times a day, but that would scarce have helped—— Well, there it is, Mary. I offer you a considerable amount of land and livestock, the Hall, myself, and precious little else. I will not prophesy whàt your married life will be like, but I daresay it will be no worse than marriage à la mode, and perhaps even a little better, for I shall have small chance of being unfaithful to you, you will have none whatsoever of being unfaithful to me, I shall not gamble away my sheep and cows, and I do not overdrink, for a good farmer cannot afford to do so. Well? What have you to say to this? You will note that I am not shouting, that I am being businesslike, reasonable and displaying a most commendable restraint. What do you have to say? You were not used to be so silent. Surely you can think of some kind of reply."

Mary said, staring at him, "If I did say no, would you go away?"

"Why, naturally," he said. "What else would you expect me to do? If one cannot sell in one market——"

"Market!" cried Mary. "Market! Is that all you think of? You would treat me like that other poor girl——"

"Poor girl! She is now married with three brats. Her heart is soldered again. I believe it was scarcely cracked. These things with women are largely a matter of vanity."

"You are a gallant lover," cried Mary more desperately than ever. "She told you to go, and you went. What kind of love is that?"

"The most practical kind. Of course I may have had some misty premonition of a pale little girl fighting rather inadequately for her virtue on the banks of the Derwent."

"I was *not*——!"

"Then you should have been. Or perhaps I heard from the future a treasonable song sung shrilly from a bedroom window. You came and looked out, Mary. It was the first time I saw you. I did not expect to meet you again so soon, but I noted where you lived. But in any case all this is irrelevant. Perhaps the whole matter is. You are going to tell me to go. I will go. Yet before I do so, I would like to know what you would have offered me in return for the largesse I have been prepared to shower on you. From a purely business point of view, naturally——"

Mary looked at him in anger and despair. She wanted to rail and cry at him—it was impossible, he was impossible, this was not how people proposed. And he still sat there, not attempting to make it easier for her. Then before her blurring eyes she saw again the small life she had despised, saw a future in which he would have no place. Her pride commanded her to say, No, most firmly; the other emotion stopped her lips so that she could scarcely speak at all.

Then she said in a gasp, "You have been very good to my family. My father—— It was all your doing."

He suddenly grinned at her. "I enjoyed myself. It was in any case the least I could do. I do not care so much for the abjuring clergy who forswear the Stuarts and keep the anniversary of Charles I's martyrdom. It was a pleasure to bully them. It is one of those occasions when it is advantageous to wear both a title and a peruke. I stormed the episcopal see. I expressed my undiluted opinion of those who take so unchristian an action for what they term Christianity. I had them cowed, well enough. It was most satisfying. Not even you could have said, yes, my lord, no, my lord, more insistently. I have never played the lord so magnificently. You could scarce approach me for my aristocratic arrogance. It is a pity they cannot see me now—— But all this is nothing to do with us. Nothing at all. You are choosing to express a preposterous gratitude. Is that all you can offer me in exchange for what I offer you? For if that is so, the sooner I go the better. I am not saddling myself with a grateful wife. I do not visualize marriage on those terms. I do not visualize you on those terms, either, unless you have changed completely, and if you have so changed, why, you and I would scarce make a match of it. I'd best go. It is growing dark. I shall be riding all the night, as it is——"

To her dismay he rose to his feet. She half put out her hand, but he seemed not to notice it. She said at last in a strangled voice, "Don't go."

He said, in the angry voice she knew so well, "Why not?"

She tried to think of a way out, could find none, so she stumbled to her feet, and ran after him. He stood there, looking down at her. He said more quietly, "You have not answered my first question. I would like an answer. I believe one should not speak of rights, yet I think I have the right to know it. What will you offer me in exchange?"

His tone betrayed him more than he realized, or perhaps he did realize, for suddenly the arrogance was swept from him, and an oddly unsure, disturbed expression came on his face. She saw this. At that moment she knew what she wanted so desperately to know. It could have been her moment of triumph; it was her chance to assert the independence she had so much prized. She put her hand on his arm. She said, a little wretchedly, "Robin, I have not much to offer. But I do love you so very much. I should like to be with you. When I thought you were not coming, I knew that I must come to you. I would have done. I could not stay without you. I daresay," she said, "that love is not much to offer in exchange for so many sheep and cattle, but then you see, I am a town girl, and I can only offer what I have. You can after all spend a great deal of time with your livestock, and I am sure you will find it very satisfactory, but you did say to me once that Wardwick Hall had been a gay and happy house, a long time ago, and perhaps—I am not sure—but perhaps I could make it so again for you. I should like to do that. I should like to feel that you were pleased to come home, and I should like more than anything to feel that I was there to welcome you; it would be a very real welcome, because—I thought this would be hard to say, but after all it is not—I truly love you with all my heart, and you must know it after all. You are not a fool. And neither am I. Not now——"

He said, in a voice she had never heard from him, "You are being very gallant, Mary."

"Oh," she said, coming closer so that she touched him. "It is not gallantry. It is sheer necessity. If you cannot do without something, then you must have it. And you seemed so very anxious to go, and I was so desperate to keep you—— You are not going, are you?"

"I must confess," he said, "I never had the least intention of doing so. I have after all ridden like—like the Chevalier himself, to get to you, and it would take the Chevalier, himself, with Cumberland's dragoons thrown in, to chase me away again. But damn the Chevalier, and pudding-George, too, for I do not give a rap for either of them. Come, Mary. I believe I have used you outrageously. Let me use you even more so. And tell me to go now, if you dare! Tell me——"

Mary did not tell him to go. She told him at this point a great many things, but going was not one of them. She did not think of the unreasonableness of men, nor did she grumble at the masculine propensity for kissing. She did not even see the reasonable world around her, for she was too enfolded to see anything; she did not even see Horace who had appeared at this instant, some twenty yards away, and who was staring blankly and amazedly at this couple enclasped in each other's arms, oblivious of anything else.

He had guessed that Mary would be by the river. He had come out to look for her. And there she was, well enough, but it was not the Mary he knew at all, the correct little vicar's daughter who had once been so angry with him for doing considerably less than this other fellow—who the devil was he?—was doing now.

Horace was not particularly intelligent, but the size of the stranger, and his curious clothes, and the fact that he wore his own hair, at last enlightened him. He stared for another moment, not quite sure whether to be furious or whether to laugh at the sight of his prim little cousin acting with an ardor of which he would not have thought her capable. Then a strange kind of gentlemanly scruple descended on him. He had thought to propose to her, himself. He had, it seemed, arrived too late. Ah, well, there were other girls—— And Mary was really too clever for him. Clever women were the devil. He cast one last, half shame-faced glance at the two of them, motionless in their embrace, plainly lost to the world, then he averted his head, and without another look set out for home. It seemed odd to him that she should love a man who was from all accounts little better than a pirate, but perhaps ladies liked pirates, and he was no pirate, only a respectable, stupid, rather overstout young man who at that moment was a little sad, a little low in his self-esteem.

And the pirate kissed his lady, and Horace sighed. And the lady kissed her pirate, and Horace was out of sight.

FIVE DELIGHTFUL
PERIOD ROMANCES FOR
YOUR READING PLEASURE